THE RIVAL ROOMIES

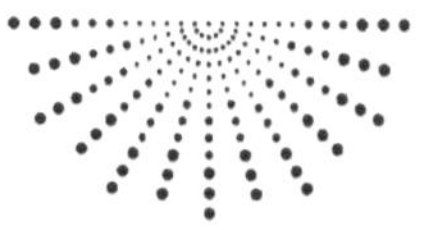

PIPER RAYNE

Cover Photo: Wander Aguiar Photography

Cover Design: By Hang Le

1st Line Editor: Joy Editing

2nd Line Editor: My Brother's Editor

Proofreader: Shawna Gavas, Behind The Writer

About The Rival Roomies

I've loved him from afar.
Though most times he's only a foot away.
I'm smart enough to know he'll never be anyone's forever.

He checks all the bad boy boxes. Tattoos. Check. Motorcycle.
Check. Chip on his shoulder. Check check.

If he wasn't my neighbor and friend I may have thrown
myself at him. Okay, yeah. I wouldn't. Because guys like
Dylan don't want a woman who writes kid's math textbooks
under him in bed. Instead, I pathetically savor morsels of
moments where I have his sole attention.

That was until his archenemy moved in with me. Now
suddenly, Dylan's moving in too and warning off the first
guy in a long time who's showing me interest. Could he
finally see me as more than a friend, or am I just a prize to
win and show off to his enemy?

THE RIVAL ROOMIES

CHAPTER ONE

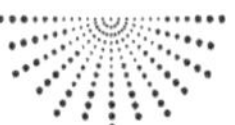

Rian

The shrill sound of my phone wakes me, and my blurry eyes focus on the screen. Only my parents ever call me before my alarm goes off. I'd ignore the damn thing if I didn't know they'd call right back or have the National Guard come check on their precious daughter.

"It's early," I answer.

"You're not up yet?" my mom asks.

"Why are you calling me so early?" I snip.

"We were out to dinner with the Fredericksons last night," she says.

I lie back down on the bed, putting the phone on speaker and resting it on my pillow beside my head.

This is going to be a long one.

"Uh-huh," I say, trying not to let my annoyance be heard.

My mom says, "Johann is working on an equation."

Johann would be the Fredericksons' son and the person

I'm constantly compared to. The one his parents named after Johann Carl Friedrich Gauss, the famous German mathematician. Imagine living in the United States with the name Johann and being the leader of the mathletes—pre bully awareness. Let's just say by the end of high school, he was walking himself into his locker and shutting the door.

I roll my eyes. "Yeah."

"Yes," my dad corrects me.

I say nothing. Obviously I've woken up on the defiant side of the bed this morning.

"It's for a contest the Mathematical Society of America is running," my mom says.

"That's great," I say with a yawn.

"They said he thinks it will take him a while to solve it." The excitement level in my mom's voice grows higher and higher while my interest wanes further and further.

"I'm sure he will. No one is better than him," I say.

"Except you, sweetheart," my dad says.

The man adds sweetheart when he wants me to do something. It's a trigger word that says this conversation will suck and I'm most likely going to commit to doing something I don't want to do. Namely this contest.

I say, "Jo is going to crush it. If he's already started it, he's as good as won."

"The contest is open, and if you win, it's worth prize money," my dad says.

"How much?" I ask.

"I didn't catch the amount. Did you, Larry?" my mom asks. "Not that it's important. You wouldn't be doing it for the money."

Uh, yeah, I would.

"You don't need money, right, sweetheart? You save a quarter of your paycheck for a rainy day like we've always taught you, right?" my dad asks.

"Of course." How many lies can you tell your parents in your lifetime? I stopped counting.

"That's my girl," he says with pride.

Mom continues. "You do it for the notoriety. Your name will grace every conversation in the industry. You could get a much better job and forget Pierson Education. They should've had you writing college-level equations by now. Fifth grade math is an insult to your intelligence."

"Mom, I don't really have the time for another—"

"Make the time. I'm emailing you all the details now. And don't tell anyone. I don't want Johann working day and night to beat you. It's about time they see how talented you are," she says.

I roll my eyes. "I'll look into it."

There's a moment of silence, and the scratching on the phone line says one of them is doing something else.

"What's going on with you, sweetheart?" my dad asks.

I glance at the phone to make sure the connection is still with my parents. Rarely do they show any interest in how I'm really doing, preferring instead to cling to the prefabricated assurances I feed them. "Good. Sierra moved out to live with her boyfriend."

"The prince," my dad says. "We saw the footage. The Fredericksons didn't know what to say when we told them that."

"That your daughter's roommate is dating a prince?"

"Is Johann's roommate dating a princess?"

"Johann doesn't have a roommate," I say.

"Exactly." My dad's tone is one of satisfaction.

Does he not realize his daughter has to live with people in order to have a nice place to live? Johann lives in New York City in a studio apartment all by himself.

"Okay, I registered you," my mom cuts in.

I sit up in bed. "What?"

"This way it's done. Taken care of."

I blow out a breath. The last thing I want to spend my free time on is a math problem, but I will say the money sounds intriguing. "Okay."

"Make sure you start on it right away. Johann already has a head start," my mom says.

"I need to get to work now," I say.

"That's fine. Your dad and I are going with a few other friends to talk to the administrators of the SAT. We think there should be different ones for gifted kids. They all shouldn't be able to score perfect."

"And that's not a knock on you, sweetheart," my dad says.

"Although you should've taken it over," my mom says.

I roll my eyes. I didn't need to take it over. I had an excellent score, she just still isn't over the fact that Johann scored better than I did. "I gotta go. Work and all."

"Bye, sweetheart," my dad says.

"Don't forget, mum's the word. No posting on social media about doing the math—"

"Got it, Mom. Bye."

"Love —"

I click off the phone, then pull up the email with all the details. The problem will be emailed to me directly by a Dr. Giroux. Once I finish, I send him my work and am only to talk to him. They don't disclose how many people are trying to solve the problem, but as soon as the right answer is given, everyone will be notified of the winner. And there's a twenty-five-thousand-dollar prize that they would prefer go to continued education but understand they cannot dictate that.

Dylan's loud voice interrupts my concentration and I rise from my bed to see what's going on. It's been only one day since my entire roommate situation took a one-eighty. I went from living with a couple to two men. One of which I still haven't really gotten to know well.

"There are rules here," Dylan says.

I press my ear against my bedroom door.

"Just relax, Phillips. I'm not looking for complications," Jax says.

None of us ever use Dylan's last name. Mostly because when Dylan introduces himself to someone, he never uses his last name. Even his business cards at Ink Envy only have Dylan in a black block font. He's always touchy about his middle name too.

"I just want to make it clear—you aren't to touch her."

Jax laughs sarcastically as my palm flattens on the door as though Dylan's recent bodyguard behavior has anything to do with romantic feelings for me. *He's your friend and only moved into your apartment so you didn't have to live alone with a guy you don't know. Do not think of this as anything more.*

Jax's laugh abruptly cuts off. "Tell me, Phillips, are you touching her?"

"None of your business."

"So this is a Naomi situation all over again?"

Naomi? I mentally mark that name to ask Knox about later.

"No. Rian is just…"

"What?" Jax eggs him on.

Dylan groans. The same tone he uses when his employees call in sick and he has to go in. "Different."

"She's into girls?" Jax asks.

"No!"

"So you want to nail her and are afraid, by comparison to me, you'll come up short?"

"Fuck no!" Dylan yells.

I slowly back away from the door. I guess that answers the question I've never asked anyone but myself.

I've wanted Dylan since he moved in across the hall with Knox. They've known each other since high school. But when the question comes to his feelings for me, the answer isn't only no—it's hell no.

I sit on the edge of my bed. Someday I need to get over this crush I have on a guy who doesn't even know I exist—at least not in *that* way. Maybe I should list all the reasons why we would never work. Perhaps our differences are too big to ever allow us to meet in the middle.

It's the classic tale—good girl wants bad boy. Cliché enough to be a romance novel. Not realistic. I shouldn't want a guy who thinks of commitment as a life sentence. He sure as hell doesn't want a girl whose only experience is a handful of half adept short-term boyfriends.

God help me.

I pick up a pillow and groan. I'd scream, but they'd hear me and I'm pretending like I'm not up yet. Which shows how much Dylan knows my schedule and routine. I'm always the first one dressed and ready.

Their voices grow softer. Dylan's door next to mine shuts minutes later.

I slide my shower cap on my head. Now's my time to escape, so I open my door and tiptoe across the living area to the bathroom.

"Good morning," Dylan says.

I jump and circle back around. He's in workout clothes and has a bag hanging from his shoulder. My gaze goes to the microwave clock in the kitchen. It's only seven-thirty. The shop was open last night, and he didn't return home until after one.

Someone hit me with a sledgehammer. It's so pathetic that I know that.

"Morning." I slide my shower cap off my head. "Where are you off to?"

"The gym." He grabs a bottle of water from the fridge. "Ethan asked me to start going with him first thing in the morning rather than later. I guess love makes you eat. Seth's supposed to come too." The way his mouth scrunches to the side on the word love means he never wants to find out. More evidence to mark under commitment-phobe.

"Enjoy." I wave and keep to my mantra to take a shower and get ready for work. I miss being able to work from home but my job changed their requirements and now I have to work from the office several days a week.

"You should be fine. Jax just got home smelling like he closed the bar down. He'll probably pass out. Shouldn't bother you."

I pause by the bathroom door. Usually I'd turn around and smile and thank him. Be polite and courteous. But a bitter taste fills my mouth—because he's acting like one of Blanca's older brothers. I never asked for, nor do I need any saving from Jax.

"Have a great workout." I step into the bathroom, shut the door, and flick the lock.

Have a great workout? Way to really give him a piece of your mind, Rian.

I turn on the shower to the hottest possible temperature so that the mirror will fill with steam and I won't have to look at myself. I need a life. One where my obsession with Dylan isn't the main focus.

Screw him. I'm baking lemon cake today.

CHAPTER TWO

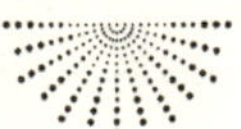

Dylan

"We don't need to go balls to the wall on the first day," Ethan says next to me, his finger hovering over the treadmill's buttons, his feet pounding on the moving belt.

"I thought you worked out?" I ask, not adjusting my speed or incline.

"I run. Occasionally. I've been blessed with a great metabolism."

I glance at him. "Until Blanca?"

He groans. "You should see what she can consume. And then there's something inside me that says I'm the man, she can't out eat me."

"Hence the gut." I pat my stomach.

He cringes. He hasn't gained enough to be that noticeable, but no harm in him thinking he has. It'll keep him coming to the gym with me and get me out of the damn apartment while Rian is getting ready for work.

Ethan looks down at his stomach and I want to bust out laughing, but I up the incline.

"Fucker," he says, clicking the button on his machine. Ethan can't back away from a challenge.

"Come on. After this, we'll do weights so you don't turn into a pansy-ass who can't lift his fiancée to fuck her against the wall."

An older woman with a displeased expression stops in front of my treadmill. I'm about to apologize before a smile forms on her lips and she looks Ethan up and down. "I bet he has no problem with it."

Winnie, my foster mom, taught me to respect my elders, so I swallow my amusement and watch Ethan smile nicely to avoid offending the woman.

She slowly walks over to the bikes and spends five minutes finding the television show she wants to watch before peddling. Even then, she has no headphones.

I turn off my treadmill, sliding back until I can hop off.

"What the hell? We can't just stop," Ethan says.

"Why not?" I ask.

"Sir! Wipe your machine," the man who works here—and wears his shorts too tight—calls to me.

I put up my hand and grab a pair of the cheap earbuds the gym offers for free. I wink at the girl behind the counter. She's been trying to flirt with me for the last two weeks, but she's got to be only twenty-one or something. The younger they are, the more attached they become.

"Dylan!" Ethan calls, his hands up in the air, his eyes tracking my movements toward the elderly lady.

I take the headphones out of the plastic disposable bag and hand them to her, plugging the cord into the television portion of the bike. She gives me a thumbs-up and a smile.

"Sir!" the guy says again.

"Relax there. Are your shorts so tight they're cutting circulation off to your brain?" I pull a sanitary wipe from the container and head over to my machine.

Tight shorts guy huffs and stalks off.

"You left me hanging?" Ethan says, shutting off his treadmill.

"You telling me you didn't want that over with?"

Ethan says nothing. Yeah, he's happy as shit I turned off my treadmill.

"Weights then." I hold up my wipe so moose-knuckle can see me dispose of it in the trash can.

He rolls his eyes and shifts his vision away.

"What's with you today?" Ethan asks, throwing his wipe away right after and grabbing a towel.

"Nothing."

"Really? Because you're being an ass to everyone but that old lady over there. Since when are you responsible for handing out earbuds? Did you get a job here I don't know about?"

I grab two dumbbells and stand in front of the mirror as Ethan follows suit. I'm not even sure if I can trust Ethan with what's bothering me, nor do I know if I want anyone to know. It's ridiculous anyway. I do a bicep curl with one arm, then the other.

"So?" Ethan asks.

"So nothing. We don't have to be like chicks and talk while we work out."

"There's a reason you're being a dick." He does a bicep curl, his eyes boring into mine in the mirror.

Ethan knows me well. I went through a lot of phases of independence in college, especially when the guilt that Winnie was wasting her savings on me made me try to sabotage my future, and Ethan was the one who set me straight.

I sit on the bench while Ethan continues pumping his arms. "I'm pissed that Knox brought Jax back here. He knows how things are between us."

He puts the dumbbells back and stacks some weights onto the bar on the bench. "What's the deal with the two of you? You're so much alike."

From the outside, Jax and I are similar. Both wounded foster kids who opted to ink their bodies with symbols and memories of harder times.

I went to college to study art and Jax headed to Los Angeles. I sold a painting out of college that earned me enough money to start Ink Envy two years after graduation. Last I heard, Jax trained under Alex Choi, a guy who'd earned his credentials on the street. Our training and paths were different, but we're still in the same fucking spot. We're both in-demand tattoo artists. The only difference now is I'm planted in Cliffton Heights and Jax just happened to follow a wind that blew him here.

"The asshole probably expects me to give him a job." I lower my back to the bench and Ethan stands above to spot me.

"Is he that kind of guy?"

No, he's not. Jax doesn't take handouts, just like me. But why is he here in Cliffton Heights? This town is too small for a personality like his.

"He's like us. You earn it yourself or it means shit."

Ethan nods, his hands hovering under the pole just in case. He's on crack. I'd need a lot more weight than this to make me struggle. I rack the weights, sit up, and wipe the sweat off my face.

"Hey, assholes, I thought we were in this together!" Seth yells from the other side of the room.

"No yelling in the facility," moose-knuckle says.

Seth looks him up and down, concentrating on his

obvious package. "I think you took your ten-year-old brother's shorts this morning."

The girl at the desk cracks up and Seth winks at her. The guy's face turns red, but he continues folding the towels. Usually we're not this big of jerks to people, so I wonder if something is bothering Seth like it is me.

Seth lays his towel on the bench and Ethan acts offended, but we both know bench pressing isn't really Ethan's thing.

"So after you dickheads deserted me—"

"We knocked five times," Ethan says.

"You have a key," Seth says, looking at me over his chest.

Ethan gets back into spotter position like he did for me.

"I overslept. It's been a shit morning all around," Seth says. "Guess who was standing on the other side of the road when I left our building?"

Neither of us answers.

"Her."

"Her who?" Ethan asks.

Seth mocks offense and stares at me like *what's with this guy*, but I'm not sure who he's talking about either. "Evan Erickson. I think she's stalking me."

Ethan smirks at me over the weight bar. "Why would she stalk you?"

"Because a few months ago, we had that altercation outside her bagel shop. Remember when Adrian worked there?"

"Yeah," I say.

"She must've liked it because after years of never running into her, she's been popping up everywhere. I found her in the gazebo with some guy last week. I mean, what would she be doing outside our apartment building that early in the morning?"

"Did you ask her?" Ethan asks.

"No!" His voice cracks like a thirteen-year-old boy's. "Why would I do that?"

Ethan shrugs. "Why wouldn't you?"

Seth pushes up his last rep and sits up, wiping his head with a towel before standing for me to take his place.

"Hello?" Ethan gives me an exasperated look and holds his hands out to the side.

"Oh, you want a piece of this?" I ask, pointing at the bench.

Ethan narrows his eyes, and Seth and I burst out laughing.

Ignoring us, Ethan lies on the bench. "Since I'm the only one who isn't hashing out imaginary problems, I think it's only fair."

"Having a stalker *is* a problem," Seth says.

"As is Knox bringing that asshole back into our lives," I argue.

I walk around the bench to act as the spotter for Ethan.

"What's your problem with Jax anyway?" Seth asks.

"He's just not someone I like to spend time with."

Seth tries to stop his smirk from forming, but I see it on his smug face anyway. Whatever is about to come out of his mouth, I'm not gonna like it.

"When I left, I heard music blaring from your apartment," Seth says. "Rian was leaving for work, and she mentioned that Jax likes to walk around naked."

I stare at him because this is Seth—he fucks around with people's heads all the time. He has to be joking.

"He-lllll… o?"

I glance down to see Ethan struggling to get the bar up. Seth hurries over to help, but between Ethan and I, we get the bar back on the hooks.

"So it's exactly what I thought then?" Seth picks up dumbbells.

"What?"

"This isn't about whatever beef happened between you and Jax years ago. This is about Rian." His cockiness grates on my nerves.

"Rian? What crack are you smoking?" I give Seth a what-the-fuck look that would make a lesser man piss himself.

"No crack. You're upset about Rian seeing Jax's schlong."

"No, I'm annoyed because I hate the asshole and I don't want to see his dick twenty-four seven."

Seth coughs out, "Bullshit."

Ethan doesn't say anything. Can he see how uncomfortable I am? That I'm trying my hardest to seem unfazed?

"Okay, so if Knox walked around naked all the time, you wouldn't have a problem with it?" I ask.

Seth huffs as he does some lateral raises. "I couldn't give a shit. Hell, I had to see his naked ass the other day when I walked in on him fucking Leilani on the couch. I just grabbed my chips from the kitchen and went to my room. The naked body isn't something to be ashamed about."

Him and his fucking mouth.

"Come on. Why the hell would you move in with them otherwise? Time to face the facts," Seth says.

I sit on the bench. "You're delusional."

"I don't think I am. We're your friends. Why would you be embarrassed to have a thing for Rian?"

The noose around my neck winds tighter and tighter, making it hard to swallow. "I wouldn't be embarrassed to have a thing for Rian—if I actually did. I love her the same as you both do. Because she's our friend and for her killer baking skills."

Seth nods like, 'yeah right.'

Ethan acts as if he's concentrating on the reps, but his glimpses at me say he's trying to decipher exactly how I feel about Rian.

"Just mind your own business and worry about your stalker," I say.

Seth throws his towel at me and we continue our workout without any more talk of stalkers or women who can bake.

LATER THAT NIGHT, after a dead night at Ink Envy, I walk into the apartment to find a half-eaten cake. Jax comes out of the bathroom, a towel around his waist.

"Clothes aren't optional around here," I say.

He spots me eyeing the cake. "She's a great baker, huh? Lemon is my favorite."

"Lemon?" I mumble. "I fucking hate lemon."

He puts his hand on my shoulder. "Oh shit, am I already taking your place?" He chuckles and stalks off to his room.

Rian knows I hate lemon. Why would she bake that?

CHAPTER THREE

Rian

I sit at the kitchen table, working away and waiting for my cinnamon muffins to finish baking. The paperwork from the Mathematical Society of America sits on the counter like a puppy starved for attention.

What would I do if I won the money? I don't think I'd go back to school. My mom texted me twice this morning, asking if I've started the problem. She's fooling herself if she thinks she wants me to win for me. She wants me to win because Johann has beat me at everything our entire lives.

A key in the door startles me and I bury my head in my project. Fractions are a bitch for kids to learn and the recipients of this textbook will be lucky if I don't take out my frustration by making them harder.

"Hey, Rian," Jax says.

I blow out a relieved breath into my papers.

"Were you expecting a burglar?" His arms slide out of his jacket and he hangs it on the hook by the door.

I take a moment to soak him in, see him in my space. We only met briefly the other morning, so it still kind of feels as if a stranger lives with me. Even so, he's not the one I was worried was going to walk through that door. But I can't be honest about that with Jax.

I stand and bury my head in the fridge. "No. I was working, and you startled me when you came in."

"Grab me a beer while you're in there?" he asks. The sound of chair legs sliding along our wooden floor rings out.

I twist off the top of a beer and hand it to him.

"My own personal waitress. I could get used to this." He grins.

I sit back down. "Don't get your hopes up."

He sips his beer, his gaze on me the entire time he rests the bottle on his lips and lowers it back down. I glance up a few times.

"So what's your story?" he asks. His approach leaves something to be desired, but he seems genuinely interested in the answer, based on the fact that his eyes haven't strayed anywhere but my face.

I place my pencil down and lean back in my seat. "What do you want to know?"

"Anything you want to offer."

He sips his beer again. Most women would probably be drooling from having Jax's attention. His dark hair and five o'clock shadow, the definition of the muscles in his arms—it all works to make him more than appealing. So although it feels nice, it's obligatory. We're sharing a bathroom now.

"I write math textbooks for elementary grade levels," I say.

He nods and sips his beer. "So you're like genius level, or math just gets you all excited?"

"Definitely not genius level." My gaze veers to the stack of papers by my purse, where the contract for the contest sits.

"You probably got some perfect score on that ASS test," he says.

I giggle. "You mean SAT or ACT?"

"Whatever." He shrugs. "I never took it."

"Why not?" I relax back into my chair and push my work to the side.

He downs another gulp of his beer. "I wasn't meant for college. That shit only gave Phillips a hard-on."

I nod, not sure if I should ask more questions or not.

"Boyfriend?" he asks.

At first, I think the question is rude, but mostly because my two good friends are now in serious relationships, which makes me wonder if I'm going to end up as a cat lady cliché. But I'm allergic to cat hair, so I'd have to be a bird lady or fish woman. Which sounds even worse. I imagine myself in a tank while my fish swim around my head or having birds resting along the lengths of my arms, their tiny claws digging into my skin, and I shudder.

"No boyfriend."

"Really?" He tilts his head and one side of his lips tip up.

Heat rushes up my neck. "Yeah. Why?"

He shrugs. "I'm surprised Phillips hasn't locked you down yet."

"Locked me down? Next you'll be calling me someone's old lady." I place my pencil in the crack of the book to keep my place and close it.

He laughs and tips the mouth of his beer in my direction.

"I think you can probably think of a nicer way to say that?"

He chuckles. "You're one of those, huh?"

"So far I'd say we're not on the best of terms with your word choices." I don't mean anything horrible, I'm mostly joking, but I don't believe anyone is going to "lock me down."

"I didn't mean any offense, I'm just surprised. You're hot in that innocent schoolgirl way. Makes me want to make you all dirty."

I open my mouth, but nothing comes out. No one has ever said anything like that to me. I never thought I was the type of girl who would get turned on by it, but my core aches with his words.

"There must be something wrong with Phillips. How long have the two of you known each other?"

I shrug. "A few years."

He nods, his gaze dipping to my cleavage. I shouldn't like the way his eyes almost sear the clothes from my body. I have no doubt he's envisioning me naked right now. I shouldn't like it, but I do.

I've found myself feeling like a wanton woman about as often in my life as I've found myself the winner of the lottery. Which is to say never. I always ended up in that middle ground.

"And you guys have never…"

We both know what he's asking.

"That would be none of your business." Luckily the oven buzzer goes off, so I have a reason to excuse myself from this conversation.

"So you write math equations and bake. Those are your turn-ons?"

I pull the muffins out of the oven and place them on top of the stove. "They aren't my turn-ons. I just enjoy baking."

"Ah, but not the math? Good girl has a secret."

I whip my head in his direction. His cocky smirk says he's already figured me out.

"I think it's time we shift the focus of our conversation to you."

He twirls his beer bottle in circles on the table, following my movements as I transfer the muffins from the pan to the cooling rack.

"Name is Jax Owens. I'm a tattoo artist. Grew up in New York City. Once I turned eighteen, I aged out of the foster care system and got the fuck outta Dodge as fast as a criminal who slipped his cuffs before being thrown in jail. Right now, I need some calm from my chaotic life. So here I am."

I lean against the counter. "What's so chaotic about your life?"

"People following me on Instagram. Everyone wanting something. You're not from my world, but I'm kind of a big deal."

I laugh but stop once his eyes meet mine. "Conceited much?"

"It's not conceited when it's fact. Why do you think Phillips hates me so much?"

"I didn't know he hated you." I'm lying, but I can't help but feel like Dylan's bodyguard and I don't like people putting words in his mouth. I have no idea why Dylan dislikes Jax.

"He does. I'm everything he wanted to be, but Winnie forced him to take one of those tests and attend college."

I say nothing. The selfish part of me wants Jax to fill in all the blanks I have about Dylan's past, because Dylan always has a way of dodging personal questions.

"The bastard got lucky with that painting."

I nod because that is something I know about Dylan's past. The painting Dylan sold in order to start Ink Envy. No one except for Ethan has ever seen it. I wonder if Jax has though.

"Talent isn't luck," I say.

He smirks, his gaze falling down my body. "You don't

have to stick up for him. He knows as well as I do that he got fucking lucky."

"Maybe by finding the right buyer, but someone would have purchased it eventually."

"So you've seen it?" Jax asks.

I place a cinnamon muffin on a plate and slide it over to him.

"Distraction by sweets. I'll take that as a no." He unwraps the muffin and chomps down.

"Are you two going to be able to play nice?" I ask, putting the muffin pan in the sink and turning on the water before adding soap.

"I don't play nice, but I do play fair." He winks and takes another healthy bite of the muffin.

"Just get along, respect each other's things, and we'll be good." I turn around and wash the muffin pan.

A minute later, the chair legs slide along the hardwood floor again. He throws the balled-up muffin wrapper into the garbage in the cupboard to my right. Then his hands land on either side of me, caging me to the sink. "Let me ask you something, square root girl, are you Team Phillips?"

Shivers rise up my neck. "I'm no one's team." My voice doesn't hold the conviction it should.

"I guess we'll see about that." He pushes off the counter. "You should make some pie," he says while walking toward his bedroom.

I look over my shoulder at him. "Why?"

He turns around in the middle of the room. "Because I'd love to eat your pie."

His smirk deepens and his gaze flows up and down my body once more with the scorching heat of a thousand flames. He walks into his bedroom and shuts the door just as the front door opens.

Dylan stands in the doorway like a German Shepherd

who just found his scent after searching for miles. His gaze meets mine then travels to Jax's closed bedroom door and wanders back to me. "Why are you so red? Is it too hot in here?"

I swallow past the dry lump in my throat. "No. I just took muffins out of the oven."

Dylan drops his stuff by the door and beelines it to the muffins. "Hot muffins? My favorite?"

He takes one, pulling the top off first like he does with cupcakes. He eats it then goes to take off his jacket but stops with half the muffin in his mouth and one arm out of his jacket. I'm too busy processing Jax's pie comment to wonder why he stopped.

By the time Dylan clears his throat after finishing the muffin, he holds a stack of papers in his hands. "What's this?"

"Nothing." I step forward, reaching for the papers, but he puts his hand on my head like an older sibling would to their younger one keeping me at arm's length. "Dylan!" I scold, my arms frantically reaching.

"A math problem?" He continues reading. "Shit. Twenty-five K?" He stares at me without releasing my head. "You're doing this?"

"No. I don't know. My mom…" I blow out a breath and give up the fight.

He releases my head and sits at the table. "You don't know? You totally should." He flips the pages, reading through the contract. "You haven't signed yet?"

I shake my head, falling into the chair next to him.

He throws down the papers and bends down to untie his boots. "Why?"

I shrug.

"Scared?"

"No."

He cocks his eyebrow.

I sigh. "I'm not scared about whether I can do it. I'm scared about what happens if I succeed."

"That makes sense."

I look at him. How does he understand what I was saying? Surely, he's never had the pressure and expectations my parents put on me. If I succeed, they'll only expect more.

"The prize is pretty awesome though. You could do a lot with it." He stands, hooking his fingers in his boots so they hang off his fingers. "Like open a bakery or something." He raises his eyebrows and disappears into his room.

My head falls to the table and I blow out a long pent-up breath of frustration. This roommate situation is ridiculous. One guy treats me like he's my big brother and protects me, pushing me like a best friend would to do something I'm scared of. The other guy makes crude comments that make me hot and horny. The latter would be great if he was the guy I was into.

CHAPTER FOUR

Dylan

I return from the gym, my legs burning from too many squats. I'll still be there tomorrow though because the gym is my excuse to get out of the apartment before anyone else is awake. Rian is a creature of habit and her alarm goes off at the exact same time every day. I wake up fifteen minutes before, giving me ample time to go to the bathroom, brush my teeth, and grab my gym bag. When I return, she's already left for work. Perfect plan really.

Until today—when I walk in after my workout to find Jax at the kitchen table in his boxers, his head in a bowl of cereal. Damn it. He usually sleeps later than this.

I'm about to bypass him to hit the shower then spend the day at Ink Envy when he slides a piece of paper toward me. My footsteps stop, but I don't pick it up.

"It's from Rian," he says.

I swoop up the piece of paper, knowing he's already read it.

Roommate dinner tonight. We're all cooking something. Initial next to your item.

Rian's initials are next to dessert and Jax's are next to meat.

"I'm left with vegetables?" I ball up the note and toss it onto the table.

"Come on, Phillips, you know I've got all the meat Rian needs." He laughs as I slam my door.

I'm not in the mood to deal with his bullshit. I strip off my shirt and grab my towel, walking back out to the main living area.

Jax is walking back to his room, so we come face to face. Both of us are shirtless, leaving the compass tattoo on the left side of his chest visible. His eyes zero in on the anchor on my left pec. At sixteen, we had them done together, for each other. I was supposed to anchor down his wild streak, and he was supposed to push me to explore and take more chances. Unfortunately, no one could tame Jax, and my obligation to Winnie kept me from seeing the world. I'm happy with where life took me so far, but I wonder if Jax feels the same.

His gaze meets mine. "Maybe you should work out twice a day." He smirks and side-steps me.

"Some of us own our own business. Well, one of us anyway," I say.

He laughs and shuts his door.

I shake my head. He's not worth the aggravation. Never has been.

Lucky for me, after I shower and get dressed, Jax is nowhere in sight.

On the elevator ride down, I retrieve my phone from my

pocket in order to text Rian.

Me: *What's up with this roommate dinner?*

The three dots appear immediately, as they usually do. She's never one to leave you hanging. It's one of the best things about her.

Rian: *Because we need to set some rules in order to get along. This whole everyone ignoring everyone thing isn't going to work.*

Me: *I'll let the other guys know.*

Rian: *No you won't.*

Rian: *It's just us.*

Rian: *The three of us.*

I send a gif of a man rolling on the floor in a tantrum.

Rian: *Funny. But still happening. See you tonight.*

I pocket my phone and walk across the street, then unlock the door of Ink Envy. My favorite part of the day is coming here in the morning when it's quiet. Sometimes I still can't believe it's mine. Walking by the stations of all the tattoo artists who want to work for me feels surreal. Heading to the back, I go to my office because I have paperwork to do that I've been putting off.

I boot up my computer then spot a note from Frankie on my desk.

I'll be out for a while. Call you when I can.

I crumple the note and toss it into the trash can. Seems I don't like any notes I receive today. I was hoping to ask Frankie for some advice about Rian.

Instead of worrying about all the bullshit that will surely go down tonight, I bury my head in the part of this business I hate—the actual business bullshit.

After an hour of recording expenses, I review last month's numbers. There's no way last month took a loss. I inch up closer as if I'm eighty and can't see the glaring red number on my computer screen that's blinking like a stoplight at two in the morning.

I knew things had been slow. Frankie was out more than usual, and let's face it, when I lost Mad Max, he took one helluva following with him to New York City. Not that I blame him for wanting to make it big. Cliffton Heights isn't where you make a name for yourself in the tattoo industry. Although I do have some clients who come from pretty far away for me and Frankie specifically, most of our customers are from neighboring towns.

Without Mad Max and Frankie working, I'm not making a cut of their jobs which has clearly hit my bottom line.

I press my palms to the edge of the desk and push myself back. The wheels of my chair slide until it hits the wall. What the fuck can I do? I need to get another artist in here.

Pulling out my phone, I scan Instagram for a newbie in the tat world who's trying to make a name for him or herself. The first artist to pop up is Jax, so I click off my phone and toss it onto the desk.

One thing's for sure—I'd better do something, otherwise I'm not making bills next month. The worst thing you can do in this industry is not have a functioning space for your artists to work in. Might as well lock your doors.

~

HOOBASTANK PLAYS on the other side of the door, which means Jax is already home. Rian is more of a country music girl.

I put my hand on the doorknob and stand there for a second. Rian's right—we can't live like this until Jax decides Cliffton Heights isn't for him. Since high school, he usually cut ties every four months from wherever he's living at least. We don't have to be best friends, but we can keep it civil.

All the kumbaya shit in my head dies when the door opens and I find Jax licking batter off of Rian's finger.

Her head shoots my way, eyes wide like I caught her doing something wrong. Jax's Cheshire Cat grin is obvious even with his lips wrapped around her finger. My jaw aches from clenching.

"Don't let me interrupt." I hold up my hands and walk through the living room toward my bedroom.

"You're not interrupting. Jax was just joking around," Rian says, but I'm already at my bedroom door.

"Let me know when you two are done, and I'll do my vegetables."

I kick the door shut and throw my bag on the bed. When I hook my phone to my radio, Papa Roach's "Scars" plays, since that's what I was listening to at Ink Envy. For a moment, I calm myself down, pissed I showed any cards to that fucker by slamming the door. I can already picture his cocky smirk waiting for me when I open that door again.

Not much has changed since high school with Jax and me. We listen to the same music, we're almost like the same person. Hell, even down to being into the same girl.

I gotta get a grip though, because Rian isn't Naomi. She's not even close to being mine. She's a grown woman who can protect herself. My reaction is just from the stress of the store. The underlying worry that I'm going to lose everything I've worked so hard to achieve.

Might as well get this roommate dinner over with. I leave the seclusion of my bedroom and thank God that it's only Rian in the kitchen.

She turns around, her blonde hair pulled back into a messy ponytail. She's wearing the apron I got her last Christmas. I still remember the blush that crawled across her skin when she read, "Warning: spooning will lead to forking."

"You okay?" she asks.

I hate that question. I've probably been asked that same question five million times in my life. It was part of the social worker's handbook. When they come to get you because you're not wanted, they lay their hands on your shoulders as they bend over to get face to face. Always the same question —are you okay?

"I'm good. Just didn't want to interrupt." I pull out the vegetables I picked up at lunch and ran up here to put in the fridge.

"You're not interrupting. You just happened to walk in when he was trying out my batter."

"Where is he anyway?" I ask.

"He's gone up to the roof to heat the grill up."

I eye her like she can cut the bullshit. "You like him?" Grabbing the cutting board, I place it on the counter and open the drawer with the knives.

"I barely know him."

I wash the lettuce, peeling back the bad layers. "He's not the ever-after type. He's not like Adrian or Ethan."

She says nothing, and when I look up from the sink, the kindness that usually radiates off her isn't there. "Who said I want that?"

I chop the lettuce as a distraction. Rian isn't a one-night-only kinda girl. She might think she could do it, but she can't.

"Are you going to answer my question?"

I scoop up the lettuce and put it into a bowl, ready to peel the carrots, but Rian's already doing that for me. She thinks I'm incapable of doing shit, which is why she always does it for me. "Even if you want a quick fuck, do you really think your new roommate is the best choice?"

She peels the carrots more forcefully now, the scraps falling into the sink at record pace. "I'm not sure that's any of your business."

"I'm your friend. It's my business."

She hands me a carrot, and I slice it into coins.

"Friends offer advice. They don't tell someone what to do." She buries her head in the fridge, grabbing the salad dressings.

The knife drops from my hand and I lean against the counter to face her. She turns around and startles.

"You'll be wasting your time with Jax."

She shakes the salad dressing and her gaze slowly rises to meet mine. "How do you know? Maybe I'm the one who changes him. Or maybe he wants someone like me. I get that I'm not what you'd consider in your league, what with me not having any tattoos or piercings, but can you really speak for a guy you haven't talked to in almost a decade?" She puts the dressings on the table, a little harder than necessary, and grabs the salad bowl from behind me.

My shoulders slump. "You're right."

"What?" she snips.

I've never seen Rian this mad.

"Anyone would be lucky to have you. Just be careful." I grip her shoulder and take the asparagus out of the fridge. "I'm going to grill this up on the roof. I'll be back."

Leaving the apartment, I rest my back against the door for a moment before heading up to the roof. The last person I want to sit down and share a meal with is Jax. Rian's the only person I'd put myself through torture for.

CHAPTER FIVE

Rian

"What's for dinner?" Seth breezes into my apartment and sits at the table, his thumb and forefinger descending into the salad bowl.

I snatch the bowl away before he has a chance to grab anything. "Nope. Roommates only."

He looks over one shoulder then the other shoulder at the empty apartment. "I'm a roommate."

"No, you're a neighbor."

He mocks offense. "I've always thought of us all as roommates."

"You don't pay rent for this apartment."

"Speaking of, you stole one of my roommates. Do you know how many extra boudoir sessions I've had to do in order to pay my share of the rent? I'm almost desperate enough to hold a sign out on the sidewalk and dress up in a suit with a rose between my teeth."

I stare blankly at him.

He laughs. "Thankfully, Blanca is giving me some free-lance work."

"I hadn't heard anything about that?" I sit down.

Poor Seth's journey toward his dream career of photography has been hard. Not horribly difficult—the man gets to see half naked women every day—but he complains about it nonstop.

"She and Ethan are doing that blog thing or whatever. She's asked me to take some landscape shots of New York City."

I grab his hand. "Thanks, great."

He shrugs. "It's something and keeps me from having to take over my parents' bagel shop for a little while longer."

"I haven't stopped in lately. How is Mama Andrews?" I stand and grab him a beer from the fridge, then I open a bottle of wine because as long as Jax and Dylan don't throw one another off the roof, dinner should be ready soon.

"Don't get me started." He sips his beer. "She asked me if I'd take pictures of her for my dad." His head falls to the table.

I purse my lips in an attempt not to laugh. His mom is very into having an active sex life and isn't afraid to talk to her son about it. I struggle to pull the cork from the bottle of wine. "What did you say?"

"What do you think? Hell. No. Then she asked if any of my coworkers would do it."

"Oh, that's reasonable."

Seth waves me over and I hand him the bottle. He pops the cork out with ease. "No, it's not. Why would I want my coworker to see my mom half naked, puckering her lips for the camera?"

I laugh and he can't help but laugh too.

"Yeah, my life is a fucking joke. My mom is worried about turning on my dad and my brother is AWOL again."

"Oh, Seth."

He shakes his head like he doesn't want to talk about it, but the way he pushes the half-drank beer to the middle of the table says he's worried about his brother.

I don't know much about his brother, other than that he disappears now and then. I think it has something to do with drinking or drugs. Seth only mentions it in passing and every time he does, he brushes the topic away before we can really talk about it.

The door to the apartment opens and we both look over.

"The girl put her finger in my petroleum jelly container and smeared it on her lips," Dylan says.

"Fuck, I'm guessing you gave it to her?" Jax asks.

"Yeah, but I charged her for it. I mean, use some common sense. Do you want an infection?"

I stare dumbfounded as the two of them walk in like they're best friends. Even Seth's eyes are bouncing between me and them.

"Shit, those steaks look good," Seth says, his eyes wide like one of those cartoons where the ribeye is hanging off a fork in front of the dog.

"Thanks. Want to join us? I got plenty." Jax places the plate in the middle of the table.

"Nope. Seth has to get home to Knox. This is a room-mate-only dinner," I say.

Dylan slides the asparagus onto the table and picks up a stalk, chomping down. "Sorry, dude, I'll leave the scraps at your door." He winks.

Seth sighs, stands from the chair, leaving his beer behind. "No need. I'm gonna convince Knox to get his dick out of Leilani long enough to go to dinner. You realize I'm the only single one now besides all of you, right?" His shoulders slouch and he exaggerates walking to the door like a child.

Dylan and Jax glance at me. I hadn't really thought about that. Blanca and Ethan, Sierra and Adrian, Knox and Leilani. Seth shoots a pair of pathetic eyes over his shoulder one last time when he reaches the door.

"Jesus," Dylan says.

"Let the guy stay, Rian," Jax says.

"Fine. But you're not to talk."

Seth straightens and smiles, walking back over and picking his beer up off the table. "I feel like I should've contributed something." He digs his hand in his pocket and pulls out some business cards. "Here. Free bagel for everyone."

The cards are for Andrews Bagels. He passes them out like a grandpa does butterscotch candies.

"Jeez, thanks. I'll add this to the stack in my room." Dylan pockets it.

I shove mine in the drawer with the others we've gotten in the past.

Jax examines it. "This is your place?"

Seth swallows his sip of beer. "My parents."

"I was at the Bagel Place this morning. They have a hot girl working there. Is there a hot girl at Andrews Bagels? You might be able to convince me to switch."

Dylan looks over his beer bottle at me and we share a look. The Ericksons own the Bagel Place. They're pretty much the Andrews' archenemies, which means Seth Andrews can never entertain the idea of Evan Erickson. Some of us think that upsets him to a degree, but we let him pretend the only thing he feels for her is hate.

Seth cuts his steak and the knife screeches across the plate. "Long dark curly hair?"

Jax's eyes light up. "Yeah. When she bent over to get me a

bagel…" He sticks his bent finger in his mouth and bites the knuckle.

Dylan and I share another look. I want him to be prepared to act in case Seth's knife dives toward Jax's throat.

"The two bagel places are competitors," I say in the hopes that Jax will read between lines.

His eyes only light up further. "Oh, I get it. So she's like an enemy of yours."

Seth shrugs, sawing into the steak again. "Andrews' bagels are better anyway."

Jax finally looks at Dylan and me and quirks an eyebrow. I don't know anything about Dylan and Jax's relationship, but they obviously have some sort of non-verbal conversation. Jax nods as if he's in the loop now.

"She's your Juliet?" Jax asks Seth.

"Owens." Dylan shakes his head.

Seth's gaze flies to Jax. "No. It's not like that."

"If you say so. You're cool if I hit on her then?" He winks at me.

Dylan growls over his forkful of salad.

"Why would I care?" Seth picks up the salad dressing and douses his salad with it. Not one piece of lettuce isn't covered with dressing.

"Cool." Jax nods, stabs the piece of meat he cut, and leans back in his chair while he chews, amused.

Dylan continues to shake his head.

"So, Jax, Knox says you're pretty famous?" Seth asks.

Dylan grunts again, stabbing at his lettuce.

"I wouldn't say famous, but I've made a name for myself."

"You're modest. Knox showed me all your Instagram followers."

"Really?" I pull out my phone and look him up on Instagram. "OMG, you're friends with all these celebrities?" I show Seth then Dylan.

Dylan never bothers to look up. Does he feel competitive with Jax? Duh, Rian. Of course he does. How do I feel about Johann? I place my phone screen-side down and pick my fork back up.

"We're acquaintances. None of them would take a bullet for me or anything." Jax eyes Dylan, who rolls his eyes.

"Super impressive," Seth says. "Maybe I'll go to you for my next piece."

He and Jax share a laugh since Dylan has yet to pick his head up from his plate. Dylan has done all three of Seth's tattoos.

"Yeah, I've always wanted to get one." I play along with the joke.

But this time, Dylan's head raises like I just announced there's a bullet coming right for him. He cocks his head to the side. "What?"

"I'll totally tattoo you. Do you have anything in mind?" Jax asks. "I've got an entire book of just chick tattoos."

"If you want a tattoo, I'll give you one," Dylan says softly, eyes focused only on me.

Jax holds his hands in the air. "Oh yeah, I'd hate to step on any toes."

"You live for stepping on fucking toes," Dylan says, looking him square in the eye.

My patience breaks. This dinner was supposed to help us figure out how to coexist, but if anything, it's made it worse.

"Okay, this entire friendship-turned-hatred thing is driving me crazy. Can you please just tell me what the hell happened between the two of you so we can clear the air?" My eyes shift from Jax to Dylan and back to Jax.

"It's Phillips's problem, not mine." Jax shrugs and continues to eat.

"It's water under the bridge," Dylan mumbles.

"Bullshit," Seth coughs out.

I'll second Seth. I cannot continue to live with all this animosity. My fork slams down on the table and all three of their heads pop up. Jax doesn't look as surprised as Dylan and Seth, but then again, Jax doesn't know me well. Which, sad to say, I kind of like.

"Talk." I lean back and cross my arms.

Dylan wipes his mouth. "It's shit from high school. I'm over it if he is."

Jax scoffs. "I came here willingly. Do you really think Knox didn't tell me you were here or that I didn't know Ink Envy was yours? Clearly, the problem isn't mine."

"It's pretty obvious you like to get under Dylan's skin," I say.

Jax laughs and rolls his eyes. "You need Rian to do your talking, Phillips?"

"Hell no, but I don't control her."

Seth looks as happy as a child watching Tom Brady and Peyton Manning throw a football back and forth.

"She's right though. You haven't been Mary fucking Poppins since you got here." Dylan pushes away from the table, rising, and grabs another beer out of the fridge.

"Why would I be nice? You act like I'm Jack the Ripper!" Jax yells.

Maybe this was a bad idea.

"I'll have a bee—" Seth raises his finger, but Dylan shuts the fridge and sits back down. "Never mind."

"Because I know how you are and things around here don't work that way." Dylan unscrews the top, flicking it into the garbage can and makes it.

"Don't act like you know me. We haven't talked in years. You have no idea who the fuck I am now."

I look at Seth. His eyes widen and he stands, holding his arms out toward both of them. Although neither of them have stood up, so they both look at him like he's a dumbass. "Let's just calm this down now."

"Sit down, Andrews," Dylan says. "I'm not going to fight him."

Could have fooled me.

Dylan stands and puts his plate in the sink, calmly finishes his beer, and tosses the bottle into the recycling container. Jax keeps one eye on Dylan the entire time. I'm so out of my league with these two. Am I going to come home one day to a crime scene?

"Thanks for trying, Rian, but our friendship died a long time ago." I open my mouth to respond, but Dylan keeps going. "And Owens, you stay out of my way and I'll stay out of yours. Got it?" Without waiting for a response, he grabs his keys and walks out the door.

"He's such an asshole." Jax heads toward his bedroom. "Thanks for planning the dinner, Rian. Sorry it's ruined." Then he shuts his bedroom door.

Seth and I look at one another. My gaze detours to the untouched chocolate-on-chocolate cake sitting on the counter. I pick it up and place it on the table between us. Seth's fork digs right in without me cutting a piece.

"Remind me to thank Knox for this," I say. Seth smiles at me over the cake. "Not." I dig my fork in the cake.

Chocolate cake always makes things better.

CHAPTER SIX

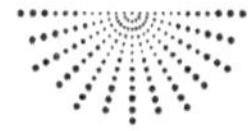

Dylan

 pack a change of clothes in my workout bag this morning because I need to head into the city afterward. But first, I scribble a letter to Rian to apologize for last night. She started the shower already, so I can slip it under her door and hightail it out of here.

I have no idea why I allow Jax to use up my last ounce of patience. What happened between us is so far in the past.

When I walk out of my bedroom, the kitchen is spotless as usual, so I notice the math problem on the table right away. I wonder what time she woke up to start working on it. I glance at it as I grab a water, but all the numbers and symbols and letters make no sense to me. Which shows how different Rian and I are. She's uber smart. The girl teachers loved and colleges begged for an application. Me, on the other hand, not so much.

Instead of sliding my note under her door, I decide to

stuff it in her book. Anyone who knows Rian knows that now that she's started, she'll be obsessing over this problem until she figures it out.

The shower turns off. That's my sign to leave, so I quietly open the apartment door and shut it behind me, turning to find Knox in the hallway.

"Shit, man." I grab my chest.

Knox is a big guy and intimidating at first glance. Plus, he holds that whole cop persona like "try me and see what happens."

He yawns. "Sorry, but I wasn't gonna miss out this time."

Like clockwork, Seth walks out of the apartment behind Knox while Ethan slowly shuts his apartment door down the hall, locking it behind him. We all look like shit—our hair up in different directions, except for Knox, who wears a baseball hat.

"Extra big bag there," Ethan says as we file into the elevator.

"I'm heading to the city after," I say.

No one says anything, but Seth shoots me a look like, "you're going to have to talk about your outburst yesterday at some point."

"Where you headed?" Knox asks after we're on the bottom level, as though his brain isn't working at full speed yet.

"The neighborhood. I need to find another artist for the shop."

We begin the short walk toward the gym, Knox and me in front with Seth and Ethan behind us.

"What about Jax? I get the history and shit, but he'd be good for Ink Envy," Knox says.

He isn't wrong. If I could tolerate Jax for more than a nanosecond, I'd ask him to come on for the short interim he'll be in Cliffton Heights. But no matter how much I love Ink Envy, I cannot work around him.

I shake my head and Knox blows out a long breath. "You gotta get over it, man."

"What exactly does he have to get over?" Seth's head pushes between our shoulders.

I turn to put my hand on his face and push him back. "Nothing."

"That's like physical abuse, dude," Seth says from behind me.

Ethan mumbles something and they both laugh. I have no interest in dealing with their shit.

"For your information, I am over it. He's the one who showed up with a chip on his shoulder."

Knox's gaze holds steady on me for a moment as he opens the door for us to enter the gym. "We both know that's not all of it. You guys were like brothers. There has to be a way to find your way back there, and I think him working at Ink Envy is a great start."

Seth and Ethan walk in, and I stop as we dig out our cards to scan in. "Hell will freeze over, pigs will fly, and Seth will nail Evan before we're ever like brothers again."

"Why are you bringing me into this?" Seth asks, handing his card to the girl at the front desk. "Just FYI, Evan is a girl," he whispers to her.

She looks at him like, "whatever, guy, keep moving." After scanning my card, she hands it to me, and I stuff it back into my wallet.

"You're being a stubborn jackass."

I ignore Knox.

I'm quiet the entire workout. Ethan and Knox talk about all the sex they're getting while Seth groans that there are no available women in Cliffton Heights. I want to call him out on his bullshit. There's just one woman in Cliffton Heights who isn't available to him and that's what he's pissed about.

But I can't very well cast stones when I'm living life in a glass house myself right now, so I keep my mouth shut.

❧

THE TRAIN IS ABOUT to pull away from the station when I arrive, so I use my last reserve of energy after my workout to chase it down. Lucky for me, I catch it, but the conductor gives me a nasty look. Like I give a shit.

My footsteps halt when I enter the train cab. I was going to use this hour and a half to nap. Now that's not going to happen. Not that I'm complaining.

"Rian," I say.

She looks up from whatever she's reading, her smile immediate. No one can put me in a better mood than Rian. Maybe because she always seems happy to see me.

"What are you doing here?"

"I could ask you the same thing." I sit down in the seat across from her.

She shuts that math book, the same one I saw on the table this morning, and holds my note. "Thanks for the apology."

"I shouldn't have reacted that way," I say.

"No. I shouldn't have pushed the two of you. It's none of my business." Her smile dims.

I owe her an explanation. I get that everyone wants to know the story of me and Jax, but it's embarrassing, which is the only reason I'm not open to share.

"Do you mind?" I nod at the empty space beside her.

She slides closer to the window. "No."

I place my duffle bag between my feet on the floor. She's wearing jeans and a jacket, her gray hat with the giant pom-pom on it still on her head. Spring will hopefully arrive soon.

"Where are you getting off?" I ask, losing the nerve to tell her about all the shit with Jax.

"The city. I have a brunch with"—she lifts the math book in her lap—"Johann Frederickson."

"Sounds like quite the intellectual," I say.

She giggles. "He's the guy my parents constantly compare me to." She rolls her eyes, looks out the window for a second, then sets her gaze on me. "Whose child is smarter? That's all my parents and his parents talk about. They're not obvious about it—that would be uncouth. It's all done covertly with a comment here, a comment there. I feel bad because my parents got the short end of the stick—Johann is way smarter than me."

I pat her thigh. "Not possible."

She laughs, but it doesn't make my heart warm. There's something off. "Johann is a math professor at Columbia. He went to an Ivy League college while I was at NYU. He's already working on his doctorate and I never even considered getting mine, much to my parents' disappointment. He's single, but I am too, so that doesn't really hold weight in their arguments. That's why my parents want me to win this contest, because it'll prove something to them."

One thing I've always liked about Rian is her way of laying out her cards like a treasure map. There's no gold or jewels hidden layers deep in the sand. There's no game with her.

"How come I've never heard of this guy?" I ask, wondering if Johann looks like his name suggests.

"Because he's not my friend. I think he secretly likes that our parents banter back and forth about who's better. I don't much care for him. He's egotistical and a jackass, truthfully."

"Then why are you having brunch with him?"

A blush fills her cheeks. A clear sign there's more to this

little brunch. "I wanted to get into his condo and see if he has any notes."

My mouth opens. "You're going to cheat?"

She's quick to shake her head. "No. I just want to see if I even stand a chance."

I tilt my head. This is so not like her. Maybe I put Rian too high up on the morals platform, but I'm more likely than her to be a cheater. She's pure. "Where's your phone?"

She narrows her eyes but retrieves her phone from her bag. I grab it, and she allows me to thumb through her phone to retrieve his contact.

I hand the phone back to her. "Cancel the brunch."

"What? No." She holds the phone and glances at his name.

"Rian, you won't be able to live with yourself if you go through with this plan. We both know it."

She opens her mouth but quickly shuts it.

"You know I'm right. Plus, you're the smartest person I know. You can solve this problem and grab that prize well before him."

"The problem is impossible. I've tried and—"

"You wouldn't even feel good about winning if you cheated to get the right answer." I grip her thigh and shake her leg.

Her shoulders slump and she nods. "I'm just going to disappoint them."

I've met Mr. and Mrs. Wright once. They came to the apartment on a surprise visit, so Rian wasn't able to shuffle all of us away. They took one look at me, all four eyes slowly perusing me from head to toe, and it was clear—I wasn't what they liked for their daughter, even as an acquaintance.

"Who the hell cares? You have a job, you're self-sufficient. What do you still need from them?" My voice is angrier than normal, and Rian's wide eyes say I've surprised her.

She glances out the window, watching the landscape breeze past. "I'll never be enough."

I fucking hate that she feels that way. It makes me want to dial up Mr. and Mrs. Wright and tell them how much they've fucked up their daughter and if they can't see how damn perfect she is, then they're the ones who need to have their IQ tested.

I put my arm around her shoulders, pulling her into my chest. The smell of her shampoo, which I've discovered since sharing a shower with her, hits my nostrils. I'm not sure if it's because we share an apartment now, but it feels like home. "You are enough. You're an amazing woman."

I pluck her phone from her hand and hammer out a text to Johann.

She sits up, seeing I canceled on her behalf. "Dylan!"

"Time for a Dylan and Rian day out, don't you think?"

Rian smiles as if I'm the keeper of her happiness. That look scares the shit out of me. I'm no one's keeper of happiness. I may hate Mr. and Mrs. Wright, but they're not wrong. I'm not who their daughter needs in her life. She can do much better than me.

CHAPTER SEVEN

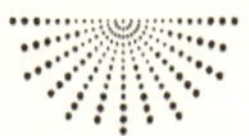

Rian

I probably need a support group. *Hello, I'm Rian, and I'm addicted to Dylan Phillips.* I'd tell my story of falling in love with a boy who will surely break my heart without ever knowing he did. The problem is that just like any addiction, there's only one thing you can do to keep clean—abstinence. The fact that I just agreed to spend the day with Dylan is the complete opposite of what I should do.

He takes me to a bagel place to kill time. It's his favorite, and I see why—though I'd never admit that to Seth.

At eleven o'clock, we approach a tattoo parlor near NYU, my old stomping grounds.

"I remember this place," I say, nostalgia hitting me. Sierra always had at least two reservations here that she canceled last minute.

"Yeah?"

"I've never been inside, but a lot of the students came

here." I glance down the street at some bars that I only went to when Sierra dragged me out. Rarely did I not have my mind solely on my grades.

"I worked here," he says. "Too bad you never came in. We'd have been friends way before."

Truth is, I remember seeing the artists and customers smoking outside. I'd put my head down and walk by, trying not to be seen. At the time, those people seemed so sure of themselves and comfortable in their own skin. That quality has always scared me. Probably because I never felt the same.

I stare at Dylan, his bright smile directed at me with his hand on the door. "Yeah, too bad I didn't."

He opens the door and allows me to walk in first.

The guy behind the counter looks me up and down, raised eyebrows to why I'm standing in front of him. "Can I help you? I'm going to start my day with tattooing a fucking flower, aren't I?"

He's intimidating just like when I was in college. Tall, big, and tatted from neck to collar, short sleeves to wrist. His blue eyes are amazing though, and I lose myself for a second.

"Phillips?" he says, his smile growing wide and welcoming when he notices Dylan at my side. He comes around the counter and the two of them hug, each hitting the others back harder and harder until they back up from one another.

"What's up, Big Man?" Dylan says.

I can see how the nickname fits. The guy has a few inches on Dylan and a lot of mass.

"She yours?" Big Man eyes me, his gaze once again flowing over my body like I couldn't possibly be with Dylan.

Bingo, Big Man.

"She's my roommate. Rian, this is Big Man," he introduces me.

The guy puts his hand out in front of me and almost bows. "You can call me Brian."

"Hey, Brian."

He studies me for a second, and I shift my weight from one foot to the other, releasing his hand.

"Virgin skin, am I right?" Brian asks.

Dylan smiles at me.

"Yes," I say, forced to answer so I'm not impolite.

"And when she wants one, I'll be the one doing it," Dylan says.

Big Man holds up his hands, laughing. "No worries, I get enough virgin canvas around here."

He walks to their waiting area and sits on the couch, holding his arm out for the two of us to follow him.

"Yeah, Rian graduated from NYU," Dylan says.

"And I never converted you then?" Big Man shakes his head like I do when I'm trying to solve the damn math problem.

"Sorry." I shrug.

He laughs. "As long as Phillips got you, I'm cool. I just hate when virgin skin goes to some asshole who will tattoo their neck before their ankle or wrist or some shit."

"Truth," Dylan says.

I had no idea there were rules in tattooing.

"So what's this visit about? Especially so bright and early." Big Man puts his ankle on his knee, and leans back in his chair.

"I'm in need of a fresh artist."

Big Man tilts his head. "Cliffton Heights suffering?"

Dylan briefly glances at me, but I pretend not to notice. "Nah. Never, but Mad Max moved on and I need to replace him."

Big Man taps his Vans. "I heard a rumor that Jax is back." His eyebrows raise in question.

Dylan inhales through his nose. "You of all people know that will never work."

"He's your best bet. All I got are people who can make a college kid happy. Ink Envy is different, you know that."

"I was hoping you might know someone up and coming," Dylan says.

Brian shakes his head. "Nah, not at the moment. Most of the people I've come across are just wannabes who watched a few YouTube videos and practiced on an orange, know what I'm sayin'?"

"Yeah, I get it. Not real artists." Disappointment rings in Dylan's voice.

"Exactly."

"If anyone comes to mind, send them my way, yeah?" Dylan asks, standing.

"I don't know a lot who'd be willing to go out to the country." Brian laughs. Dylan pretends he's going to hit him, but they end up doing that man hug again. "But we both know people will go out there for Jax. You should do it even if it's temporary."

Dylan shakes it off like he doesn't agree.

Brian turns to me. "And you're welcome any time." He holds his hand out to me and I shake it. "Although I do have to refuse your virgin skin. Dylan's claimed it, I suppose." He acts as if that's a big loss.

I laugh and Dylan's hand finds mine. Even Brian looks down and a shit-eating grin appears on his face. We leave the tattoo place and walk down the road toward the subway station before he releases my hand.

"Why won't you just hire Jax?" I ask. It's the million-dollar question because it'd surely help out his business. "You love Ink Envy. Do it for the company."

"It's not that easy." He runs his hand through his dark hair.

A few college girls walk by and snicker to one another

about Dylan. At least I'm not the only one who wants to climb him like a tree today.

"I just spilled all my family shit on you."

He looks at me from the corner of his eyes. "Up for a field trip?"

"I thought we were already on one?"

We continue walking as he laughs. "Today's destination is to visit the part of the city that fucked up Dylan Phillips. You in?"

Am I ever. "I'm in."

He doesn't smile—if anything, he looks nauseated—but we head to the subway, and once again, he pays for me. Which makes me get all swoony.

Come on, Rian, it's a train fare, not a romantic dinner for two.

"JUST STAY CLOSE TO ME, OKAY?" His voice is hard and lacking any type of affection.

We're in his old neighborhood. Needless to say, it's very different from where I grew up. The concrete buildings are all decorated with graffiti, and homeless people line the sidewalk.

"So, you and Jax and Knox all grew up here?" I ask.

"Yeah."

My heart sinks to my stomach. This wasn't an easy place to grow up. The lack of anything green and alive pulls on my heart.

We walk by a high-rise apartment. Some guys are hanging out by the doors, and others are playing a basketball game across the street.

"That's where Jax and I grew up." He turns me by putting his hands on my shoulders to face a building kitty-corner to us. "That's where Naomi Jennings lived."

I nod though I don't understand. "Who is Naomi Jennings?"

"The wedge that came between Jax and me."

He signals with his head for us to walk. "Winnie, my foster mom, took me in my freshman year and Jax our junior year. I already knew Jax before then because we went to the same school, ran in the same circle. We were both foster kids and had been thrown together a few times when we were younger."

No wonder they can still have non-verbal conversations across a table like they did last night.

"The first day Jax moved in with Winnie, I thought it would be cool to live together. I think that's a big part of the reason Winnie agreed to take him in. Jax was labeled as a troublemaker. Technically, we both were, but Winnie got me under control, so they thought they could give her the tougher cases, I suppose."

The farther we walk, the farther we move away from all the concrete. There's some grass, but most of it is still recovering from the long winter.

"Jax had a giant chip on his shoulder from day one. He constantly called me momma's boy, which pissed me off because although I loved Winnie, she wasn't my mom. And Jax knew that all I knew about my parents was that they didn't want me. He, on the other hand..." Dylan stops and looks at me. "Well, that's his story to tell."

I entwine my arm through his and lean my head on his shoulder because I feel like an idiot for complaining about my parents. Parents who only want me to succeed. They gave me shelter and food. Who cares that they gave me extra homework on top of my school requirements? I had parents who cared for me.

"Don't pity me," Dylan says in a low voice.

I remove my arm and stand up straight next to him. A rush of guilt hits me.

Dylan stops us on the street corner. "I'm sorry. I didn't mean to upset you, but I've had people pity me my whole life."

"I don't." Although I kind of do, I'll keep that to myself.

"I made a life for myself."

"You did, and you've done amazing."

He offers me a soft smile as I take the familiar role of his cheerleader. "I wouldn't have been able to get out if it wasn't for one person, and if you want to know the true reason Jax and I are where we are now, a lot of it has to do with her." He nods toward the cemetery across the street.

"Who?"

The light changes and we walk across, dodging the pedestrian traffic on the other side. When we come together again on the other side, we enter the small cemetery attached to a Catholic church. He's quiet as we walk a path through the rows of burial plots. This cemetery doesn't have huge granite headstones carved with quotes about their lives. There are no statues of angels or crosses. Everyone has a small rectangular marker with their name and birth and death dates.

He walks a path he definitely has memorized until he stops under a tree and shoves his hands into his pockets. "She's the one who helped me, and that's why Jax hates me the way he does."

My heart breaks as I read the name.

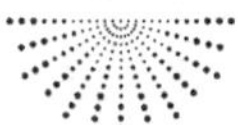

CHAPTER EIGHT

Dylan

Bringing Rian to Winnie's burial plot isn't what I had on the agenda today. I wanted us to have a fun day. But after another asshole brought up the problems between Jax and me, I knew I owed her some answers. Especially since she opened her chest and let her heart fall out on the train ride here.

"She died our senior year. I'd already aged out of the system, but she let me stay through graduation. Hell, she would've let me stay after too. But Jax was a month shy of aging out, so he had to go to another family." My mind floats back to that time. Jax and I were best friends, along with Knox, but we fought like brothers. "She left me her savings with the stipulation that I had to use it on myself to attend school."

I look at Rian and she nods.

"Jax went to a shitty house for his last month of high

school, but again, that's his story to tell." I've never told anyone Jax's story and I won't start now, even if our relationship is in disrepair.

She nods again. "I thought it was whoever that Naomi girl is who came between you?"

My head whips in her direction. "No. The Naomi situation wasn't good, but it was only a symptom of the problem."

I've told her enough at this point. Time to take a turn off memory lane. Rian's and my childhoods couldn't have been more opposite. The pity in her eyes is driving me insane, making me want to punch the trunk of that nearby oak tree.

I stare at the grave marker and read her name. Winifred Ann Carlson. Although it doesn't say mother, she was one. To so many kids, but most of all to me. Everything I've done since the day she died in that hospital bed, I've done for her.

I bend down and run my hands over the etching, removing the dead leaves from around the small stone.

"Ready?" I say to Rian when I stand again.

"Yeah." Her voice cracks.

More reason to get the hell out of here. I'm probably not going to find myself a new tattoo artist in New York City who wants to live in Cliffton Heights anyway, even if I was still in the mood to do so.

We walk out of the cemetery and stand on the street corner, waiting for the light to turn. A couple walks over to wait near us. They have a dog and Rian bends down to pet it, asking its name. They tell us how they just adopted him down the street from a shelter that didn't think it'd be able to keep their doors open.

"Oh, that's so sad." Rian looks at them with sad puppy eyes.

"There are two more there. She tried to get me to adopt all three," the man says with a nod to the woman. "We can barely put food on our table. We can't feed three dogs."

I laugh, remember Winnie saying she couldn't take any more kids because the government pays shit and if she can't feed herself, how can she feed others? But she took in Jax even after she had been laid off, and she made it work.

The woman bends down to Rian's level. "They're so cute. The people at the shelter said they aren't getting enough donations. I'm not sure how anyone with a heart can just walk by."

The light changes, so the guy tells the woman to pick up the dog so they can cross.

Rian looks at me. "Are you allergic to dogs?"

I shake my head, wishing I could lie to her. "No, but—"

"Do you know if Jax is?"

"I'd like to say yes."

She pulls out her phone and dials him up while walking in the direction the couple came from. "Hey, Jax, are you allergic to dogs?"

My blood shouldn't boil that she has his number, but I feel it heating anyway.

"You'll have to pay that ridiculously high pet deposit to the landlord," I say.

Rian turns around, putting the phone to her chest. "I have some savings."

"What's happened to you?" I ask. First, she's going to cheat on the math problem and now she suddenly wants a dog?

"Great. And you don't mind?" She smiles at whatever Jax has said. "Oh, Dylan and I are in the city and there are these dogs at this shelter that might be closing." Rian finishes her conversation and hangs up with Jax while we walk another block.

"Do you really think any of us can take care of a dog?"

She shrugs. "I don't know, but it sounds like fun and they need homes."

I put my hand on her arm to stop her and she steps out of the way of pedestrian traffic, moving to the edge of the sidewalk. "Are you doing this because I'm a foster kid?"

The excitement drains from her face. I feel like I just told a kid that Santa Claus isn't real. Fuck.

"No. That's not why."

"Okay, just making sure." I step back onto the sidewalk and she joins me, not nearly as excited as she was before. "I want to make sure you're not on some do-good kick now that I told you about Winnie. It can be contagious, you know?"

"What can?"

"You hear a story about how someone did good and you want to replicate it."

She pulls me aside by the sleeve, closer to the buildings. "That's not why. For the first time, I wasn't thinking of the consequences of something. I saw the dog. The dog was cute. I wanted the dog. That was all. But let me ask you a question…"

"Spit it out," I say.

She still hems and haws for a moment.

"Rian, I can take it."

"Well… don't you ever want to repay what Winnie did for you?"

I chuckle. Out of everyone, I never would've thought it would be Rian to call me out. But actually, paying it forward is something I feel guilty about. Like someone saved me, so shouldn't I save two more people and keep the good deeds going? I understand her bigger point, but I'm not sure this is the situation to step up.

"So because Winnie saved me, I should let a shelter dog shit and piss all over the apartment? You have the dog for its entire life, not until it reaches adulthood or its parents sort their shit out."

Rian bites her lower lip and stares at the sidewalk. "True. Maybe this is a bad idea."

Her disappointment hits me square in the chest, making it tighten. But the more I think about it, she's kind of right. Adopting a dog who's hours or days away from death sounds pretty damn appealing right now. And yes, I'm fully aware I'm probably more willing to do this because I just left Winne's grave. Plus, dogs piss off Jax. He's never liked them. Naomi had one that would always hump his leg.

"Maybe not," I say.

Rian's eyes light up. Shit, to see that excitement from her, I'd adopt ten dogs. "Really?"

"Yeah, come on." I tug her sleeve and we walk a little faster now. Our excitement escalates the farther we make it down the sidewalk.

"How far away was it?" she asks.

"I don't think they said."

"They didn't act like it was this far, did they?" She bites her lip again and her sunshine smile dims.

Finally, I see the shelter's sign on the corner, but we have to wait to cross when we're met with the big red hand. When we reach the animal shelter, a couple is walking away with a dog and Rian claps her hands in front of herself. But when we look in the little pen, all that's there is shredded newspaper with some dog shit.

"Where are the puppies?" Rian asks a woman who approaches us.

"That couple just took the last one. Thank goodness. Did you see our flyer?"

I put my arm around Rian's waist because we're not going to be dog parents today.

"They're all gone?" she asks with a strangled voice.

The woman finally understands and touches Rian's hand. "I'm sorry. They are."

Rian splashes on a fake smile, something she does often. "That's good. I'm glad they all have homes." She steps away and out of my hold.

"There are a lot of other shelters. Would you like a list?" the woman calls.

I take the piece of paper from her since Rian isn't listening anymore, then I catch up to Rian down the street.

"Hey." I duck to meet her eyes. No tears, thank fuck. I have a hard time dealing with tears.

"We should probably head back, huh?"

And just like that, the dog subject is abandoned.

WE WALK OFF THE TRAIN, neither one of us accomplishing what we wanted. I've never seen Rian so depressed. Like she owned a puppy and someone ran over it.

I stop us outside our apartment building. "I've gotta go to Ink Envy, want to join me?"

"Nah. I'm going to try to work on that equation."

I nod. "Cool. I'll be home in a little bit. Let's order pizza tonight?"

A slight smile creases her lips. "Sure."

After she gets in the front door, I walk across the street. The parlor is dead. Of course, that's because neither Frankie nor I are working and we're what keep this place going.

Lyle takes his feet off the front desk and sets his sketchpad on the table. "What's up, boss?"

"You can relax," I say, beelining it to my office, but I stop midway and turn back to him. "Do you have an Instagram account?"

Lyle is my newbie. He's still trying to find clients, but you find lots of those through walk-ins. It's why he has the crappy shift. But he needs to produce on the crappy shift too.

"I don't take pretty pictures, boss," he says.

"Start taking pictures of your drawings and posting them on Instagram, tagging Ink Envy. Same if you do a piece on someone. Friend every eighteen-plus person in Cliffton Heights. Find a way to bring in some business, or you're out."

His face pales. Once I'm back in my office, I feel like a jackass. I can't pressure him like that—he'll never produce what I need him to through fear.

Rian was wrong when she suggested I'm not into repaying my debt for what Winnie did for me. I take in the artists people won't give a chance and try to teach them the way of old tattooing—not the nuevo way of get a client and do whatever the fuck they want no matter what reputation you get from it.

I'm all about the no face until chest and no hands until arms. If I don't think I can give them what they want, I send them to someone I know will. Tattooing is about the art, not the ink. And not solely the money.

I pick up the phone and buzz to the front.

"Yeah, boss?" Lyle says, his voice apprehensive.

"I'm not firing you. But I think the Instagram thing is a good idea. It might drum up clients who like your stuff."

"Okay, I just joined on my phone."

I chuckle. "Okay."

I hang up and press my fingertips to my temple. I should be worried about my bottom line, but all I see is Rian's frown.

Instead of posting my own sketches to Instagram, I start a group text.

Me: *Game night tonight. We're playing Drawing Without Dignity because it's Rian's favorite and she needs cheering up.*

A whole slew of messages come in.

Sierra: *We got the pizza.*

Blanca: *Ethan says he'll get her favorite wine.*

Seth: *I'll pick up a dessert.*

With that settled, I open up another chat box.

Me: *Hey, Rian needs some cheering up, game night tonight at our apartment.*

Three dots appear. Guess I shouldn't be surprised that he never changed his number.

Jax: *Your dick would cheer her up. On second thought mine would do a better job.*

Me: *This was a peace offering so you weren't excluded. Now you can fuck off.*

Jax: *Aw, don't be such a sourpuss.*

I toss the phone onto the desk, regretting extending him an invitation. One thing I need to figure out soon is whether Jax wants revenge or friendship. Because he's back for a reason, and I need to find out which one it is.

CHAPTER NINE

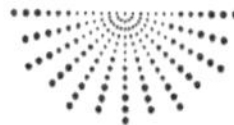

Rian

I got about ten percent through the problem today and I feel as though I'm on the right track, but I've had enough for one day, so I shut the notebook and swing my purse over my shoulder.

Jax comes out of his bedroom in a pair of jeans and a faded T-shirt that hugs his muscled shoulders and chest. "Where are you going?"

"Grocery store," I say. "Do you need anything?"

It's been an entire week since Dylan planned a game night to cheer me up after my out-of-body experience when I couldn't get a puppy, and since then, he and Jax have been civil enough. There's no watching television at the same time or eating at the table together, but there are no more mean words being spat at one another.

I'm still embarrassed when I think about how that puppy thing threw me into a funk in front of Dylan, but it warms my heart that he planned a night with our friends to cheer me up.

"Do you mind if I go with you?" Jax asks.

"Um… no." I wouldn't mind the company. Dylan works late on Saturdays, so it'll just be Jax and me around the apartment tonight.

"You sound unsure. You worried Phillips will have a problem with it?" He grabs his phone off the charger and pockets it.

"No," I say in a tone that would convince a senile eighty-five-year-old dementia-ridden grandma.

"Right." He opens the door and holds it, not hiding his smirk.

We walk down the hall and ride the elevator down.

"You guys don't use that roof nearly enough," he says.

"Yeah, I know. But it's just getting nice out again. We will."

I don't necessarily feel uncomfortable around Jax. He's an easy-going guy who doesn't bite his tongue. But we haven't spent that much time together since he moved in. Usually because I'll go to my bedroom if he's watching television when I come home.

"We should watch a movie tonight," he says.

I nod and rock back on my flats. "Yeah, that's a good idea."

We walk out and he's a gentleman, allowing me to go first and holding the door open for me.

"So we'll make something to eat and watch a movie on the roof?"

"Um…"

I'm not sure what has my tongue tied? Is it because part of me worries I'm going against Dylan? Like I'm picking Jax's side over Dylan's?

"I'm not asking you out, Rian. This is strictly a platonic thing."

I yank the cart at the grocery store, but the damn thing

won't separate from the one in front. I move to the next row, and it's the same fucking thing.

Jax puts his hand on mine to stop me. *Stay True* is inked across his knuckles. "I've got it."

He fixes the child seatbelts so they're not interlaced with the metal openings and a cart slides out easily. Instead of handing it to me, he takes control, pushing it ahead. "What should we make tonight?"

"Um…"

"You know, for a girl, you sure don't talk a lot." He chuckles.

I giggle because I'm still tongue-tied. Jax is intimidating in the same way I found Dylan to be when he moved in with Knox across the hall.

"I'm just…" I'm what? Finish the damn sentence, Rian.

"How about we ask each other questions? You ask me one and I'll ask you one?"

I pick up a head of lettuce and put it in the cart. "Okay."

"Ladies first." He stops the cart and throws in a bag of pistachios.

"How long are you staying in Cliffton Heights?"

"Man, right for the jugular, huh? I underestimated you." His head moves side to side. "At least six months. We'll see how it goes."

"You signed a year lease…" I say. Technically it was a sublease through Sierra.

He tugs on my ponytail. "I pay all my debts. If I leave before a year, I'll pay you."

"Okay." I push away the reoccurring fear of me living alone like Ms. Merrigold on the first floor. Except for the cats, since I'm allergic.

"My turn then." He rubs his hands together and looks me over as though he's trying to think of something that will embarrass me. "Why on Earth do you write math textbooks?"

I chuckle. "That's your question?"

"Would you rather me ask how long you've had a female boner for Phillips?"

My cheeks heat.

"Relax, your secret is safe with me." He grins.

"It's not like that."

He holds up his hand as though he doesn't want to talk about it. "I simply asked you why you chose your profession."

I nod and put some apples in the cart. "I was always good at math. I don't have to interact with many people. And it pays the bills."

He nods. "But you don't love it?"

"I like that I'm good at it."

"Interesting." He grabs oranges and puts them in the cart.

"What does that mean?" I ask, pulling my list out of my purse, along with my pen.

"It means it's interesting. I always like to hear why people chose to do what they do." He pushes the cart and rides it to the deli counter, where he tosses in pita bread and pulls a number from the red ticket dispenser.

I stop since I don't have meat on my list. "Why did you become a tattoo artist?"

His smile is wicked and cocky and drop-dead gorgeous. "I love art, but I hate confinement. I love giving people ways to express their beliefs or celebrate the life of a loved ones or just make a statement. It's an honor when someone lets me put my art on them permanently."

I'm stunned silent. Those are all good reasons. I have nothing like that for being a math textbook writer. He winks when he realizes I'm second-guessing why I do what I do for money.

"I love baking," I blurt.

"I've noticed. Do you do that because you're good at it too?"

My mouth hangs open. Few people have ever talked to me like this. I guess it's his don't-give-a-shit attitude. "I enjoy tweaking recipes. I love the preciseness of it. Baking is really mathematical and scientific when you get down to it. And I love seeing people enjoy something I made."

He taps my nose with his finger. "Then why aren't you doing that?"

His number gets called and he holds up his hand without looking away from me until he absolutely has to. As he requests from the nice lady an order of every processed meat that's doing absolutely horrible things to his insides, I peruse the baked items. None of them look half as good as mine.

"Ready?" he says, and I nod. "Round two?"

"You have more questions?"

"I have lots of questions. But it's your turn."

I look him over and decide to stay away from his childhood. "Why are you here?"

"I thought I'd get some groceries to eat so that I don't die from starvation." I tilt my head, and he laughs. "My life was getting out of control. I don't like that feeling. I called Knox at the right moment to snag the opportunity for a place to stay."

"You're so honest," I say.

He looks over the meat in the coolers. "I noticed you didn't have any steak the other night. Are you only a chicken gal, or do you eat red meat? Please don't tell me you're the tofu girl." He dodges my comment, so I let it die.

"I eat all three, although if you ask my mom, I only eat red meat once every two weeks and I prefer fish over anything." I pick up some organic chicken breasts and put them in the cart.

He laughs, picking up a package of steaks. "Oh, I love you parent-pleasers. You guys amuse me."

I roll my eyes. "Steaks again?"

"If I'm cooking for you, you can't complain."

"True enough."

"And it's my turn now. You're digging deep here, so I feel like I should nail you with something you don't want to answer." He makes an exaggerated effort of hemming and hawing.

My stomach stirs. I wonder what I should tell him if he does ask me about Dylan. While I anxiously wait for what he's going to ask, we turn down the bread aisle.

"Have you always had a thing for bad boys?" he finally asks.

My entire body heats. "I don't have a thing for bad boys."

I'm such a liar. If I didn't already want Dylan, I'd probably be looking at Jax like every middle-aged woman we've passed in the store has. Like they want him to jump on the end cap and do a striptease.

"So that's how it's gonna be? We're going to lie to one another?"

I pick up English muffins and hold the package in front of my face so he can't see me blush.

"Rian?"

"I swear if you tell him, I will come into your room at night and cut off your balls."

He crosses his legs and puts his hands over his junk. "Ouch. You're not that kind of girl. Don't say things that will make me hide all the knives under my pillow at night."

I laugh and he does too as we walk down another aisle, each of us picking up things and tossing them in the cart.

"I won't say anything, but you know Phillips knows, right?" he says.

"No, he doesn't, and it's just a crush. Not like anything would come from it."

He stops the cart and backs me up to the end of the aisle, plucking my paper and pen out of my hand and tossing them behind him. I try to weave to the side to see where they went, but he moves in the same direction. "I guarantee you, Phillips knows how you feel and so far he's done nothing about it, so why don't you give this bad boy a try? I promise to check all your boxes." His hand lands on my hip.

There's nothing terribly inappropriate about what he's doing. But I can't help but notice that he smells different than Dylan. It's muskier.

"My boxes?" I roll my eyes and look away.

His forefinger lands under my chin and forces me to face him. He is gorgeous. All chiseled jaw and sharp nose. Scruff like he doesn't care, and his hair gelled into a mess of perfection. Lean muscles that could have him front and center in a Calvin Klein ad.

"Yeah, your boxes. Don't-give-a-shit attitude. Check. Fuck you in public. Check. Dirty talker. Check. Know how to make a woman orgasm five times one after the other. Check."

With the last pluck of his tongue, my lady parts are scratching their heads saying, *Phillips who?*

But that's not totally true, because all I can think about is Dylan giving me those things. Maybe Jax is *too* bad boy for me, if there's even such a thing.

"Okay, playtime is over." I push his hard chest and he backs up, laughing.

I bow my head at an elderly lady who's blatantly gawking from down the aisle.

"I thought playtime was just starting. Man, Phillips really has his grip on you." He places a box of Triscuits in the cart.

I do admire his ass as he heads down the aisle though.

"If you aren't taking me up on my offer, then you can't enjoy staring at my finer qualities," he says, turning the corner and leaving me in the cookie and cracker aisle in stunned silence once again.

I grab all the E.L.Fudge cookie variations and follow him.

We reach the frozen foods section without making another scene, although I really need to get home to make good use of my toys. I think I'll imagine Dylan caging me in in the supermarket like Jax did.

Standing in front of the ice cream, I debate between Ben and Jerry's and a gallon of store brand since they're the same price. Jax grabs a gelato pint.

"So far, your Triscuits and gelato aren't supporting your bad boy claim," I say with amusement.

"Then take a chance and go out with me. If for no reason but to drive Phillips crazy."

There's no smile or amusement in his tone. He's serious. All I can think is, does Dylan really know how I feel? Does he have any interest other than remaining friends? Because if he did have any interest in me, wouldn't he have hit on me at some point? Or asked me out?

I bite my lip. I might not have feelings for Jax like I do Dylan, but maybe it's time I put Dylan aside and see what else is out there. I don't know Jax well. Maybe I could end up liking him in that way.

"Okay," I say.

Jax's eyes widen. "I'll pick you up tomorrow night at six. Dress casual."

My heart flips-flops. Here's a guy who knows what he wants and isn't afraid to go after it. All that needs to happen now is for the universe to shift so that I want him instead of the guy who doesn't see me as anything other than a friend.

CHAPTER TEN

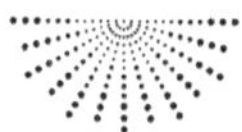

Dylan

Saturday nights are always long. Not that I have any right to complain. Lyle actually had two girls come in after they saw his designs on Instagram. One got a piece and the other one said maybe next week. And the line that never died down is a good thing. Most of Frankie's regulars trusted me to do theirs. Still, it was a nonstop night that required stellar concentration and my brain is fried.

As I trudge down the hall to my apartment, all I want is to strip bare and crawl into bed, but the giggling on the other side of the door when I insert my key says Jax brought someone home.

When I enter the apartment, all I see is Jax on top of someone on the couch. I'm half tempted to shut the door and crash on Seth's couch until the blonde peers up to see who it is.

My gut twists in one giant knot as Rian says, "You're home."

"You're up." I take off my jacket and hang it up on the hook.

"We couldn't sleep, so we started watching wrestling. Jax said he once wanted to be a wrestler and was showing me what his signature move would've been."

She's all happy and now I'm grumpy. Jax's arrogant smile rises my blood pressure, and I swear I can feel my heartbeat in my neck.

"I guess I don't have to ask how your Saturday night was?" I reach inside the fridge for a beer, torn between staying out here so that maybe Rian will feel uncomfortable letting Jax be all over her and locking myself in my room to continue to live in denial.

"Jax set up the rooftop to watch a movie, so we ate dinner and watched *The Wedding Singer*. You know, the one with Adam Sandler." Rian's giddiness grates on any nerves I had left after my last client didn't feel the need to tip me since I'm the owner.

"Yeah, I know it." I sip my beer in the kitchen. "It was a long night. I'm going to head to bed. Enjoy the night, you two."

Rian sits up and looks over the back of the couch. Surprisingly, no smartass comment comes out of Jax's mouth, and the two remain quiet as I walk through the apartment to my bedroom.

After closing the door, I sit on the edge of my bed, finishing my beer and overhearing their laughter from the other side of the wall. How the hell did I ever get here? Usually I'd be out at the bars after work. I should've accepted Lyle's offer after we closed up.

I kick off my boots and slide up to the headboard of my bed, putting in a pair of earbuds and grabbing my sketchpad.

Rian's giggling can be heard over the music while I sketch the design that's occupied my mind since we were in New York last week. A peony with shedding petals—meant for Rian if she ever comes to me for ink. She needs something as beautiful as her and she's like a peony—a symbol of beauty and fragility, but also a happy life and prosperity.

While my pencil sketches the design, I imagine where I'd ink her if the choice was mine. Her right ribcage would hurt more than somewhere else, but as I curved it around and under her breast, it would be beautiful. Even if I'm only going off of the few times I've seen her wear a bikini when she and Sierra sunbathed on the roof.

As soon as that thought comes to mind, I reprimand myself for thinking about that part of her body. I need to get a grip on my feelings for her. The attraction remained in that box I kept under double locks until Jax arrived. The more he flirts with her, the more a King Kong version of me wants to kidnap her.

What bothers me is that I have no idea if this is Jax's way of reliving the past or if he truly likes her. If he does, he's more man than me to pursue her without any guilt that she's too perfect for him to mess up.

But that's Jax—he does now and thinks later. It's the greatest difference between us. Where I get lost in my head, he acts without thinking, hurting innocent people.

I can't protect Rian, but if I want her, I'd better be able to suffer the consequences.

THE NEXT MORNING, I'm sure that Rian won't be up. It's Sunday, and the only dumbass who will work out with me is the other single guy in our friend group, Seth. So when I come face to face with Rian as she opens the bathroom door, I'm surprised.

She doesn't see me at first, probably still half asleep. Her matching T-shirt and shorts pajama set clings to her figure. Her hair is thrown up in a messy ponytail and a chunk of strands have fallen out of it. There's even a dry line from drool off her mouth. She's adorable.

"Dylan!" She startles, her hands releasing her ponytail holder, allowing her hair to cascade down her shoulders.

"Go back to bed. I'm heading to the gym." I walk by her and grab my water from the fridge.

"So early? Take a day off." Her voice is still rough from sleep.

I say nothing, but she's waiting by her door as I shove the water into my bag. Her gaze follows me, but as soon as I look her in the eye, she stares at the floor.

"You okay?" I ask.

"Yeah. Um…"

We stand across the room from one another, me waiting for her to say what she needs to. "Is something wrong?"

She shakes her head. "I just wanted to let you know—I mean, it's not a huge deal. But with this roommate situation, you need to be in the loop. You probably don't even care—"

"Spit it out," I say.

Her eyes fix on mine. "Jax asked me out on a date. We're supposed to go tonight."

My stomach drops. He's made the first move. I'm surprised, but I'm not. This is how Jax works.

I smack on the fakest smile I can at this time in the morning. "Cool. Have fun."

Her hands twist in front of her. "You're okay with it?"

"Does it matter?"

She's quiet but observant. Her deep inhales suggest she's not sure how she should act right now.

"It's great. Have a great time. Seth's waiting for me." I thumb at the door and hightail it out of there before I climb over all the furniture to smash my own lips to hers and beg her not to go out with him. The problem with that move is, what the hell do I back it up with? Wait for me? Wait for what? For me to get my head out of my ass?

I rush out the door to find Seth sitting on the floor outside his door, waiting for me. His gray hoodie is over his head and his phone is in his hands. I glance at the screen to see an Instagram post of a curly dark-haired girl holding a tray of bagels.

"Good morning," I announce myself.

He looks up, quickly turning off his screen. "This is ridiculous. It's Sunday." He pushes up off the floor. "I was up half the night listening to Knox fuck like a damn porn star."

I laugh because back in high school, Knox earned the nickname Ron Jeremy. He's a cop now, but back then, indecent exposure wasn't something he had an issue with. He'd screw a girl on the park bench if she let him. Then again, back then he was going through as much shit as the rest of us.

"Well, get ready for a good workout. Rian just told me Jax asked her out." I step into the elevator.

Seth stands idly in the hallway, his jaw hanging open. I grab his sweatshirt strings and drag him into the elevator.

"That's low."

I press the ground floor button. "Is it really? I mean, she's not seeing anyone."

"Yeah, but anyone who's around you guys knows…"

His words drift off because this isn't something we've ever talked about. I flirt with Rian, and yeah, I've felt that maybe she might like me. But I've kept my feelings close to my chest because anyone can predict the outcome of the two of us in a relationship.

We head out of the apartment building and down the street toward the gym.

"I think it's time you're truthful with her," Seth says, repositioning his bag over his shoulder.

I want to ask him if he's ready to admit why he's following Evan Erickson or the Bagel Place on Instagram if he hates her that much. "I'm not into losing friendships at the moment."

We walk into the gym. A guy who's roughly our age takes our cards and says good morning. We return his greeting and make our way to the locker room.

"You'd rather risk the chance that she and Jax start dating? What are you gonna do? Watch them make out during *Blue Bloods*?" He strips off his track pants and sweatshirt, shoving them into the locker.

I shrug. "I'll move back in with you and Knox." Easiest solution ever.

"Sorry, man, Leilani is paying your rent now. I guess she needed a place and Knox offered her your old room."

I lock my locker, grab my towel and water, and follow Seth to the treadmills. "Why didn't I know this?"

He shrugs, positioning all his shit exactly where he wants it. He pins his key to his shorts. "Because it didn't matter. Not like you consulted us when you moved out to protect Rian from Jax. The same guy you're laying down on the pavement so he can turn you into roadkill."

I up my speed and incline. Screw warming up.

Seth's not like Ethan though, so he doesn't compete with me. The fucker takes a leisurely Sunday stroll on his machine.

"I have no right to stop her." I'm talking more to myself than Seth.

He waves to the girl who's always folding towels. "You do

have a right. You're her friend. You have her best interests in mind. It's piss or get off the pot time."

I shake my head, starting to sweat. I can't admit that I'm being a pussy here. She's the only one of my friends that I've told about Winnie and my upbringing. There's a reason for that. Somehow, I know I can trust her with the information, and I know it'll never be slung back at me. To put a relationship like that in jeopardy for a few orgasms seems moronic.

"Let's talk about something else. How about the Bagel Place?"

Seth rolls his eyes, slowly walking as he waves to everyone as though he's running for office or something. "Don't turn this on me. You're the one with the girl problems. Which is funny when you think about it. When we first moved in together, I idolized you and all the women you got. Now you're wound up tight over one. I'm enjoying sitting on the sidelines." He waves and says hello to Joe, an elderly man who's here on the bicycle every morning.

I up his speed without him realizing and he fumbles to keep up, falling off the back of the treadmill.

Payback is a bitch.

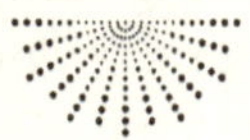

Rian

"A date?" Blanca's eyes light up.

"With Jax?" The disgust in Sierra's voice tells me where her allegiance lies.

"He asked." I sit in Sierra's plush living room on Sunday afternoon. I guess when you date a prince, you end up living a cushy lifestyle.

"Is that the only reason you're going out with him?" Blanca asks. She's sitting cross-legged and reading a bridal magazine. They've yet to set a date, though I know she's getting pressure from her mom about having a big Italian wedding.

"No." I fall over on the couch, clutching a pillow to my stomach. I wish Dylan was the one who had asked me out, but I have no control over him. The look on his face this morning when I told him made me think for a second that he didn't want me to go. Then he smiled and said it was cool. "He's a funny guy actually."

"I ran into him in the elevator the other day. He asked me why I would want to get married." Blanca's face shows no emotion, I'm not sure where her mind is. "I had three commitment-phobe brothers. I'm familiar with the type."

"See!" Sierra refills our glasses of wine.

Blanca raises her hand. "But I've also witnessed what happens when they find a woman who brings them to their knees, so I can say with confidence that sometimes the playboy falls."

"Hardly ever—except in a romance novel." Sierra sits next to Blanca and points at the open page of the magazine. "Beautiful."

"Too revealing." Blanca flips the page. "Shall I remind you that you're with a prince who didn't exactly keep his dick in his pants?"

Sierra smiles as if she's remembering something. It's common knowledge that she and Adrian slept together their first night together. Not that any of us care, but if he was like that with her, I'm sure there were girls before her.

"Where is he anyway?" I ask.

"Sandsal. Gets in tonight." Another million-dollar smile is on Sierra's lips. Adrian has to go back and forth to his country on occasion until everything is done and the new rules of the monarchy are official. Long story that I don't care to get into. Sierra points at another page in the magazine. "Oh, I like that one."

Blanca turns the magazine so that I can see it and we both laugh.

"What?" Sierra asks.

"That's you, not Blanca." The dress is a skintight mermaid-style design. Blanca is more a fairytale Cinderellastyle dress girl. As for me, I have no idea what I would want to wear.

"Sometimes you have to go outside your comfort zone," Sierra says. "You have the body." She stands and disappears into the kitchen.

A little of the tension releases with Sierra's departure, though it's not because of her. Sierra and I met in college, and I was intimidated. She had a quick tongue, never afraid to tell people what she was thinking. Her personality was loud and boisterous. You either hated her or loved her. I guess you can be drawn to your opposite, because I never cared if I stood in her shadow or was drowned out by her ability to control everything. In some ways, I envy that side of her. If Jax had cornered her in the grocery store, she would've known exactly how to react. Whereas my comebacks come twenty minutes later.

"I'm kind of nervous," I say to Blanca.

She looks up from her magazine, shuts it, and scoots closer. "Why?"

I shrug, sipping my wine. "He's forward."

Blanca's lips turn down. "I'm not sure this is such a good idea. I mean, if you still like Dylan and you're trying to get a reaction from him, what if you don't get the one you're looking for?"

She sips her wine as I recall my day with Dylan in New York City. When he took me to his foster mom's grave. How much he divulged to me. More than he has with anyone else as far as I know. I almost understand how someone growing up like that could leave someone scared to lose anyone they care for.

"I'm not trying to get a reaction out of him." The words feel like a blatant lie coming off my tongue, but I have to save some face. "I think maybe it's time I move on."

There's a little truth to my words. I've been pining away

for Dylan for years, and though I did hope for a reaction from him, maybe it really is time to accept that nothing's ever going to happen between us. I can't put my life on hold forever, hoping that will change.

Blanca nods. "True enough. See what else is out there."

I twist my hands in my lap. "But Jax doesn't bite his tongue, and you know me. I'm slow on the uptake. I'm polite to a fault."

"Oh, Rian." She puts down her wine and slides over, wrapping her arm around my shoulders. "If you're not comfortable, don't go. If you want to go, then just be straight with him. If you're uncomfortable, call me. I grew up with three brothers—I know exactly where to hurt them."

I laugh, understanding what she's saying. "It's just… what am I going to wear? A cardigan and mom jeans?"

"Dramatic much?" Blanca says.

Sierra comes out with a tray of cheese and crackers and grapes.

"We're not royalty," Blanca says, laughing and sharing a look with me. "I'd happily take chips and guacamole."

"Well, this is what I have. Believe me, if I served this to the queen, she'd probably turn her nose up at it." She falls into the couch and appraises Blanca's arm around my shoulders. Her finger waggles between us. "What's going on?"

"Rian's a little nervous."

Blanca says it nicely, but in truth, my heart has drummed all day whenever I think about the date.

"I'm not his type," I say.

"You don't even know his type," Sierra says, which I guess is technically true, but I checked his Instagram account. There's definitely a specific type of woman he hangs out with.

"I have no tattoos. There's nothing edgy or sexy about

me." I could keep going, but Sierra's eyes widening with excitement stops me.

"Uh oh," Blanca says, laughing because we've seen that look on Sierra's face more than once. The last time was when she decided to enter a contest to win a date with Prince Adrian Marx. Of course, that worked out pretty well for her. "What are you thinking?"

"Makeover!" Sierra tosses the rest of the cracker into her mouth and springs up off the couch, her hand on my arm pulling me up. "Come on."

"Like what kind of makeover?" I say, allowing her to tug me off the couch.

Blanca follows us.

"Nothing crazy. We'll just show off your amazing body a little more than you usually do. Maybe some more dramatic makeup."

Before I can blink, I'm on Sierra's bed and she's lost in her closet. Blanca runs her hand down my arm, shooting me a sympathetic smile before joining Sierra in her closet.

This could go two ways. Either I'm more confident—like the time in college when Sierra dressed me for a party and the star quarterback actually cornered me to talk the majority of the night—or it goes bad. Like Halloween of our junior year, when she convinced me to dress in a slutty nurse costume and I ended up getting a taxi home midway through the night because I couldn't handle all the stares and inappropriate touches by asshole frat boys. Sometimes it's a curse we're the same size.

Sierra comes out with a stack of clothes on hangers. "Did he say what to wear?"

"Casual," I say, shaking my head at her gown. "Let's get back to reality here. I'm not dating a prince, so no need for an actual ballgown."

Sierra laughs.

"Casual, so jeans?" Blanca asks.

I nod.

"But heels," Sierra says, holding her finger up and diving back into her closet.

"I haven't worn heels since I got dragged to that frat formal in college when you made me be Trey Longfield's date because you were going with his best friend."

Sierra comes out with a pair of black suede boots with a stiletto heel that will probably snap the first time I twist my ankle.

"Why can't I wear my flats? That's casual."

Sierra blows out a breath and Blanca nibbles on the inside of her cheek.

"Come on, it will be fun to dress a little outside of your usual," Blanca says. "Sierra promises not to go too crazy, right, Sierra?"

"Definitely. You're gorgeous. We're just upping the look a little because it's a first date."

I release a breath. Maybe a new look will give me more confidence. "Fine. But no crazy makeup. I'm not Sandy from *Grease*."

They both laugh.

Sierra pretends to stomp out a cigarette and says, "Tell me about it, stud."

Then she saunters back into the closet, and I succumb to her and Blanca's suggestions.

Two hours later, I emerge from the bathroom. The girls jump off the bed.

"Are you ready?" Sierra asks.

I nod. I haven't looked at myself in the full-length mirror yet, so I turn to check myself out. I'm wearing ripped tight jeans with a tight body suit. Somehow, I'm managing to walk in Sierra's black boots that have an opening at the toes, but they make me about three inches taller.

They both look at me from behind through the mirror.

"I'm not sure. I'm super tall," I say.

"Jax is huge. You're fine," Blanca says.

My hair is curled in long tendrils and my makeup is smokier and darker than I ever wear it, but my lipstick isn't nearly as dark as I anticipated Sierra would go. All in all, I love the look. Not that I'd do this daily, which makes me feel as though I'm falsely advertising myself.

"Sierra!" Adrian's voice booms through the apartment, and her eyes go huge.

"I'll be right back," she says and rushes out of the room.

"Let's go before they start having sex while we're still here and we end up stuck in this bedroom," Blanca says, grabbing her purse off the bed.

I collect my stuff and we walk out of the bedroom. Sierra is attached to Adrian like a koala bear, casting kisses on every part of his face, his hands plastered to her ass.

He glances over her shoulder. "Ladies."

"Hey, Adrian," Blanca and I say in unison.

"We'll be leaving the two of you alone," I say.

Blanca slides by them to the front door.

"No. Wait." Sierra slides down Adrian. "What do you think? Rian's going out with Jax tonight."

Adrian's eyes roam over my body, but in a polite way, never stopping on any one part, even though my boobs are the first thing anyone would see when they look at me.

"Very nice. Jax?" he asks with a wrinkle on his forehead as he glances at Sierra.

"I'm escorting her across the street." Blanca swings her arm through mine.

"Really it's so I don't break my ankle," I say.

Blanca laughs, knowing I'm telling the truth.

"Have fun with… Jax?" Adrian says as though maybe he has the situations wrong.

has the situations wrong.

"Thanks." I smile.

Adrian slides out of his jacket and puts his phone on the wireless charger by the couch. I wonder what it's like to go from country to country at least once a month.

Sierra pulls me into her body. "I want a detailed report tonight."

"No need to call tonight, Rian." All of us look at Adrian. "I've been gone for five days, babe."

Sierra blushes. I love seeing that look on her face because she's so smitten, more vulnerable and in touch with her feelings. "Oh, yeah. Tomorrow morning is fine."

Adrian comes up behind her, his arms around her waist. "After eleven though." He winks.

I smile at the two of them. So in love. Although I'm slightly jealous, I'm happy for my friends.

Blanca and I say our goodbyes and take the elevator down their expensive apartment building to the main floor. We're out on the street and about to cross to our own apartment when we spot Dylan at the door of Ink Envy. He glances over then does a double-take.

"Hey, Dylan," Blanca waves.

He stands there gawking. "Hey, you two," he says, his voice sounding distant and far away.

We cross the street and I glance over my shoulder, but he's walking into Ink Envy. I guess that's all I'll see of Dylan tonight.

CHAPTER TWELVE

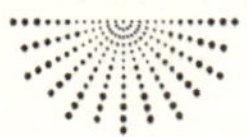

Rian

"I heard Frankie's been gone and Dylan's had to work extra shifts," Blanca says once we're in the elevator.

I nod. Of course she knows all this because of Ethan. "Yeah."

"Okay, so let's go over some things." The elevator reaches our floor but she holds the door closed button.

"What?"

"First of all, he asked you out. Remember that. *He* wants to date *you*. Do not think he is at all above you in any way. You are at his level, got it?"

I nod.

"Good. I can't stress this enough, Rian, and I would never lie to you—he's the lucky one. Lucky to go on a date with you."

I nod again.

84

"And if he tries anything funny, you get ahold of his wrists." She grabs my wrists, forcing them down to my sides. "Dig your nails into the inside and thrust your knee as hard as you can into his balls."

I laugh.

"I'm serious. You never know. Then you call me, and I'll handle the rest."

I stare at her little five-foot-two body and raise my eyebrows.

"Don't underestimate me because I'm small. All my brothers are over six foot and I've had them on their knees, praying for mercy." I laugh again, and even her lips tip up. "This last piece of advice is the most important part though."

My shoulders fall. "What?"

"Have fun. Just enjoy him. Enjoy his flirting and flirt back. This is your night. Make the most of it." She hugs me and sways us back and forth. The doors slowly open.

"Thanks, Blanca."

We turn to leave, and Seth and Ethan are standing there.

"Don't mind us. Continue as you were," Seth says with a grin.

Ethan takes no time at all to corner Blanca in the elevator. "Come on, we're headed out to grab a pizza and a beer."

"We said no chicks," Seth says.

Blanca looks around the small space. "I don't hear any chirping, do you, Rian?"

I laugh, stepping out of the elevator. "No."

Seth gets in and looks me up and down. "Looking good, Rian." He nods at me as the doors slide shut between us.

I inhale a deep breath and glance at my watch to see it's five fifty-five. Using my key, I open the apartment door and find Jax in the kitchen, opening a bottle of water. He doesn't look much different than he does on any normal day. A pair of jeans and a gray T-shirt with a jacket over top. His hair is still mussed up perfection any girl would want to run her fingers through. He really is hot.

The bottle stays tipped to his lips as his gaze floats over me like a feather, pausing at my breasts, my hips, and my shoes. He's blatantly and unapologetically checking me out. All those doubts and worries vanish.

He stops drinking, securing the top of the bottle. "I thought you were standing me up." His vision won't stop dipping to my chest, and I can't deny that it feels good to be wanted. "You look fucking hot."

I laugh, which spurs his own deep chuckle.

"Let me just put this away." I head to my room and toss a bag with the clothes I was wearing onto my bed. I check that everything I need is in my purse, adding a phone charger just in case.

When I come back out of the bedroom, Dylan's sitting in a chair with a water bottle in hand. I glance around not finding Jax in the room anymore, which only makes this even more awkward.

"Hey," Dylan says. He's still wearing his boots, one ankle resting on the knee of his other leg. He takes pull after pull off his water bottle. His eyes move the way Jax's did over my body, but instead of the lust that filled Jax's eyes, distaste fills Dylan's. "Nice look."

"Is that your way of complimenting me?"

Dylan's gaze shoots up. Even I'm surprised I had the balls to ask him, but I'm stepping out into the world with the possibility of getting hurt. When's the last time he did that?

"Good luck holding a conversation with him. He'll be staring at your tits the entire night."

I say nothing, every retort running through my brain not nearly good enough.

"Is that what you want, Rian? A guy who just wants to fuck you?"

"You're being ugly tonight." I beeline across the room to the kitchen. "Have you seen Jax?"

"He got a call. In his room."

I turn around to find Dylan's gaze still on me. He can act like he doesn't like what I'm wearing, but this is the first time he hasn't been able to take his eyes off me. Our eyes lock and he quickly diverts his, raising his water bottle to his lips. Those luscious lips I dream of kissing. Ugh. Maybe going on a date with Jax is a bad idea.

Before I have a chance to really think about why I'm doing this, Jax comes out of his bedroom. "Phillips." He nods and shuts his door.

"Owens."

The two are cordial.

"Ready, angel?" Jax asks, holding out his hand for me.

I nod and slide my hand into his. I'm surprised by how smooth it is.

"See you, Phillips." Jax never turns around as he leads me to the apartment door.

"Have a great date. Just put a sock on the doorknob if you want to be alone later." Dylan waves his water bottle.

Jax laughs, opening the door and waiting for me to walk through. His hand guides me by the small of my back, and we walk down the hall in silence. The elevator arrives quickly so I don't have to force conversation, but Jax has a different idea once we're alone in the small space.

"Was that as painful as it was to watch?" he asks.

I peek up. "What do you mean?"

"You pretending that you didn't want Phillips and me to switch places?"

I smile at this man I barely know but who can somehow see through me as though I'm as transparent as a piece of glass. "I'm happy to be going out with you."

"Bullshit."

The elevator stops on the bottom floor and we file out. "I'm sorry. I'm not using you to make him jealous or anything."

He nods. "I didn't figure you were the type."

"Do you want to call this thing off?" I ask.

A wicked smile crosses his lips. "Hell no. You're looking smokin' hot and Phillips is about to rage right now. We're going out and staying out. You might not have an agenda to make him jealous, but I like to torture the shithead." He grabs my hand again and pushes through the front door of our apartment building.

"Where are we going?" I ask.

"That's for me to know and you to find out." He winks and we stop by a motorcycle. "Have you ever ridden on one?"

I shake my head.

"Never with Phillips?"

I shake my head again.

He blows out a breath. "I guess we're walking then."

I tear my hand out of his. "Wait, why? I can ride it."

He smirks and stuffs his hands into the pockets of his jeans. He looks up at the apartment then down at the bike. "Your first time on a motorcycle shouldn't be holding on to me. Everyone needs a great memory of the first time they ride, and if I allow you on my bike, you'll regret it like girls do their virginity—always wishing they'd saved it for someone else."

I step toward him, my hand on his cheek, and stare into his beautiful blue eyes. "You're sentimental?"

"No. I'm just letting Phillips pop that cherry of yours. Contrary to what he might think, I'm not a complete asshole." He removes my hand from his face and entwines our fingers.

The door of the building opens and Dylan walks out, his eyes falling to mine then to where my hand is in Jax's. He walks in the opposite direction, climbs on his bike that's a few spots down from Jax's, secures his helmet, then he's gone, turning right before the yellow turns red.

"If he's going to be a pussy, the least I can do is show you a good time."

Jax tears my attention away and we walk down the sidewalk to begin our date.

～

JAX TAKES ME BOWLING. Which would be fine if I was wearing socks. But the gentleman he is, he buys me a pair for six dollars through the vending machine.

"What a prince you are." I rest my cheek on his chest and flutter my eyelashes at him.

He shakes his head.

It turns out that Jax isn't intimidating once we figured out nothing would happen between us. Although he is just as big a flirt.

We each get our shoes on and Jax asks the guy to put us at the far end of the lanes, away from other people. The kid tries to say he's not supposed to do that but ultimately gives Jax his way. I'm pretty sure the sixteen-year-old was intimidated by the big Jax Owens.

I slide off the heels, which is a relief. I worry for a second that I won't be able to get my feet back into them to go home. After I tie my shoes, I jump up to pick a ball. "I haven't bowled since I was, like, eight. There was a birthday party and it was boys versus girls."

Jax smiles and shakes his head as he ties his shoes. "And you kissed a boy by the bathroom?"

"No," I screech, and he laughs as though he expected that to be my answer.

"How old were you when you had your first kiss?" I ask, then wave off the question. "I don't even want to know."

He grabs a sixteen-pound ball and I grab a respectable ten. "You probably don't want to know."

I type in our names on the electronic screen while a waitress comes over. I'm happy for the distraction. Comparing sexual conquests isn't really a conversation I want to have with Jax. I'm pretty sure I know how I'll stack up against him. He orders us a pizza, a pitcher of beer and two waters, and stops her before she leaves to add on an order of wings.

When Jax slides into the chair next to me, his arm brushes mine. For a moment, I wonder what would have happened if I had met Jax before Dylan. Would I feel differently?

"Ladies first." He leans back, stretching both his arms long the back of the booth.

I stand, pick up my ball, and prepare as best I can to mimic what the couples with matching shirts a few lanes down are doing. As I walk up to the line, I pull back my hand with the ball.

"Man, you do have a great ass."

My foot slips, my fingers almost lodging in the ball as I bring it forward to release it. A terrible scene flashes through my mind of me splayed on the wooden lane with my arm outstretched and the ball still attached. But at the last minute, my thumb pops out and the ball slides straight into the gutter.

When I walk back to wait for my ball to return, Jax is standing there. "Let me give you some pointers."

"Is this your way of getting your hands on my hips?"

He smirks. "You're smarter than I give you credit for."

"Thanks?"

"I see what Phillips sees."

I turn away from him and he grabs my ball before I can, showing me where to put my fingers. He walks me up the line with one of his hands on my hip and the other on my hand holding the ball. His palm is so big, it fits over my hand.

The ball careens down the lane and six pins go down. I jump up and Jax high fives me.

"See? Only good things happen when my hands are on your hips." He winks and busies himself getting his ball while I sit back down and sip my beer.

Jax and I play two games while eating our pizza. He eats more wings than me and probably drinks more beer too. But I see why Jax and Dylan were best friends at one point. They're so similar. They each put themselves last. Jax asked me five times if I wanted the last slice before cutting it in half and demanding we split it.

I'm on Jax's back when we step out of the bowling alley because as I assumed my feet are swollen and I couldn't get the boots back on my feet.

"Shit, it's raining," Jax says, raising his hand for a cab. "Looks like I don't get the opportunity to have you on my back the whole way home."

A taxi that was waiting down the street parks along the curb and I slide in, Jax joining me. He gives the driver the address of our apartment and I pull out my phone for no reason but to look like I have something to do. I sit up straight when I see the first text in an exchange in our group.

Knox: *Dylan was in an accident. He's headed to Memorial. One of you need to come because I'm still working.*

A huge boulder lands in my stomach and my lungs stop working properly. I put my head through the open space in the plastic divider and the cab driver startles.

"We need to go to Memorial Hospital," I say.

Jax glances at me.

"Dylan was in an accident."

His face pales for a moment, but he quickly recovers. "That asshole will do anything to ruin my date with you." He stares out the window, leg bouncing now.

I say nothing, tapping out a text to our friends to find out who is already there, but no one answers.

CHAPTER THIRTEEN

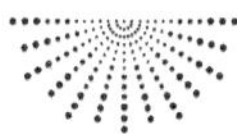

Dylan

"**I**'m fine. Let me go home," I repeat to the nurse who says I need an MRI of my head.

"Just relax, will you? You're making their job, like, ten times harder." Seth sits in the chair to my right, watching *The Bachelor* and eating a bag of Funyuns.

"I'll be back in a few," she says and leaves the room.

"I hate hospitals. It's bad enough I fucking broke my arm." I lift my arm that's in a temporary soft cast until some of the swelling goes down and they put on a hard cast. My *left* fucking arm. The one I write with, the one I wipe my ass with, and most importantly, the one I fucking tattoo people with. My head falls back to the bed. "I have no choice. I'm going to have to offer Jax a job."

It doesn't seem like Seth hears me when he looks away from the screen. "Do you think you could be on this show and kiss some girl one night and another one the next?

Seems a little sleazy the way the guy leads them all on, no?" He chomps down on another onion ring chip. "That probably makes me sound like a pussy. It's probably most guys' wet dream."

Knox walks in. Thank fuck I get a reprieve from *Bachelor* talk for a moment. He's in full uniform, gun holstered to his hip. If someone had told me when I was sixteen that Knox Whelan would be a cop, I would've asked them when their rocket leaves for Mars.

"You're being cited." He hands me a ticket.

"You're ticketing your best friend?" Seth asks.

"No. The other officer did. I'm just delivering the ticket." Knox glances at the television, where the rose ceremony is beginning, and his eyebrows scrunch. "Failure to yield, which means this hospital bill"—he circles his finger at my arm—"is on your insurance, not the guy who hit you."

My head drops back to the bed again. What has happened to my life?

Knox pulls up a chair next to my bed.

"Hey, Knox. Do you think you could be the Bachelor?" Seth asks.

Knox glances at the television again. "Go to exotic places and have twenty gorgeous women vying for me? Yeah, I think I could." His tone says, "Is that even a fucking question?"

"So I'm the pussy." Seth brings his Coke to his lips.

Knox leaves Seth to watch television. Knox has those same eyes I got when Winnie died. The same ones he gave me when I watched Jax make stupid-ass decisions and did nothing. Strike my earlier comment—Knox Whelan was meant to be a cop.

"The witnesses said you were reckless," he says. "That with the rain, you took the corner faster than you should have."

He's telling the facts instead of asking me questions. It's his way. He wants to know what's on my mind. Out of everyone, Knox knows I don't share my problems because people try to fix them and give me those damn looks of pity. That's not changing now.

I could tell him it's about business, which isn't a complete lie. Add on this hospital stay and my insurance deductible, the fact that I'll be out of work until my arm is out of the cast, and it all leads to one word—*broke*!

But the reason I sped through that light was because Rian was stunningly beautiful when she left our apartment to go out with another guy. And not just any guy. Not the smart accountant I always envisioned her marrying. My archenemy. A guy who hates me so much, he'll do anything to hurt me. Jax is a smart guy. It probably took him five minutes in a room with Rian and me to figure out there are hidden feelings there. Jax also knows me well enough to know why I've never done anything about it.

Everyone gets dealt their hand in life. I've made the most of mine. I've been blessed in many ways I wouldn't have thought of, based on the shit hand I was dealt at birth. The one thing I love the most in my life is the friendships I've made. Friends that are like a family to me. Something I've never really had. If I start something with Rian and we can't make it work, which I've never been able to do with anyone, then we split up the group just like a divorced couple would.

I watched it with Sierra and Ethan. The jagged line that divided our close-knit group of friends. Ethan on the outskirts, forced to move out even if he says he did it by choice. It's not worth the risk. What are the chances a guy like me could make Rian happy long term?

"Dylan," Knox says, drawing me from my internal thoughts.

"Like, think about it. When you kiss someone, you're

kissing everyone they've kissed." Seth shakes his head, crumpling up the Funyuns bag and tossing it in the trash can. "And how come the women don't care? Where do they find them to sign up for this? It's kind of sexist." He turns his attention to us only because the show has gone to commercial. "What?"

"Get off the *Bachelor*," Knox says.

Seth props his feet up on my bed and relaxes back into his chair with his fingers laced over his stomach. "I'm just saying—"

Knox shoots Seth the stern dad look before turning to me. "We're your friends, Dylan. You can talk to us."

I blow out a breath and stare at the ceiling.

"Just fucking tell him," Seth says.

My head shoots in his direction. Knox's attention shifts between Seth and me, obviously waiting for one of us to spill.

"Shut up," I say and kick Seth's feet off my bed.

He props them back up.

"Rian went out with Jax tonight," Seth says, smirking as he wiggles his ass to get comfortable in the chair.

"Why are you here again?" I ask him.

"Because I'm your in case of emergency. Which I should say, I feel honored about." Seth's hand covers his heart. "No offense, but mine is my mom, but you know, she'll baby me if something bad happens."

I stare blankly at him.

"I feel oddly offended I'm not your in case of emergency. As pussy as that sounds." Knox looks down as if he's examining himself for thinking that.

"You're a cop. You'll know when something happens to me. Seth's got nothing going on in his life."

"Jeez, thanks." Seth gives me the stink-eye.

"And no offense, I'm changing my in case of emergency

now," I say.

He flips up his middle finger, his attention back on the television. "Man, I'm surprised there aren't any cat fights. One rose left. Even my heart is pounding."

"Is this about Rian going out with Jax?" Knox asks me.

I shake my head. "No."

He looks at me long and hard. Is this what he does with the people he pulls over?

"You're trying to intimidate me into confessing. Not ethical, man."

He chuckles.

"Shit, I hate how they drag out this last rose," Seth says.

"Do you always watch this show?" Knox asks Seth.

They might live together, but they're on opposite shifts most of the time.

Seth scoffs. "No."

Knox picks up the remote from the bed and turns off the television.

"You fucker, he had the rose in his hand!" If looks could kill, Seth just murdered Knox.

"Give me a damn break. Why do you give a shit? There will never be twenty women vying for your heart."

"That's insulting," Seth says. "I like to think I'm quite the catch. Case in point, I don't think the show is very ethical."

I let them go on as long as they want even if it's annoying the shit out of me because who the hell cares at this point? The longer they argue, the less likely the conversation will turn my way again.

Then Knox's radio squawks and his hand raises to the walkie on his shoulder. Thank goodness—he'll have to go. I'll let Seth watch *The Bachelor* and hopefully the nurse will take me for my damn MRI. After Knox is done talking, he stands.

Perfect. Just as I predicted.

"I gotta get back on the road," he says. "Seth, take him

home. You can stay in Leilani's bed if you don't want to stay with Rian and Jax. She can sleep with me."

"I'll be in my bed."

"It's just an offer. You haven't driven your bike crazy since Winnie died." He pins me with a stare.

My hands clench on the sheets. Seth looks at me too. He knows about Winnie. Not everything, just that she was my foster mom who died.

My driving crazy after Winnie died was completely different. I'm actually surprised I'm still alive after all the races I took part in.

"I'm fine in my own bed," I say. "And please let's not make some big deal about this."

"Sure," Knox says.

"Of course not," Seth says.

Just as Knox is leaving the room, Rian appears in the doorway. All the rage from earlier refills the empty well inside me when I see her in that outfit and makeup again.

"They didn't want to let me in." She rushes over to the bed, taking me in as though she's examining where all my injuries might be.

"Where's your date?" I snip.

"Dylan," Knox says, sighing.

"He's in the waiting room. I told the nurse at the front that I was your sister."

"Um… Rian?" Seth asks.

She turns to him, but then looks back at me quickly, looking as if she's mentally checking off each part of my body that isn't harmed.

"Where are your shoes?" Seth asks.

I lean over the bed to see her white-sock-covered feet.

She looks down at them. "I couldn't get my shoes back on. Long story."

"So where are they now?" Seth asks.

I want to take the shortbread cookies they gave me after taking my blood and shove them down Seth's throat when I picture the boots she had on earlier on the floor of Jax's room.

Rian shrugs. "Jax has them."

Knox waves from the doorway. "I'll see you at home. Glad nothing more serious happened."

"Yeah, thanks for the ticket." I hold up the piece of paper.

Rian plucks it from my grasp.

"Hey, you do the crime, you do the time," Knox says.

"Har-har, Officer Knox," Seth says.

Knox flips him off, walking out of the hospital room.

"So is it just your arm?" Rian's hand on mine pulls my attention back to her.

I hate all the makeup Sierra and Blanca put on her. Rian doesn't need to change for Jax. She's beautiful. "Yeah, six weeks in a cast."

Her shoulders fall. "It's your left."

I nod. "Yeah, which means no tattoo unless you want to be my first right-handed attempt." I laugh.

She doesn't. "This is serious. What happened?"

She reads over the ticket, her tongue sliding out as she reads. I desperately want to tell her how cute she looks when she does that. Like when she's trying to tweak a recipe and she thinks about it for most of the day before, her tongue teases me like that the entire time.

Seth clears his throat. "I'm hungry. Anything?" He stands and points at us.

"Nah," I say.

Rian doesn't answer.

"How was your date?" I ask once we're alone so that no one is a witness to me losing my balls.

She puts down the paper. "Failure to yield? The bike is so dangerous."

I wait because I know she heard me and we're not going to play this game.

She sighs. "It was good. We went bowling."

That explains the shoe thing. I'm relieved it wasn't what I was envisioning.

"I'm not sure why you had to put on all that makeup or dress like that." My gaze falls over her body. She's so damn hot, my dick is already on board with banging her. Her tits practically beg for me to grab them, her hard nipples poking out through her bra. "It's way too much."

She stands and heaves a breath. "Thanks for the advice. Next time you can do my makeup."

Of course she takes it wrong.

I grab her hand, my thumb running along her inner wrist. She doesn't pull away, which has to be a good sign. "I've been a bastard."

"Yeah, you have." She doesn't look at me.

"Okay, you ready to ride the MRI train?" A woman I haven't seen before comes in. She smiles sweetly at both of us. "He'll be right back." She unlocks the wheels on the bed, and before I have time to say anything or stop her, I'm being taken out of the room. "You can wait here or go down to vending. We'll be about thirty or forty minutes."

Rian says nothing, and I can't see anything since the bed is already rolling.

On my way down the hall, I get a glimpse of the waiting room. I see Knox and Jax in deep conversation by a vending machine. Seth is with Ethan and Blanca. Adrian and Sierra are just walking in, both with just fucked heads of hair.

It all reconfirms not to fuck with this. It wasn't that long ago when I was laid up in the emergency room with a horrible case of the flu and there was no one to call. I waited for discharge and I left the hospital all by myself. Back when my in case of emergency was an empty box.

CHAPTER FOURTEEN

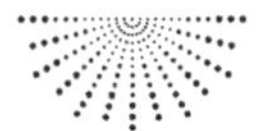

Rian

I sit in the chair in Dylan's hospital room. I'd never admit to anyone how scared I was when I saw that message from Knox. How does a police officer not tell you exactly what's wrong? If he would've said Dylan's conscious, I wouldn't have been nearly as worried that something horrible had happened.

"Oh, did they take him for his MRI?" A nurse comes in, sanitizes her hands, and stops by the door.

"Yeah."

Her smile dims into a sympathetic look. "Oh, don't worry. I'm sure he's fine. He's one of the smart ones who wears a helmet. But he'll need some help until that cast comes off."

"Of course."

"My husband slipped on the ice at his job last winter and had to have surgery on his shoulder. As you know, men can't handle things like this quite like us women can. He whined and complained his whole recovery. I chalked it up to him having the 'man flu.'" She puts man flu in quotations. "But turns out he got so depressed, we had to get antidepressants. It's hard for men like them to sit back and allow their loved ones to care for them."

She talks as though she knows Dylan. My gut twists when the question pops in my head, and I'm not even prepared to hear the answer. She's only a few years older than us and I spotted a tattoo on the inside of her wrist when she raised her hands to sanitize them. "Do you know Dylan?"

"No. I just know his type. A replica of my husband." She picks up the papers on the tray. "Mind if I go over the care instructions with you?"

I sit up straighter. Should I tell her we're not a couple? Then the haunting thought that might be going through Dylan's mind right now triggers in my own. Who will help him? He doesn't have a girlfriend to see him back to health. He's definitely too proud to ask.

"Sure," I say, knowing that Dylan's rehabilitation is up to me.

"My husband loved the sponge baths." She laughs. "But just wrap his arm in plastic and use a scrunchie to secure it at the top of the arm. If you need to, a bigger rubber band will help. He obviously can't swim in a pool. No scratching by sticking a pen or ruler or anything down there. He'll probably go through some itching as it heals, so keep an eye out for that." She shrugs. "Other than that, it's just a broken arm. He did say it's his dominant though, which means he'll have to relearn to do stuff with his right, I suppose."

She stands and tucks the doctor's chair under a table with a computer on it. She scans her badge and types away.

Seth walks in with a Snickers bar in hand. "What's up, buttercup?" The nurse looks at him and he raises his hand. "In case of emergency contact." He points at himself with a big grin then sits next to me and holds the Snickers bar in front of my face.

"No thanks."

"Oh, you look sour like Knox did earlier. All these people vying to be Dylan's in case of emergency. I know. I was shocked too."

I stare blankly at him, and even the nurse is eyeing him from the corner of her eye.

"Should I go over the care instructions with him?" she asks, closing up the computer.

"Care instructions?" he asks.

"No, I'm Dylan's roommate," I say.

"What kind of care instructions?" Seth asks again.

"Sponge bath techniques," the nurse says, picking up the papers and handing them to him.

The Snickers bar drops to his lap and he holds up his hands in front of him like a ten-year-old boy.

The nurse laughs. "I think you need to have a conversation about that in case of emergency thing. As soon as his MRI comes back clean, the doctor will be in and you guys can get home."

"Thank you," I say.

She smiles and walks out of the room.

Seth picks up his Snickers bar and blows on it. "What're your thoughts on the *Bachelor*?"

AN HOUR LATER, Dylan is released and being wheeled out in a wheelchair by an orderly. Seth is on one side and I'm on the other. All our friends stand as we push through the doors of the waiting room. Each of them hugs Dylan or shakes his hand. Jax is even there, having stuck around, and the two do a handshake thing I've never seen Dylan do with anyone.

A few minutes later, we're all outside and Adrian's car pulls into the circle.

We shuffle Dylan into the car and the orderly goes back into the hospital. We all split up between Ethan, Adrian, and Seth's cars. Somehow, I end up with Blanca and Ethan.

"This is a nice car, Ethan."

"Thanks. It's nothing like Adrian's, but it gets us from A to B," he says with a big smile. It's not a brand new car, but it's his first. I know how proud he was when he purchased it last month.

We aren't even out of the circle driveway of the hospital before Blanca peers at me between the seats. "So?"

"So what?" I ask.

"How was the date?"

Ethan says nothing. I've actually known him longer than I've known Blanca, so even though it feels a little odd, talking about Jax in front of him isn't weird.

"It was good. He's a really nice guy."

"Nice?" Blanca looks at Ethan for a moment before her brown eyes land on me again. "Did anything happen?"

"Blanc," Ethan says.

"I'm just asking." She waves. "You don't have to answer if you don't want to."

"I didn't kiss him. We were just leaving the bowling alley when we got the call about Dylan," I say.

I'm not sure if I want to tell Blanca, and Ethan, that Jax saw right through me. That he knows I'm pathetic and have fallen for a man who will never feel the same about me. It's embarrassing even if Blanca knows my feelings for Dylan. But to deny the attention of another guy because of that crush feels ridiculous. Like I'm holding out for something that's never going to happen.

"Oh, I bet he knows how to kiss," she says.

"Blanca!" Ethan yells.

Blanca bites her lip. "Not as good as you, babe." She kisses his cheek before whispering something in his ear.

"Better," Ethan says.

"Do you think you'll go out with him again?" she asks.

I shrug. "I'm not sure. We're roommates, and I don't want to mess that up either."

Blanca turns back around to face forward. Ethan looks at me in the rearview mirror, and our eyes meet. I can tell by his expression that I'm not as transparent as I like to think to him either.

"Dylan's going to need some help until that cast comes off," he says, giving me an out of the conversation about Jax.

I mouth, "Thank you," and he nods.

"Yeah, we'll all have to pitch in," Blanca says.

"I'm sure I can handle most of it," I say. "Who knows? Jax stayed around the hospital, so maybe those two can kiss and make up now."

"Yeah, what's up with them?" Blanca asks.

Ethan looks at me again through the rearview mirror as if he knows everything.

"I have no idea," I lie because it's not my business to share.

Thankfully, Blanca isn't Sierra. She gives up. Sierra's like the dog that never lets go of the tug toy until you give her something bigger and better.

We pull up to the apartment building and Ethan lets us out before he goes to hunt for a parking space. Dylan and Sierra are already waiting at the doors since Adrian gets to park in the lot designated for his building across the street.

"Here, take your boots." I pass her the boots I have in my hand. "You can go, Sierra," I tell her, inserting our key into the building.

"Are you sure?" she asks.

"God yes. Please carry on with your sex fest," Dylan says, walking over with a mumbled thanks after I open the door.

"Okay, I'll come by and check on you tomorrow!" She's already about to cross the street.

"I guess we don't have to tell her twice," Blanca says, following us inside.

We ride the elevator, Blanca asking Dylan a million questions about what happened. He only offers one-word answers. She shoots me looks behind his back.

Dylan digs his keys out of the pocket of his jacket and tries to open our door with his right hand, but the tip of the key keeps missing the hole.

"Struggle to get it in? That's probably a first for you," Blanca says, laughing on her way down to her apartment.

"Here." I hold out my hand even though my keys are in my purse.

"I have to figure it out eventually."

He doesn't release them, and I watch the tip of the key keep hitting the lock. I think whatever pain killer they must've given him at the hospital is affecting him. Finally, it goes in the hole and he unlocks the deadbolt, but we still have the bottom lock. Amazingly, it only takes four tries until we're in, but by the time we enter, Jax, Seth, and Ethan are in the hallway with us.

"Just call me if you need me. Remember, I'm his in case of emergency," Seth says and Jax slams the door in his face.

"I'm going to make him a badge," Jax says, moving right to the fridge. He pulls out two beers and one water bottle, untwists the caps, and hands the water to Dylan, a beer to me, and downs a huge sip of his own beer. "Well, this sucks, huh?"

Dylan says nothing and downs his water. I take off and throw the white gym socks in the trash.

"Hey now, I paid good money for those socks!" Jax laughs, and I join in.

Dylan grunts and stands. "Listen, you guys, don't worry about me. I'll be fine."

"Let me help you get settled in bed. I have some extra pillows," I say.

But Dylan is already halfway to his room. When he gets to the door, he turns to us again. "I'm good. Promise." Then he disappears into his room.

Jax steps over to me. "He's such a martyr, I swear."

"He's too proud."

Jax rolls his eyes and puts his empty beer bottle in the recycling. "I'm going to head to bed too. It was nice going out with you tonight even if…" He leans forward and I wonder what I would do if he did try to kiss me. "It was platonic. I don't usually welcome second place, Rian."

I bite my lip, unsure what he wants me to say.

"But if you ever get lonely at night, my bed is open." He winks.

I'm not sure if he's serious or just has no idea how to handle the situation we find ourselves in.

After his door shuts, I dump my beer down the drain and add the bottle to the recycling bin, lock the apartment door, and go into my room. Once I'm completely ready for bed, I knock on Dylan's door. He mumbles a come in and I twist the doorknob.

"Just checking on…" My words trail off as my gaze falls to his bare chest.

I've seen Dylan shirtless plenty of times, but never have I seen him only in his boxer briefs. They're lime green—which seems odd to me because the majority of his wardrobe is black and gray. I would've placed money on them being a neutral color. Maybe navy blue. But never lime green.

"Eyes up here, Rian," he says.

As my vision sweeps up his hard chest to his eyes, I find his attention centered on my chest. It's then I realize I'm not wearing a bra and I'm nipping. They're like two flashlights seeking attention.

"I could say the same."

He laughs, licks his lips. "I've never seen you in that," he says, nodding toward my silk-and-lace tank-and-short pajama set.

"I change before coming out in the morning. I wasn't thinking."

"Are you telling me you're a closet lingerie wearer?" he asks, his smirk so big my stomach flip-flops nonstop.

"No, it's just not appropriate to wear…"

His gaze descends down my body one more time and I really wish I would have grabbed my cardigan. I just thought I'd pop my head in.

"You're right. I don't want Owens to see you like that."

His words warm me, and I nibble on my bottom lip. "Do you need another pillow or anything?"

"No. I'm good."

I nod with one last look at him. "Okay then. Goodnight."

"Goodnight, Rian," he says, and I shut the door.

As I hustle back to my room, I've never felt sexier. Maybe my lingerie needs to come out a little more often.

CHAPTER FIFTEEN

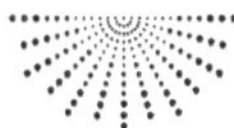

Dylan

Monday. Ink Envy is closed, but the minute my alarm goes off because I should be getting ready to go to the gym, I groan. My permanent cast was put on yesterday and it's even more awkward and uncomfortable than the temporary one was.

Sliding my ass to the edge of my bed, I stand then open my dresser drawer and pull out a pair of track pants. Sitting back down, I open the right side to step through successfully, but opening the left is somehow impossible. After sweat beads along my hairline, I get my leg in, but now I have to pull them up.

"I look like I'm doing some kind of chicken dance at a wedding," I mumble, shimmying them up my legs.

Forget the damn T-shirt.

I walk into the living room and toward the kitchen. Rian's

just getting out of bathroom. Shit, did it really take me that long to get the pants on?

"How are you this morning?" She tightens her robe.

It's not the first time I've thought about her being naked under that puffy thing. But after I tried unsuccessfully to beat off with my right hand after she came in wearing those short silk shorts and tight cami that outlined her tits last night, I have to try to ignore the thought of her naked. Going six weeks with blue balls isn't going to help my mood.

Again, her eyes fall to my chest. It makes me want to walk around without a shirt on all the time.

"I'm good. Sore." I'm not sure sore from the broken arm. The bruises and scrapes all demand more attention at the moment.

"Well, eat something before taking the pain pills." She walks across the living room.

"Got it, Mom, but I need to take a shower before I do anything."

Her feet stop and she turns around. "Your nurse told me that you have to wrap the cast up in plastic." She comes toward me. "She said we could try one of my scrunchies."

"Yeah, I read the instructions last night."

She grabs a garbage bag, not listening to me, and puts it over my arm. "Like this, I think. Maybe I should YouTube it?" She leaves the bag on my arm and turns to head back to her room.

"I got it, Rian, no worries."

"Are you sure?"

I nod.

"Okay." Her expression reminds me of the day she couldn't get the puppy. "Well, my scrunchies are in the drawer on the left."

She disappears through her bedroom door and I feel like an asshole for not allowing her to help me, but somehow, I think she's probably not surprised. I chomp down on a granola bar and take two of my painkillers before taking my garbage bag to the bathroom.

I open up the left drawer and there's a stockpile of hair stuff. I put my arm through the garbage bag and roll the scrunchie up my arm, although it feels like my circulation is cut off.

Taking a shower without the use of your dominant hand sucks. My right hand feels as if I'm a robot and it's short-circuiting every minute. By the time I'm finished, I still don't feel completely clean. And drying myself off? It's a damn joke. I can't wrap the towel around my waist with only one hand. My track pants are my only hope of walking out of here covered.

I stick one leg through the pants, though my skin is still damp because I apparently have no muscle strength in my right arm to even dry my skin. Shimmying them up my legs like I did this morning is ten times harder with wet skin, and I end up falling on my ass with a huge bang.

"Fuck!"

A knock sounds on the door immediately.

"I'm good, Rian," I say.

"Okay. I can cover my eyes if that makes you feel more comfortable." There's a long pause. "I mean, if you need help."

I look between my legs, my dick limp and flaccid. No way in hell is she coming in here.

But the track pants aren't an option either.

"I need you to close your eyes because I'm going out with only a towel covering my dick."

"Oh… okay." Then there's nothing for a second. "My eyes are closed."

I shrug off the track pants. Covering my dick with a towel, I open the door and walk out.

Rian's at the kitchen table with her hand covering her closed eyes. "I'm not looking. Swear."

"She might not be, but I am. Great bod, Phillips."

Jax shuts the fridge door with a smile. He's actually dressed in a shirt and pajama pants on for once.

"Fuck off, Owens." I slam my bedroom door like an angry teenager.

THIS FUCKING SUCKS. I look at the zip-up hoodie I laid on my bed. I need to cut the left sleeve to work with my cast, but I have no scissors. Not to mention if I try to cut it with my right hand, it will never work out. Having no other choice, I open my bedroom door, looking for Jax.

What I find is Rian still at the kitchen table.

"What are you doing here?"

She glances up then down then back up. I'm still shirtless. If I'm not careful, she'll become immune to the image soon.

"I'm working from home. Pierson doesn't have a problem with it."

"Why?"

"To help you." She stands from the chair. "What do you need?"

"I was going to have Jax…"

"Jax just left. Went to do his laundry."

He's never up this early. And laundry? Likely excuse. Where did he really go? If it was the city… I stop my mind from assuming anything. Jax isn't my business. He never really was, and if he wants to look up old acquaintances and get into trouble, I can't stop him.

"I just need someone to cut off my sweatshirt sleeve."

She turns and opens her junk drawer that's not really a junk drawer. It's more like an organized miscellaneous drawer. All her different types of tape are lined up according to size. Coupons stacked neatly in the corner. She turns back around with a pair of scissors. "Got it."

Before I can blink, she's in my room. Although this hasn't always been my room, I've made mine since living here and it feels weird to have her in my space.

She eyes the sweatshirt on my bed. "Do you know where I should cut it already?"

"I never put it on, so no."

She picks it up and unzips it. With her feather-light touch, she pulls it over my good arm. Her wet hair is twisted into a bun on top of her head and her face is bare of makeup. She's beautiful, pure, and natural. How does she not see that? Allowing Blanca and Sierra to give her a makeover was unnecessary.

She arranges the other side of the sweatshirt to rest on my shoulder, the sleeve hanging down empty. She reaches for my casted arm and eyeballs where she'll have to cut. Her eyes follow the track of her hands until our eyes connect.

I swallow past the dryness in my mouth. "Thanks for doing this."

She steps closer, tearing her eyes from mine and touching the part of the sweatshirt we'll be cutting off. "Do you have a pen?" She moves to my dresser where my sketchbook is and stops, staring at the picture. "Dylan…" A sigh falls from her lips. "It's beautiful. Did someone request this?"

I admire the peony tattoo I'm sketching for her. "No. I just sketched it for someone who I think it would be beautiful on."

Her ass falls to my bed and her hands run down the paper. "I love it."

"Really?" I seek out the confirmation that I really do know her as well as I think I do.

"Yeah. I never knew if I'd have the guts for a tattoo.

Seeing all the girls who go into Ink Envy and pick a generic tattoo that could be on anyone else's body never appealed to me. This is unique. When you do something like this, do you ever resell the image?" She stares at the picture in her hand.

"No. Not if the client asked me to draw it."

"So you could draw something for me that's just mine and no one else would have it?"

My mind screams *tell her*. Tell her you drew the peony for her. Let her eyes soften and her lips part. Open yourself up and allow her to climb in. Rian is safe, she'd never destroy the friendship you've built.

Instead I say, "Definitely. As soon as I'm out of the cast, I can sketch something. Any ideas?"

Coward, my conscience screams.

She glances at the sketchbook. "Just something beautiful like this."

"And you'll really let me tattoo you?"

She nods and stands, abandoning the sketchbook on the bed and picking up the scissors and the pen. She marks a spot on the sleeve, and I suffer through her closeness while she helps me take off my sweatshirt. She cuts off the sleeve and puts the hoodie back on me.

"Thanks," I say.

"Zipped or unzipped?" Her fingers hold the edge of the zipper dangerously close to my dick that's at half-chub from the scent of her soap and her being so near.

I'm screwed. Why now, after all these years, is she like a drug and I'm an addict? "Zipped."

After she's done, we go out to the living room, her heading to the kitchen table and me to the couch.

"How's that problem going?" I ask, clicking on the news.

"It's okay. I think I might have part of it right, but this might be above my intelligence level. No matter what my parents believe."

I slide on the cushion so I'm turned in her direction, resting my broken arm on the back of the couch. "You're the smartest woman I know." And that's the truth.

She rolls her eyes. "Thanks."

"Does my opinion mean nothing?"

She stands from the chair and refills her coffee cup. She pulls another cup, fills it, and comes over to me. "You get a coffee for the compliment."

I sip the black coffee. "Is this how we'll work it?"

She laughs. "Sure."

"In all seriousness, you know you don't have to stay home. I'll manage."

She picks up her coffee and joins me on the couch. "I get that you're not used to having people to count on, but you have us. We all want the best for you."

"Thanks, but—"

"No, Dylan. I can do the same work here as I can at the office. After a few weeks when you're used to the cast, I'll go back, but you'll have to suck it up for now. This is the way it is." She tucks her legs under her body and sips her coffee.

My chest gets a warm funny feeling in it. "Listen, about last night…"

I want to say what I should have told her a long time ago. It's time she knows how I feel about her and why I've ignored the telltale signs that maybe she likes me more than a friend.

She glances away from the television to me. "What's up?"

I open my mouth to tell her, but the buzzer from downstairs goes off.

She places her coffee on the table, standing to answer. "I have no idea who that would be." She presses the intercom button near the door of the apartment. "Hello?"

"Hey, it's Frankie."

"Come on up." Rian presses the button to allow her in

then opens our apartment door a crack. "I'm going to bake some cookies or something. I'm sure you'll have a lot of visitors today."

Just like that, I lose the nerve to say lock the door, keep Frankie out, and let me be straight with you.

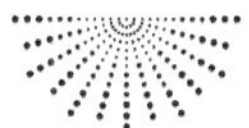

CHAPTER SIXTEEN

Dylan

Jolie's sings as she and Frankie come through the door. Rian's giddy to see the three-year-old and already cleared the table of her work. I'm fairly sure she can't bake cookies when she's at the office, but I'm not saying anything. I fear I'll need Rian's help, so her being around is probably a good thing.

"Uncle Dylan!" Jolie runs toward me but stops. She points at my arm. "Hurt?"

Frankie follows right behind, closing the door and saying hello to Rian with a hug. She's thinner than she was a week ago.

"Hey, boss," Frankie says, sitting in the chair beside the couch, Jolie's bag between her legs. Her jeans and T-shirt hang off her. She's always been thin, but she's gauntly now.

"Jolie, want to help me make monster cookies?" Rian asks.

Jolie's eyes widen and her mouth forms a small O. She

stares at me as though she's wondering if she heard Rian ask that or if she's hearing things.

"Whoa, did you ever come on a good day, huh?" I say.

She unzips her coat as she circles around the room to reach Rian.

Frankie sends Rian a look of appreciation before she leans back, her eyes wide on me. "Fell off your bike, huh?"

"Yeah, I'm out for six weeks."

"I heard," she says. "And what are we going to do about it?"

I sit up, sliding down the couch toward her so we can talk with a little more privacy, although Jolie's excitement is so loud, I doubt they can hear us. Rian probably wouldn't care or judge me anyway, but the alpha in me would prefer her not to know business is bad. "Are you back now?"

She nods. "He's locked up." Her worried eyes venture to Jolie.

I touch her knee. "How long?"

Frankie lives a complicated life and I try not to pry, allowing her to dish out information as she sees fit. I guess it's because of how I grew up.

"Six months, I hope."

At least she should be in good shape to take over Ink Envy for me. "I need to find a replacement for myself. I went to the city before this happened and nothin'. Lyle is progressing, but I don't want to rush him."

She laughs. "He told me you lost your cool the other day. I thought he was going to piss his pants when he called."

Good to know my employees gossip about me.

"Yeah, not my finest moment. Neither was getting myself in this situation." I lift the cast.

"And how exactly did you do that?"

I glance over my shoulder to where Rian is tying one of her aprons on Jolie.

"Rian, it's okay if she gets dirty," Frankie says.

"Yay!" Rian looks at Jolie and they toss the apron away. "How about I sit down and just read you the directions?" Rian sits and crosses her legs, but Jolie grabs her hand to pull her back up.

"We'll talk about it later," I say and try to move my left hand up to my hair. Fuck.

"Oh, I gotcha." Frankie winks. She's been giving me hell about Rian for a while now.

We shoot the shit about nothing important. I fill her in on the shop. She asks about the arm and the accident. Jolie and Rian have fun making cookies.

I head into the kitchen to get Frankie a coffee, where I catch a glimpse of the cookies. "I thought they'd look like monsters?"

Rian pours out a container of sprinkles on top of the drops of batter she already has on the cookie sheets. Jolie watches on with wide eyes.

"No, they're just big cookies with a lot of sprinkles and candies."

She really is great with kids. Another damn checkmark for Rian.

Frankie and I chitchat the entire morning. Once Jolie gets bored baking cookies, she pours the contents of her bag on the table in front of the television. Soon the news gets replaced by a talking dog show.

Frankie and I move to the kitchen to help Rian with the cookies. Mostly Frankie though.

"So what's he paying you to nurse him back to health?" Frankie asks Rian.

"He'd prefer to be left alone. You know how he thinks he always has everything under control." Rian rolls her eyes.

"Oh, I can only imagine. What's he had you do so far?" Frankie asks.

Rian tells her about the bathroom and how she had to close her eyes after my shower, then tells her about the sweatshirt situation, not mentioning the sexual tension. Unless maybe she didn't feel the thick as smoke pull in the air.

They like to talk about me as if I'm not there. I guess Rian knows me the best out of all the girls we hang out with and Frankie is stuck with me at work, day after day. They openly complain about me when we're all around each other.

Right before Frankie packs up Jolie because she has to take a nap, Jax walks in with his laundry bag over his shoulder. Frankie eyes him as he stops just inside the door, his large duffle falling to the floor in front of him.

Jolie runs over, her feet sliding to a stop in front of him. "Who are you?"

Jax peers down at Jolie, then at us standing around the kitchen. "Did I just walk into the wrong apartment?"

Rian laughs. "Jax, this is Frankie." She places her hand on Frankie's shoulder as Frankie nods a hello. "And that's her daughter, Jolie."

"I'm Jax," he says to Jolie, picking up his duffle and swinging it over his shoulder. He walks to his room.

"Friendly guy," Frankie says.

"He really is a nice guy," Rian adds, which bothers me to a degree I'm not comfortable with.

"Oh, Rian." Frankie puts her hand on Rian's shoulder and shakes her head.

"What?" Rian asks, packing up cookies for them to take home.

"We're just different. You always see the good in people and I always see the bad." Frankie puts her purse over her shoulder.

That's all I need to hear. Rian sees the good in me, and she won't see my bad until I've already hurt her. Without even asking for it, Frankie gave me the advice I needed to hear.

"I'm going to walk them out," I say to Rian.

Frankie hugs Rian goodbye. "Don't let him talk you into any sponge baths or anything."

Rian's cheeks redden. I love that look on her. Before I was restricted to only using my right hand, I'd imagine telling her all the things I wanted to do to her and that blush hijacking her body when I beat off.

"Thanks, Rian." Jolie hugs Rian while consuming a cookie that's bigger than her face.

"Bye, Jolie." Rian hugs her tightly. "You're welcome any time you want, okay?"

Jolie nods, hugs my knees, and I tug on one of her pigtails.

Outside in the hallway, Frankie lets Jolie have her phone and sit against the wall so we can talk.

"So what's really up?" she asks.

"If I don't find anyone soon, I'm going to ask Jax"—I nod toward my apartment—"to come in on a temporary basis."

"Wait." She shakes her head. "Who is that guy?"

I blow out a breath. Frankie wouldn't be impressed by the people Jax has tattooed. She's strictly does it for love, not money. But she follows enough artists that she'll know who he is.

"Jax Owens."

Her mouth drops open. "Shut the front door!" She moves to beeline by me, but I grab her arm and pull her back. "Why didn't you introduce me to him?"

"Rian introduced you."

She cocks her hip. "No, Rian introduced me to a new *roommate* of yours named Jax."

I shrug. "Not my fault you didn't recognize him."

Technically it'd be Jax's. He's not big on his picture being on Instagram. He showcases his artwork more often than not.

"So you're going to have me manage *him*?" She points toward the door.

I nod.

"You're insane. And please tell me why you're allowing the business to suffer when the solution is right inside that apartment?"

I stare at her for a moment. "He went to high school with Knox and me. We aren't exactly on the best of terms."

She pats my shoulder. "Time to kiss some ass, Dylan. And since I was going to bring this up later anyway, you should be kissing Rian's ass too while you're at it. Literally." She glances at Jolie, who's watching something uber loud that echoes through the hall.

"My mind is so fucked up right now."

"Good." She smiles sweetly.

Frankie isn't a sweet girl. She's the girl other girls are afraid of. She's got a sharp tongue and her insults cut deep. She can come back with a snappy retort within a second and she honestly doesn't give a shit what you think of her.

That's why she says, "I'm going to be your working mind for the time being. You're going to go in there and ask Jax to come work at Ink Envy. Give him whatever the hell he wants. And then you're going to tell Rian exactly how you feel."

"What the hell are you talking about?"

"Make a good deal. Tell him you want a percentage of who he brings in. It happens all the time."

I shake my head because the Jax thing I can handle. And she's right—I'm sitting on my gold mine, fiddling with my limp dick.

"And the Rian thing." She places her hand on my heart. "It's a good thing. You're a good guy. Stop pretending you don't like her, because if I had to guess, this experiment of the two of you together day in and day out, alone? It's gonna blow up in your face if neither one of you will talk about it, and it'll kill the friendship. Be mature and talk it out."

"You seriously want me to tell her 'I like you' as though I'm some twelve-year-old adolescent boy who just got his first boner?"

She laughs and shakes her head. "You have to get out of your own head first. For now, save your company. No one wants to date an unemployed loser," Frankie playfully smacks me on my cheek. "Let's go, Jolie."

They disappear into the elevator, and I walk back into the apartment. Frankie's words aren't helping me in the slightest. When I get inside, all the baking stuff is put away, replaced with her work stuff on the kitchen table now. Rian smiles at me, and I beeline across the apartment, knocking on Jax's door before I lose my nerve.

"Come in," he says.

I open it to find that he hasn't really made the room his. It still has Sierra's cream-colored bedframe she left behind. There are no posters or pictures or anything personal, and his clothes lay in piles on the floor as though he'd just have to stack them together to pack into his bag to leave.

He tosses his book aside and pulls his Air Pods out of his ears. "What's up?"

"Ever think about taking some shifts at Ink Envy?" I should ask nicer.

He glances at me from the corner of his eye and his smirk shines bright. He knew this day was coming. "I have been kind of bored lately. Who was that girl here with the kid?"

"She works there. We can do this one of two ways. You work and she'll manage you, or you rent a chair."

"I'll rent a chair."

"Okay."

After we negotiate price, we reach that awkward point where I should probably thank him. He knows exactly why I came in here. I'm screwed and we both know it. He's my only hope of keeping Ink Envy.

He says, "I'll post on my Instagram and tell them by appointment only. Can they book through your place?"

"Yeah. Maybe I'll take over the schedules. I can at least do shit like that." I raise my arm.

"Sounds good," he says.

"Okay then. Are you starting tomorrow?"

"Yeah."

"Any days off you want?"

He shakes his head but then stops. "I'm good as long as Mondays are always off."

"Yeah, shop's closed Mondays so no worries." I'm actually impressed we're being so civil to one another.

I go to leave, and my hand is on the doorknob when I look at him over my shoulder. "Thanks," I say, not nearly loud enough.

"Happy to help your sorry ass out." He grins.

I huff. One day we'll have to converse more than we are right now, but I'm at max capacity for touchy-feely shit today.

CHAPTER SEVENTEEN

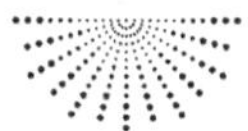

Rian

Five days after he came home from the hospital, Dylan is fully wallowing in his own self-pity.

"Look at you," I say, coming out of the bathroom.

Every day he comes out of his bedroom and plants his big body on the couch, where he watches daytime television. Yesterday I stole the remote when he put on the soap opera channel.

"What?"

"You should be at the shop. You're not unable to walk. It's just a broken arm. That adorable scruff you love so much is now a full-on mountain man beard. And the whole not showering thing?"

He stares at me as though he can't understand the words I'm saying.

I pick up a pillow and throw it at his head. "Hello?"

He whips it back at me as though I'm his annoying

younger sister. I wouldn't be surprised if that's all he sees me as.

"Want to help me make up math word problems?" I sit in the chair by the couch, cross-legged with my computer on my lap.

"Sure. If I sleep for five hours and Rian sleeps for zero hours for the next six weeks, how many more hours of happiness do I have?"

"Now your lazy mood has affected your brain because that's a stupid word question."

He glances at me then looks back at the television. "Aren't you kind of like an educator? There are no stupid questions?"

"There are stupid questions, and I'm not an educator."

He props up his head on his good arm. "Fine. How about if I lay here for ten more hours and do the same thing for the next three days, how long until the couch smells like ass?"

"The couch already smells like ass. Plus there's not enough information to logically answer that question."

He grunts and his head falls back on the pillow. I pull the pillow out from under his head and his head crashes to the arm of the couch. I hate this whole "feel sorry for myself" version of Dylan. Not to mention being alone with him in our apartment day in and out kind of sucks. Jax is working at Ink Envy now. Other than when he pops in between clients to grab something to eat, it's just Dylan and me. Time I would have cherished before he turned into this man I don't recognize.

"Well, if I didn't have a concussion before, I have one now." He sits up and rubs the side of his head, staring at me like a confused boy.

"Why don't I start a shower for you?" I close my laptop. "We could go for a walk or go visit Ink Envy. Get lunch."

"Or I could sit here and find out if Jake really *is* the father."

I shake my head, concentrating on my computer as I try to find some other way to get to him. I'm not strong enough to get him into the shower. Even if I did manage that feat, how would I keep him there? Then there's the whole thing about wrapping his arm in plastic.

"Can I bribe you?" The words fall out of my mouth as soon as they pop into my mind.

"Bribe me? I never figured you for bartering sexual favors, but…" He laughs, hooking his thumbs into his track pants.

My eyes betray me before I can look away. Damn them. "I was thinking more with my baking. Chocolate cake with Oreo crumbs between the layers with the chocolate frosting." Surely that will make him stand and take a shower.

"Eh."

I swear I've entered another dimension. Dylan loves chocolate more than sex. I think. I'm not exactly sure, of course.

"Seriously?"

He glances up from the television. "You think you own me when it comes to your baking, don't you?"

I roll my eyes and concentrate on the same question I've been trying to form for the past hour. "No."

"You do." The familiar lilt to his voice that's been void since the accident is present and my stomach flutters.

"Well, you usually do go gaga over my chocolate desserts."

He laughs. "So all these years, you've been using them to get what you want?"

I scrunch my eyes. If I got what I want, I would have him and I would have used my naked body to persuade him to get into the shower. "You act like I've swindled money from you."

He shakes his head. "No, but remember that time we were arguing about what new series to start watching? You wanted *Blue Bloods* and I wanted *Hawaii Five-O*. What do we watch now? *Blue Bloods*."

"You're absurd. We put that to a vote."

"You made chocolate on chocolate cake that night."

"How do you even remember that?" I close my laptop because I can't concentrate right now.

He snaps his fingers and points an accusatory finger at me. "And what about that time we were talking about going on a weekend trip? And it was a split vote between skiing in Vermont or Portland, Maine?"

I bite my lip to not smile. "Those are just coincidences," I say with as straight of a face as I can manage.

"Bullshit. You use your baked goods like a pair of brand new tits."

I cough out a laugh. "You're delusional and that's disgusting. I would do no such thing."

He shakes his head in a joking manner. "To think I thought I could trust you, that you were different, but all women use tactics against men to get what they want."

The buzzing of someone calling up from downstairs interrupts us.

I place my computer on the coffee table and make my way over to the door. "You're very wrong. Cake is not the same as sex."

"Maybe to me it is. Maybe I like your chocolate cake as much as I love tits." He winks.

I pretend to roll my eyes. But the idea that Dylan thinks about my tits does weird things to my insides.

"Imagine if I licked chocolate frosting off a pair of tits. Best of both worlds."

Thank goodness I'm no longer right in front of him because my entire body feels as if an inferno is ready to engulf me in a ball of flames.

I press the intercom button and say hello.

"Hey, it's Lyle. Is Dylan there?"

I pretend to laugh. "Of course he is, but plug your nose when you come in."

I press the button to let him in downstairs, then I open the door and walk back to the chair, picking up my computer.

Dylan's hand lands on my upper thigh, way too close to the center of my legs. "Your chocolate cake doesn't control me anymore."

I stare at his hand, his warmth leaking through my leggings and spreading across my skin like a brush fire. I set my computer on the table again and lean toward him. "Okay, so if I bake one right now, you wouldn't take a shower for one slice?"

His fingertips grip my inner thigh a little tighter and all I can think about is how if they inched a little higher, they'd be exactly where I want them.

"Not on your life."

"Only one way to test the theory," I singsong.

He wraps one arm around my waist and pulls me into his lap. With only one arm, he still manages to tickle my ribcage as I squirm out of his hold.

"You're going to hurt your arm," I say.

Between his track pants and my leggings, I'm sliding around his lap. His lips are right at my ear, my body over his. It's then a hard ridge slides against the seam of my ass.

We both freeze in place.

"Is this what you guys do for fun?"

Our heads whip up to Lyle gawking over the couch. I scurry off Dylan's lap. He grabs the pillow and places it over his crotch.

"Rian," Lyle says, his eyes scanning my body as if he has X-ray vision.

"Lyle," I say, though not in the same flirtatious tone he said my name.

Not that he's a bad kid, but he's just that—a kid. Lyle's nineteen and has followed Dylan around since he was sixteen, begging for him to take him on as an apprentice. Dylan finally had a moment of weakness last year and took him under his wing.

"You two could add Jell-O or oil to your wrestling routine," Lyle says with a smirk.

"What do you want?" Dylan asks.

Lyle sits on the opposite end of the couch as I busy myself in the kitchen, trying to convince myself that my ass wiggling didn't give Dylan a hard-on.

"You gotta come down to the shop. Frankie and Jax argue nonstop. It's bringing back memories of my childhood, man." Lyle's voice cracks as if he's going to cry.

"What are they fighting over?" I ask, my interest piqued. I thought for sure they'd work well together.

"Everything. His clients. Her clients. What's for lunch. The candy Frankie brought in for clients. The magazines in the waiting area. Everything and anything. It's like they secretly enjoy it." Lyle pinches the bridge of his nose.

"And you're here why?" Dylan asks.

"Because you're the boss. Fix it. I can't be creative in that type of environment."

Dylan looks at me and I shrug.

"Jax actually says things?" Dylan asks, which would be my question.

Frankie definitely speaks her mind and I can see her going crazy about certain things. But Jax is pretty laid-back, allowing stuff to roll off his shoulders.

"He mostly grumbles and grunts. But they went in the storage room to hash it out when this group of girls came in last night. They came for Jax, but as you know, he's booked."

Dylan nods.

"He told them they could stay and observe if they wanted. Frankie lost it because she had a client booked and there was nowhere for them to sit while they waited."

As Lyle tells the story, he's so dramatic. Like they're his parents having fights all over again.

Dylan raises his hand. "Okay, I'll head over and see if I can't get this straightened out."

Lyle looks him over. "After you shower, right? Because they'll probably just team up on you if you come in looking like that. How much food has fallen into that shag carpet on your chin?"

Dylan peers down at the track pants and T-shirt I think he's been sleeping and living in, then he looks at me.

"And I didn't even have to make the chocolate cake." I smile sweetly.

He grumbles and stands, heading to his room. "Give me a half hour."

Lyle stands. "You guys are into some kinky shit." He leaves, shutting the door.

Dylan walks out of his room. "Well, lucky you. You get to shave me."

My stomach catapults like I was shot out of a cannon. "Shave you?" I follow him to the bathroom. "I said I would start a shower for you."

"I'm not going to use my right hand because I don't care for the 'I just got mugged in an alley' look." He peeks over his shoulder. "You're the only one here, so you're the lucky lady."

"But… I could call Seth or Knox. I've never shaved anyone before."

"You shave your legs?" he asks.

I nod.

"And your pussy?"

My eyes widen. "That's none of your business."

He holds out the razor. "I'll walk you through it. Just imagine my face is your pussy. Be gentle as fuck."

He grins and pats the bathroom counter, stripping off his T-shirt with his good arm. He's really getting used to the one arm thing. My eyes zero in on his tattoos. I slide up on the counter, my heart racing a million beats per second. He starts the water and pulls out the shaving cream.

His hand glides up my inner leg, spreading my thighs. My breath hitches.

"Come on, make room for me," he says and laughs.

"Are you sure?"

He locks eyes with me, and I swallow the lump in the back of my throat. He's the most gorgeous man I've ever known. "You're the only person I would trust to do this."

I slowly take the razor from his hand and nod.

So we're doing this then.

CHAPTER EIGHTEEN

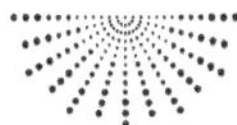

Dylan

After Rian uses my trimmers to trim off the excess hair, I debate whether I should have her shave the rest completely off. I could keep the scruff I've perfected over the years, but being this close to her feels good. If I have to look like I'm fifteen all over again to prolong this feeling, so be it.

Rian's hands are soft as she puddles water in her palms and runs it through my beard. I ignore the droplets falling to my bare chest. Once what's left of the beard is wet enough, she cups her hand and dishes shaving cream in it, then uses both hands to lather it on my skin.

"It's now or never," she says, her gorgeous blue eyes shining under the lights in the bathroom.

My hands are on either side of her hips, my body between her open legs. We're so close, it's nearly impossible to ignore the pull my lips feel toward hers.

"Let's do it. Just go slow and steady," I say in a gravelly voice.

I'm a little worried about how this will turn out. But if I've figured out anything in the past five days, it's that I'm not ambidextrous. Rian had to open up the pickle jar for me yesterday. Hold on while I hang up my man card until this cast is off.

"Tell me about your tattoos," she says. "I can't do this in silence."

"Which ones?"

"All, any, whatever." Her hand shakes as she raises the razor to my face.

I grip her wrist, my thumb smoothing along the surface. "Relax. Nothing horrible is gonna happen."

She nods, but the worry is alive in her eyes, so I do as she requested. I talk about my tattoos.

"The ones on my legs, I did to myself mostly. When I was practicing."

"You did them yourself?" Her eyes are on my sideburns, watching the razor move down my face.

"Yeah." I move my jaw as little as possible when I speak so I don't mess her up. "A few of my friends, like Big Man, trusted me to tattoo them. But to get the feel of the needle to know how deep to go, you have to feel that for yourself."

"I've never really looked at your legs," she says, pulling the razor down my skin.

"Funny, I've checked out yours."

She glances at me as she washes off the razor. "I don't have any tattoos."

"Your legs, Rian. I've checked out your legs."

Her flush is the most gorgeous thing I've seen on a woman. She believes that she's not beautiful. If I confessed to her how many guys I told she wasn't available, she'd be pissed, but truth is, none of them were good enough for her.

They would have broken her, and seeing Rian broken? I'd rather gouge out my eyes.

"Stop the flirting and let me concentrate. Tell me about your arms."

I want to glance down to know which specific tattoo she's asking about. "They all have different meanings. The apple is for Winnie, because she made a killer apple pie in the fall."

"Not for a teacher, huh?"

She rinses the razor. "Nope, although I did have some teachers who had an impact on my life.

"The phoenix on my back is self-explanatory. I think every foster kid gets one." I laugh to settle her sympathetic heart from giving me that pitying look. "The wolf is to remind me to be noble and loyal to those who are to me. A lot of the roses, stars, and other things are just filler. Things my friends thought would look killer. But all of them have a memory of some kind. Whether it's who did it or what it represents."

Her gaze skates across my chest. "What does the anchor mean?"

"Anyone tell you that you have a knack of digging crap out of people?"

She smiles softly, the razor grazing along my cheek. "I think only you. Maybe you want to tell someone. Have you ever thought of that?"

I'm not sure if she purposely doesn't look at me after that comment. She might be right. Maybe I've held all this shit in for so long, I want to purge to someone. Maybe it's a way to prove to her that I might not be good enough for her—but then look how far I've come. Maybe in my lifetime, we'll be equals.

My hands slide closer and rest beside her hips.

She wiggles, washing the razor off in the sink. "So the anchor?"

"The anchor." I nod. "Jax and I went into a tattoo place when we were sixteen. We knew a kid who was working under someone, so they didn't card. He got the compass and I got the anchor. It's not our most brilliant plan. I was supposed to see the compass on his chest and that'd tell me to explore the world. Don't stay in one spot. And if he looked at my anchor, he should remember to have a place to call home."

"So in truth, maybe you should've gotten the compass and he should have gotten the anchor?" She chuckles.

"Yeah, which is exactly why I make sure to tell my clients if their ideas are stupid. I'm blunt and have insulted more than one customer, but I won't have it on my conscience. Plus, if you knew how many calls we get days after we do a tattoo." I shake my head.

Regrets. People with regrets. I've never wanted to have them, which is probably why I've never ventured too far from where I grew up.

"And do you want to travel? Be like Jax?"

There's a hitch in her voice. She doesn't know if she wants the answer. I don't blame her, because I'm not sure I want to give it to her.

I shrug. "I don't want to be like Jax, but sometimes I wonder. Who doesn't wonder, right? Either about some old boyfriend or girlfriend. The what-ifs life leaves you with. But then I never would have come here to Cliffton Heights or moved into the Rooftop Apartments. I wouldn't have met Ethan or Sierra, or Seth, or you. You've all given me a sense of family."

She swallows, and the small room grows quiet except for the sound of the razor against skin.

"Rian?" I say, and her gaze dips up from my chin.

The tension in the room becomes a living, breathing thing.

A fake smile lands on her lips. "What?" She's trying to be flippant.

"Me and you. I can't imagine you not in my life."

Her smile turns real as her entire face beams. "You don't have to worry about that unless you're going to travel the world like Jax."

I say nothing. Jax's life isn't for me.

We go through the motions without saying much more. I'm not sure if we're both lost in thought. I hold court in my head on whether to tell her that there's a reason I never made a move on her. That fear paralyzes me. But then she'll look at me like I'm weak, which I am. She swipes up the last strip of my neck and looks over my face.

"It's coming though," she says, never making eye contact.

"What is?"

"Ethan's engaged. Sierra's not far behind. Knox and Leilani are practically moving in together. Eventually, every one of us will find someone to share our life with."

I doubt Knox and Leilani have any happy ever after in their future if the past is an indicator, but I keep my opinion to myself. "Doesn't mean we won't still be in each other's life."

She nods and wets a washcloth, wiping it down my face. "Not every day. Not like we are now. You don't hear about married couples who all live together with their kids." Her hand pauses. "But you don't plan on getting married."

She says it like a fact. I've never said that, but I guess I've never disputed it either. Mostly because I never thought marriage was for me. Not because I'm into juggling a million girls at one time. It's mostly because the girls I've dated aren't the marrying type and girls like Rian... I'm not even going there.

"True. I guess it's inevitable for me to be the fun uncle, huh?"

Her hands fall to her lap as though the washcloth is now too heavy to hold up. "Why don't you want to get serious with anyone?"

I step back, shift over, and look in the mirror, my hand sliding over the smooth skin. "Wouldn't you like to feel this along your inner thighs?" I pull her hand up to my face.

No smile creases her lips. "Don't do that." She jumps off the counter, snatching her hand back.

I follow her out of the bathroom. "What?"

She whips around. "Don't use sexual advances to keep from answering the question."

"It's not some new revelation. I've always been upfront and honest about my feelings on commitment. Plus, you like my sexual advances." I step closer, locking her to the wall. "You blush when I say them."

Her hands land on my chest and she shoves me back before stepping over and jumping off the arm of the chair to get to her room. At the last minute, she circles back around, up on the chair and back down again, poking her finger at me. "You know what I think? You're scared. The whole no commitment thing is so you can keep everyone at arm's length. I think you really want a wife and kids and the whole package, but you'd rather act like you don't than let someone in here." She places her hand over my heart.

I desperately deny the urge to cover her hand with mine.

"As far as the sexual advances. Yes, they make me blush because I want those things from you. I want to feel the smoothness of the skin I just shaved run up my thigh. I want your hands and lips to explore my body. And you can act like you don't want those things, and until recently, I believed you. I thought I was invisible to you." Tears well in her eyes and my heart splinters as if it took a blow from a sledgehammer.

She's never been invisible to me.

"Rian," I whisper.

She shakes her head, and strands of hair fall from her ponytail. The tears magically disappear, and fury transforms her blue irises. "Go ahead and deny it. Tell me you don't want me, and I'll box you up and put you on the top shelf." She pulls my good hand up to run my fingers over her lips. "Tell me you don't want to taste these?"

I stare at her lips, but I say nothing.

She tips her head back and runs my fingers down her throat and through the valley of her breasts. "How much do you want to truly feel me?"

I'm stunned into silence because I never thought there was a woman like this living inside Rian. She's putting her hand out for me to see. Everything the pansy inside of me hides.

All my muscles tense, trying to deny the urge to give into her. The thick air around us makes dragging in a breath impossible.

"It's now or never. Take me now or never." She rests my hand between her breasts, her eyes glued to mine.

When I say nothing, she shifts away, but I grab her wrist. "Do you have any idea what you're asking me to do?"

"Do you have any idea the agony you're putting me through?"

The cord of tension between us snaps like an elastic pulled to its limits, and I push aside the thought of all consequences. Whipping her around so her back is plastered to the wall, I cradle her cheek with my good hand and I lock her against it with my hips.

"Just remember you asked for this," I say and slam my lips to hers.

My entire body feels as if it's floating ad I'm having an out of body experience. That this is a dream would make sense, because Rian's never complained to anyone about anything. She's the least confrontational person I know.

But as our lips melt together and she opens for my tongue, all the worries that fill my life every day vanish and all I feel, see, and smell is her. The sweetness of her perfume, the softness of her touch, the blush that goes from her neck to cheeks. I'd die kissing her and be content. She's everything and nothing like I imagined she'd be, but one thing she is, is perfect.

Someone knocks on the door, but it doesn't stop us. I've waited too long for this, so whoever it is can go the fuck away. Rian's grip on my shoulders must mean we're in agreement.

"Holy…" Seth says from somewhere behind us.

My tongue only deepens the kiss because if Seth's smart, he'll walk back out that door. Rian's moan says she's on board with my plan.

"Rian Isabella Wright!"

Fuck. Our lips fly off one another's and look toward the door to find Rian's mom with her hands on her hips. Seth can't hide his amusement—laughing, stopping, then laughing again. Eventually he covers his mouth with his shirt.

"Mom!" Rian says, wiping her mouth while I back away from her.

My heart that was flying like a balloon in the blue sky with white clouds pops, landing in my stomach like a semi-truck. Time to get the hell out of Dodge.

CHAPTER NINETEEN

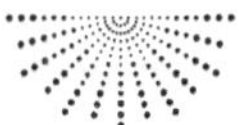

Rian

You'd think someone screamed fire with the speed that Dylan shakes my parents' hands, heads to his room for a second, says goodbye and is out the door. Seth follows him.

As soon as they leave, my mom says my name like a question, as though she doesn't need to ask me the actual question of why I was lip-locked with Dylan when she walked through the door.

"What?" I ask.

"You know exactly what. Am I to assume you finished that math equation if you have time to kiss your roommate?"

My dad sits at the kitchen table, grabbing an apple out of his pocket and biting into it. I'm not even going to ask where he got the apple.

"I haven't figured it out yet. Well, the first part I have, but that's it." I grab a water from the fridge. "Do either of you want anything?"

"Water would be great," my dad says, smiling. "You look good, sweetheart. Your cheeks are rosy like when you were a baby."

"Because she couldn't breathe with Dylan suctioned to her face like that," my mom says, sitting. "Do you have coffee? I didn't have enough this morning and I have a horrible headache."

"I can make some."

Which I will gladly do in order to not have to sit at that table. It's much easier for me to roll my eyes with my back turned to her.

As my mom rambles on about Johann, all I can think about is how I had the nerve to pressure Dylan into kissing me. I was so angry with his flirty behavior, knowing he wasn't planning to back it up with action. I also can't stop thinking about what his lips felt like on mine. The way he didn't want it to end—just like me. Although he barely touched me, it felt as if he was everywhere on my skin.

"Hanging out here isn't the type of environment you need. A tattoo artist? And then that Seth gave me a business card of what he does. Nude pictures." She purses her lips and shakes her head.

"I don't know, Barbie. Maybe we should give it a try."

I glance over my shoulder to see my mom's reaction to the thought of having her picture taken in lingerie. My dad waggles his eyebrows as my mom looks at him as if he's lost his mind.

"It's not nude, Mom," I say, turning back around.

"There's a picture on his business card."

"Let me see it," my dad says.

"I dropped it by mistake in the hallway."

I huff. Does she really think Seth won't figure out what she did?

I'm not sure what look my dad gives my mom, but she sighs. "I did. Sorry. I didn't realize you wanted to lower your IQ by looking at nude pictures. Next thing, you'll be asking me to have plastic surgery."

Mom is the most dramatic person I know. I always chalked it up to her growing up gifted with the name Barbie. Had to have been hard on her.

"Did you stop in here just to ask me about the equation?" I let the coffee pot work as I lean against the counter.

"We wanted to get out of the city for a while. Figured a day trip to check on you would be nice." My mom forces a smile.

She really wants to see where I am on solving the problem. She's not opposed to me cheating to win, I'm sure. Imagine my surprise when I turned in a paper my sophomore year in high school and my teacher pulled me aside to talk about plagiarism, only for me to find out my mom had switched her paper for mine during the night. Talk about feeling inadequate.

"I'm not showing you the problem," I say, pouring her a cup of coffee.

"Then let's take this time to talk about some of your life decisions. Like you working from home in order to care for your delinquent roommate who crashed his motorcycle, probably from driving recklessly." She sips her coffee. "This is too strong. Do you have milk?"

I stand and pull the milk from the fridge.

"Do you have almond or soy?" she asks.

"We're not Whole Foods," I say, grabbing the regular whole milk.

My mom has a specific look when I've annoyed her. So

far, I've seen it three times in this short visit. I like to count because the child inside me enjoys pissing her off.

"Are you dating him?" my dad asks, which is surprising. He didn't even come out of his office when I went to prom.

"We're friends, and I'd rather not talk to you about it right now." I sip my water.

My dad pats my hand. "Okay, sweetheart, but I will agree with your mother. A man like him might be easy on the eyes, but he's going to be hard on the bank account."

I stare blankly, and he chuckles. Another stupid joke.

"He runs his own tattoo parlor," I say.

"Rian, you cannot be serious. Is this some phase you're going through? You need to be with someone with goals and dreams and... money." Mom nods the entire time like a bobblehead. Barbie the bobblehead. No one would buy one because they'd be nauseated by how much it bobbles.

"I told you I don't want to talk about it."

"That's not an option. We're your parents," my mom says.

"And I'm not twelve."

There's the look again. We're up to four times now.

"What on Earth do you talk about? Surely you have nothing in common." My dad continuing this line of conversation makes me want to bash my head on the table.

"Another topic please," I say.

My dad looks at my mom and they nod in agreement, but it won't be the last they have to say about Dylan.

But if they can't talk to me about the math problem or Dylan, there isn't a ton left.

"Looks like you haven't baked in a while?" my dad says, scanning the counters. He wants a sweet since my mom limits them as though he's a child.

"Not in a few days."

My mom exaggerates leaning over as she examines my

body in the chair. "You looked thinner over there." She motions to the wall that Dylan had me pinned against.

Reliving that moment, my body warms like I've sunk into a hot bath. "Is that a compliment?"

"You're very touchy today. I think you're probably getting your period," Mom suggests. "Johann is going to beat you if you don't start making smart decisions. I feel like we raised you well."

And here we go. Same old same old.

She stares at my father with her trembling chin. He puts his hand on hers on the table, leaving the apple core in the middle.

"We did great," he says. "She has a job and supports herself. What else can we ask for? I think we knew at three there were no Nobel Prizes in our future."

Cue my mouth drop.

I must make a noise because both of them look at me as though they're surprised I'm in the room. My dad's other hand reaches for mine and I'm too dumbstruck to care.

"No offense, sweetie. It's like winning the lottery."

I stand so fast my parents' eyes widen. "Did I miss the part where the two of you won a Noble Prize? Is it hidden in a box somewhere?" A strangled laugh erupts out of me, which is good because at least they won't see me cry. "You two get off on how smart you are. Well, I'm sorry that two smart people didn't make an uber-smart person, but I am smart. And if I choose to write textbooks for a living, then so be it. And if I run out and marry Dylan, then that's my choice." I point at myself. "Me, because I'm an adult."

"I doubt Dylan is the marrying type. And even if he did, he screams cheater." My mom rolls her eyes.

My hand flies out, pointing at the door. "*Out!*" I inhale a deep breath. "Out. Leave."

"Sweetie, you're overreacting," my dad says.

"We'll talk after you're done with your period," my mom says, standing and tucking in her chair. "You're obviously emotional."

My arm drops and my fists clench at my sides.

"It wasn't a knock on you," my dad says, but my mom pushes him toward the door.

"You're lucky to have us, and you need to realize that one of these days," my mom says. "Poor Sierra would probably love to have her mother here."

It's game over. All I see is red. Words and phrases flash in my mind. I could use the classic fuck off, or I could go into detail about how she's the worst mom ever.

"Just please leave before I say something that would hurt you like you've hurt me all these years," I say in a calm voice.

That sentence makes her stop. "Rian." She sighs.

I shake my head, swallowing the lump and pushing back the tears.

The apartment door opens, and my parents rear back, the door barely missing them. Jax slides by, nodding his hello but never stopping to converse.

"Who's this?" Mom asks, but I don't answer.

Jax looks at me standing near the kitchen table and stops on the way to his bedroom. His gaze flickers from my parents to me and back to my parents. For once not one smart comment comes out of his mouth.

"Just go, Mom," I say softly.

My mom looks at Jax. "Just another horrible decision. Let's go, Larry." She squares her shoulders and walks out the door.

"Bye, sweetie. We love you. I never meant—"

"*Larry!*" my mom screams.

"Call us after you're done menstruating."

He shuts the door and I collapse into a chair, throwing

the apple core at the door. My head falls into my folded arms and I weep for everything I'm not in my parents' eyes.

"Hey," Jax says, running his hand over my back. "You okay?"

I sit up and wipe the tears from my eyes. "You know, you and Dylan think your lives are so hard because you don't have parents, but not all parents are good people."

He slides the chair beside me out from the table and lowers himself into it. "I get that."

"They expect me to be perfect. I was valedictorian." I swipe a tear. "I was dean's list every semester in college. I never did anything bad. Never got arrested or in trouble. I respect my elders. I'm polite and courteous to everyone I meet. Do you think any of that is enough for them?" I point toward the door. "No, because all they care about is whether I get some award they can brag to their friends about."

My voice shakes, and my anxiety is through the roof. The tears won't stop piling on top of one another as they spill down my cheeks.

"Hey." Jax slides his chair closer. Gripping my one arm, he pulls me to him. "It's okay. Parents suck. I mean, I don't have any, but mine would have hated me. Talk about a disappointment." He pulls me into his chest and his large hand runs down my back.

"Don't make me laugh. I want to be mad," I say.

His chest rumbles with laughter. "I'm serious though. You are what parents hope for when they decide to have kids. I'm the nightmare. If your parents don't see that, then fuck them. I'm also proof that you don't need a parent to survive."

Oddly enough, his words help me. I know my parents and I were coming to a crossroads. That eventually our relationship would change as we moved in different directions like a fork in the road. I just hoped we could be headed in the same direction.

The apartment door opens behind me, and Jax's body stiffens. I turn my head and find Dylan standing there. I sit up straighter as Jax releases me almost with a shove.

But it doesn't matter because Dylan walks right back out and slams the door.

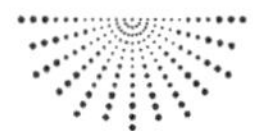

CHAPTER TWENTY

Dylan

I press the elevator button, and when it doesn't come right away, I race down the stairs. I'm pissed at myself for being a coward when Rian's parents showed up, but damn, I'm confused about that kiss and where we stand. How would I sit and talk with her parents?

How naive of me to assume whatever happened between her and Jax was over. I never asked her after my accident.

I walk into Ink Envy.

"Boss." Lyle slides off his stool.

I raise my hand as I pass him.

"We need to talk," Frankie says.

"Later," I mumble.

She's in the middle of a tattoo, so that gives me time to lock myself in the office. I slam my door, lock it, and sit in my office chair. Staring at my cast, I want to take a pair of scissors and cut it off. I want to go out there and take a client and lose myself for hours in art and ink. Get my mind off all this shit swirling around.

All I can think of is Rian's lips and the softness of her touch.

Then I picture her in Jax's arms.

He was the one consoling her after her parents said something else to hurt her. Hell, they have their opinions on me too, I'm sure. With them witnessing our first kiss, she probably took a heavy dose of disappointed looks from both of them.

That's why I stayed at Seth's, waiting for them to leave so I could go back in and apologize for running out. Joke's on me though, because once again, Jax sneaked in and got the girl.

A knock sounds on the door.

"Not now," I yell.

"Okay, boss," Lyle says.

But no less than a minute later, another knock sounds on the door. When I say nothing, a key is inserted and the door is unlocked.

Frankie stands there, dangling her keys in front of her. "Why are you locking yourself in the office? And you look like shit, by the way. Like a fifteen-year-old boy who got his heart broken. What the hell happened?"

I run my hand down my face. "Rian shaved me." Her eyes light up with intrigue, so I raise my hand to stop her mind before it gets too carried away. "Don't worry, I'm pretty sure she's into Jax."

Her eyebrows shoot up and she shuts the door before coming over to the chair on the other side of the desk.

"You're with a client," I say.

"She needed a breather. I'm giving her a five-minute break." She sits. "Talk to me. What happened?"

Before I can respond, the door busts open and Jax stands there. "You're a fucking idiot, you know that?"

I put my hand up to stop him. "Just, everyone, leave me the fuck alone."

"You need to leave," Jax says to Frankie.

Her eyebrows shoot up. "In case you missed it, I'm the second in command around here." She dangles her keys in the air.

"This has nothing to do with the business." Jax holds the door open and gestures for her to leave.

"I'm not in the mood to rehash our fucked up history right now." I boot up my computer.

"Too fucking bad. I'm done with this shit." He squares his eyes on Frankie. "Kindly leave."

Frankie straightens her back and crosses her legs, getting comfortable. "I've been here a long time and they're both my friends. I'm sure as hell not going to leave a man like you in charge of him seeing the error of his ways."

"A man like me?"

"Yeah. A man who probably thinks commitment is for the weak. A man who dates a younger version of the same woman he's always dated because he has some warped sense of self-image when in reality, people look at him like he's pathetic."

"You know nothing about me," Jax says. "You've known me less than a week."

Frankie crosses her arms. "I know your type all too well."

A hollow and bitter laugh falls from Jax. "Don't take out your heartbreaks on me. I wasn't the guy who fucked you over."

She laughs right back.

I roll my eyes. Thankfully, she doesn't say anything else. Jax bows dramatically and ushers his hand toward the door. Frankie shakes her head.

He slams the door. "Fine, you're about to find out a lot of things about your boss and me then."

"Can we please do this another time?" I ask.

Frankie looks at me with concerned eyes. That's when I make the decision that Frankie shouldn't be in the room right now. Jax is right on that. Whatever is going down behind this door, she doesn't need to know about it. No one does but us.

Jax leans against the wall with his arms folded across his chest.

"Just give us ten minutes," I say to Frankie.

She inspects my face. Oh, how she's used to being a bodyguard for everyone but herself. Standing, she touches my shoulder and walks to the door. "Don't listen to his bullshit about relationships."

Jax shakes his head, and she flips him off. Whatever is transpiring between these two isn't good. Which is weird, because if someone would've asked me to bet money on how well they'd get along, I would've said they'd be best friends within a week.

She leaves and shuts the door. Jax pushes off the wall and sits in the chair Frankie just occupied. He leans his forearms on his knees and clasps his hands together.

His head hangs low and he speaks to the floor. "I don't want her, man."

I lean back in my chair, my casted arm lying on the armrest and my other hand fiddling with a pen. "Could've fooled me."

He peeks up. "I've been an asshole. I thought it would be fun to fuck with you, but that all ended the night of your accident. That isn't to say if she wasn't so hung up on you, I wouldn't have banged her."

My jaw clenches.

"But that's all she would have been," he says. "Just like Naomi was."

There were times I wondered if Jax and I would ever mend our rift. Could there ever be a time when we could get back to being friends? What would the conversation consist of? Would we skate over the Naomi situation or dissect it? I guess by him bringing her up, he wants to get it all out in the open.

"I never wanted her. It's no excuse, but she was consoling me about Winnie and it just kind of happened," he says. "She loved you. She did."

I'm surprised he's ready to show his vulnerability. I huff. "I think she loved both of us."

He looks at me and shrugs. Naomi wanted us to be morphed into the same person. She loved my stability and the fact I was headed to college. She also loved Jax's wild streak and tendency to get into fights. To say I was surprised when I walked in on them would be a lie. Which is probably why I felt more betrayed by Jax than Naomi.

"But Rian is different, Phillips. She likes you, and for some fucked up reason, you keep pushing her away." He looks at me, expecting an answer.

"Man, you know just like I do that Rian isn't anything like Naomi."

"Which is a good thing." He leans back.

I nod. True enough. "You know her type. She's meant for an accountant who works nine to five and is home every weekend. A guy who gives her the American dream of a house and two point five kids and a dog running around the yard. A guy who gets excited for pizza nights on Friday and movies on Saturdays."

"Nah," Jax says. "She doesn't want some douche who only screws her missionary and can't work his tongue on her."

I huff out a laugh. "Her parents hate me."

"Sounds like she hates her parents." He locks his fingers together over his stomach. "Keep coming up with excuses. We both know you're more the settling down type than you want to admit."

Have I ever thought about marriage? Yeah. But did I ever think I could go through with it? I'm not sure.

"I haven't seen any other girls hanging around you," he adds.

"Are you trying to diss my game?"

He laughs. "No, I'm saying you're not interested in anyone but her."

He's got a point. Somehow when Jax moved in, my fear of losing her overruled my fear of ruining our friendship. "If you hadn't come back, I'm not sure I would've ever acted on my feelings."

A smirk crosses his lips.

Son of a bitch.

"You did it on purpose?" I ask. "You purposely asked her out just to get me to act on my feelings?"

He holds up his hands. "Truth?"

"Yeah."

"I liked her when I first moved in, but I saw how protective you were of her. You've always been transparent," he says, his smirk grows wider. "I thought I'd just give you an extra push if you were toeing the line. I didn't think you'd need a bulldozer."

"So much could go wrong."

"So much could go right," he counters.

I nod. He's right.

"You can sit here and be a pussy, all scared in your boots and worried about what-ifs, or you can go over there and own your feelings for her." I stare at him, and he sighs. "What are you worried about?"

What am I not worried about?

"Our friendship. Hers and mine. Other than Naomi, I've never had anything serious. What if I don't like it? What if I feel suffocated and screw it all up? It's not just our friendship at stake. It's all our friends. We're in an interconnected cobweb and if Rian cuts one strand, it rocks the entire group."

He nods. "You guys do have a little family here, don't you?" He nods toward the door. "Even that spark plug out there."

There's longing in his tone. I first heard it in ninth grade when Winnie would make me come home for dinner at six. Then he had to do the same once he moved in with Winnie. Maybe that's the one thing Jax hasn't gotten since he left—a sense of home, family. Which is why he thinks it's okay to throw yourself to the wild and deal with consequences later. I can't do that with Rian.

"They're all really important to me."

This is usually when Jax would cut off any sentimentality. When his jokester side would prevail, and he'd make a snide remark so the person believes he doesn't really care. But this time, he looks me square in the eye. Something he hasn't done since he returned. "Let me ask you a question."

"What?"

"Do you really think the two of you will survive being friends forever? Was it just that you didn't want to lose out to *me*? You were going to sit through that wedding to the accountant? Be the godfather of her baby? Where does it end? How long do you torture yourself?"

The things he mentions flash in my mind. Me sitting in the pew, watching her give me one more look before saying I do to some other guy. Or me coming to her house to celebrate my godchild's milestones. I'd no doubt be wondering what could have been if I hadn't been a pussy. Could it have been me she was saying I do to? My hand she held as she went through labor?

"You're a fucking asshole," I say, standing from my desk.

He smiles.

I walk to the door but turn around. "I'm sorry. I should have allowed you at Winnie's funeral."

I was so angry about him and Naomi that I forbid him from attending her service. Looking back, I think I was just angry at the world and the fact that Winnie had died more than I was at Jax. But he was as good a target as any to direct my fury at.

He shakes his head. "Forget it." He pauses as though he has something more to say, so I wait. "I shouldn't have blamed you when Winnie left you that money for your future. I understand now why she did. Anything that came my way I would've just blown through. Probably would've done more harm than good."

I nod. I figured that out a while ago. Jax was always wilder than I was. I think Winnie trusted that I would put the money to good use. Jax, not so much, as harsh as that is.

I open my arms. "Hug it out?"

"Fuck you. Go get your girl." He nods toward the door.

I laugh all the way through Ink Envy until I'm outside our apartment door.

CHAPTER TWENTY-ONE

Rian

Some people clean. Others cook. Others might exercise. I either do math or bake when I'm upset. Today it's math. When my mind is scrambling with a million uncontrollable thoughts swarming like bees, the precision of math, the fact that there is only one correct answer, calms me.

So after Jax runs after Dylan, I take my stuff to my room and pull out the problem.

Okay, yeah, I would love to solve this problem just to prove to my parents that I'm not some stupid child. A psychologist would probably say that proving it to them is still seeking their approval. But I don't really care. To me. it's like a middle finger to them.

The apartment door opens and my math bubble pops. Suddenly, all my issues are front and center in my mind again. Either Jax or Dylan is home, and I'm not sure which one I'd rather talk to right now.

Footsteps pound across the hardwood, making my heart race as though I should be hiding under the bed. It feels as if everything stable in my life is about to crash down.

The pencil slips from my grasp with the rap of knuckles on my door, falling from the paper to my mattress and rolling to the floor. "Yeah?"

"Rian." A thud sounds on the wood.

My shoulders fall at the sound of Dylan's voice. "Yeah?"

"Can I come in?"

"Sure."

My eyes lock on the doorknob as it turns, and the door pushes open. And there he is, his cleanly shaven face making him look more innocent and youthful than normal.

He shuts the door and stands with his back pressed to it.

"I'm sor—" I say, but he holds up his hand.

"I'm the sorry one. I never should've left when your parents showed up."

I shake my head. I'm used to it. My house was never the hang-out house. I quit asking for birthday parties when I was nine years old and my parents made the girls do a hundred question multiplication sheet. Whoever completed it the fastest and most accurately won the prize—an abacus. "It's okay."

"No, it's not. Do you want to talk about what happened with them?" He pushes off the door, and I suck in a breath the closer he moves. Before I can soak in everything that's happening, he's at the edge of my bed.

"Nah. Same old."

He eyes my book and picks up the pencil from the floor, handing it to me. "I'm jealous of Jax."

"Why?" It's a stupid question. The kiss sealed the fact that whatever is lying dormant under our friendship isn't just on my end. But maybe because I've waited so long, I want to hear the words from him. How badly does he want me?

He stares at me for a moment. It's all there in his gorgeous light brown eyes. "Do I have a reason to be jealous?"

The silence is deafening, the tension wound tight. "No."

His eyes close for a second and his chest rises and falls. Leaning forward, he tucks a strand of my hair behind my ear. "Good."

It's clear that he wants to kiss me again, and after the wall incident, I know that one kiss is going to end with both of us naked in this bed, my math book forgotten. Part of me wants to tell my conscience to allow that to happen, but what if he only wants me because Jax made him jealous?

My hand presses on his chest.

His eyebrows raise in question, but Dylan's a good guy, so he backs up and my hand falls to the mattress between us. "Are you sure I shouldn't be jealous?"

"This has nothing to do with Jax, but are you sure whatever competition you have with him isn't the reason you want to be with me? Can you honestly say we would be here if Jax had never showed up?"

"We've always been friends who wanted more."

I shake my head. "You were content dating other women. Having sex with other women. Why now?"

He looks as if I slapped him, but we can't live in a bubble and not face the truth. Something bad will happen and that bubble will pop. "Jax made me realize that I could lose you."

I nod. "Because you guys compete over everything. This would be your way of winning."

He shakes his head. "No. That's not it at all."

I stand, unable to be so close to him while I put on hold something I've wanted for years. "Put yourself in my shoes."

His head falls and he stares at the floor. Slowly, he nods.

"Believe me, Dylan, I want nothing more than to strip down and beg you to take me right now. To fall under the covers with you and do all the things I've masturbated to for years, but I can't do that with the prospect of heartbreak once you win me."

He nods again. "I get what you're saying, but I'm telling you that's not it. I've always felt like I wasn't good enough for you."

He stands and I step back, which stops him from approaching. My forehead wrinkles. "Why?"

"Come on, Rian. Why do you think your parents have a problem with me? They see it. I bring you down."

I don't care what my parents think, and I've never thought that about Dylan. "That's not true."

When I don't move, he welcomes that as his opportunity to continue toward me. "But I don't care anymore. I mean, I do, but I'm not going to lose this opportunity. I was so hung up on the what-ifs, I never thought about three or five years in the future—the what-ifs I'd feel then. The regrets I'd live with if I never tried to see if we can work this out." He cages me against my dresser, our chests pressed together and his hands on my hips as though he's afraid I'm going to run. "I'm scared of losing your friendship or messing up our friends' circle, but I'll take the chance because the other alternative is too painful to bear."

I've loved him from afar for so long, I never took into consideration the impact on our group of friends. What happened to Ethan and Sierra could happen to us. But I decide right then, "I'd never let that happen—unless one of us did something stupid." Like cheat.

"I can't say I'm going to be the best boyfriend at first. There's a learning curve." I tilt my head, and he chuckles. "I'd never fuck it up by cheating. I meant other things."

I stare at him and he steps closer, his chest pushing

against mine. When I woke up this morning, I never thought we'd end up here. "Why don't you take a shower? Think it over some more."

He chuckles. "I have a better idea. Why don't *we* take a bath?" His hand slides down and he links his fingers with mine. "We can talk this over while naked and wet." He winks and my heart somersaults.

Who am I kidding? I want this as much as he does, and I don't want regrets in a few years either. All I can do is trust him when he says that this isn't because of Jax and their competitive nature.

"That's tempting," I say. "One condition."

"What?" He squeezes my hand, stepping back toward the door.

"You tell me about Naomi."

His face falls, but he nods, tugging me forward so I fall into his chest. He wraps his good arm around me, stares into my eyes, and bends down for a kiss.

Just as it did hours earlier, my heartbeat skyrockets the minute his soft lips land on mine.

But he ends the kiss too quickly. "Let's get me clean so I can show you exactly how dirty I can get."

I bite my lip, and he chuckles.

"I guess it's time for me to see what I'm getting, huh?" I unzip his sweatshirt and help him pull it off his arm. My hands run along his bare chest, over all his ink. He groans as my fingers hook on either side of his track pants, pushing them down his legs until they pool at his feet. "My boyfriend doesn't wear underwear?"

"Not since the accident. Too fucking hard to put on."

He stands there and allows my gaze to drift over his body. He's not embarrassed or self-conscious, nor should he be. He's lean, muscled perfection and it makes my mouth water.

His hard dick is pointed north. Nice for me. I step closer, taking his dick in my palm and rubbing.

"Whoa." His hand covers mine. "Don't I get to see my girlfriend?"

I smile and bite the corner of my mouth, sliding my tongue over my bottom lip.

"Don't be embarrassed. I can't wait to see you."

He knows me so well. Of course I'm embarrassed. The heat in my cheeks says I'm wearing that emotion like a flashing stop sign. I step back, taking the hem of my T-shirt and pulling it up over my body.

"Slowly," he says, and my eyes rise to meet his. "I want to savor this moment."

That's all it takes for my embarrassment to fade away.

I raise the shirt over my stomach and my bra until I lose sight of him as I pull it over my head. I drop the shirt onto the floor and his eyes are on my ribcage, not my breasts like I assumed. I reach back with both hands and unhook my bra, then I slide the straps off each arm.

He grunts, and his attention moves to my breasts. "Jesus, I can't wait to have both my hands on them."

A maddening look fills his face. I forgot about his arm and how trying sex is going to be.

I unbutton my jeans as his vision zeros in as though I'm giving him the code to a vault holding millions of dollars. My forefinger and thumb glide my zipper down and his breathing becomes labored. His rapt attention boosts my self-esteem. He's making this so easy for me.

"Turn around," he says.

I circle around, pushing my jeans down. As I get them halfway down my ass, he puts his hand on the side of my hip.

"Slow it down for me."

I look over my shoulder to see that he's wrapped his hand around his dick, tugging and nodding for me to continue. I shimmy instead of pushing my jeans the rest of the way down. When I stand up straight again, he's closer to me. One hand slides around from my ass to cup a breast. His dick digs into my satin panties.

"You're so damn beautiful," he whispers. "Mouthwatering tits, and an ass I want to slap until it looks like a strawberry." His hand slides down my torso, under the hem of my panties, and cups my mound. "I'm not sure I can handle seeing this without spreading you open right here for a taste."

My entire body is Jell-O, willing to bend and shift, molding to whatever he wants to do to me. I want to experience it all with him. The screams, scrapes, and moans. The gentle graze of his knuckles along the lips of my pussy make my head fall back on his bare shoulder and his mouth casts small bites along my flesh, working his way up to my ear.

"I want you so bad," he whispers.

"Take me," I whisper back and tilt my head to the side.

He captures my mouth, his tongue diving in. His finger runs the length of my center, pressing the smallest, lightest circles along my clit, and I moan into his mouth.

"You like that?" he asks once he stops kissing me. "Let's go."

His hand slides out from between my legs and I miss it already. "Can we take a shower rather than a bath?"

"Why?"

"Faster."

His eyes light up. "I love the way you think."

He guides me across the living room, and we lock the bathroom door once we're inside. Best. Day. Ever.

CHAPTER TWENTY-TWO

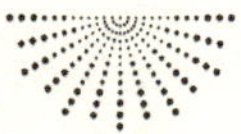

Dylan

Rian's body deserves a reaction like that cartoon character whose jaw hangs low and drags on the floor. I've gotten glimpses throughout the years. A shirt that rode up a little high or a button that popped open. Pajama shorts where I could tell she wasn't wearing panties. All of those pieced together to give me a vision of what I thought Rian looked like naked. Turns out I was dead wrong. She's flawless and beautiful in a delicate way. Like when a tattoo is done and nothing more needs to be added. Her body is perfect.

"What about Jax?" she asks with the click of the lock.

"Don't worry, Jax isn't coming home for a while."

He understood exactly what I was going to do when I left Ink Envy, so if he's the guy I've always known, he'll crash somewhere else, at least for tonight.

My arm slides behind the shower curtain and I turn on the water.

"Oh, your arm," Rian says.

"Shit. I'll be right back."

She laughs as I slide out of the bathroom and head to the kitchen to grab a garbage bag. I'm more upset that one set of my fingers won't be able to participate today. Being restricted to only one hand is a lot to expect from a guy during his first time with a girl. She might think I'm a horrible screw.

"I got the scrunchie!" she hollers.

I grab the garbage bag and shut the cabinet right as the apartment door opens. I swear to fucking God. We have to start locking that thing.

"Oh shit, I'm blind!" Seth screams.

I scramble to escape to the bathroom, but Rian screeches and slams the bathroom door.

Seth still didn't take my nakedness as his clue to leave.

"What the hell are you talking about?" Knox bumps Seth out of the way.

I slowly turn around, covering my junk. Knox nods at me and sits on the couch, pressing the power button on the controller.

"What are you guys doing?" I ask.

Seth joins Knox on the couch. "It's, like, channel five hundred or something."

When *Superbad* plays on the television, they both relax with their feet up on the table.

"Perfect," Knox says.

"Don't you two have jobs?" I ask.

"Day off," Knox says.

Seth raises his hand. "I cut out early."

The bathroom door behind me slides open. "Dylan," Rian whispers, "I have no clothes in here."

I nod. "You two need to leave."

The bathroom door shuts again.

That seems to alert Knox that something isn't normal. "Oh, I thought you were just finally showering." He nods toward the bathroom. "You got someone in there?"

Seth turns to look at me.

I didn't think I'd be telling everyone about Rian and me this soon, but they'll find out anyway. "Yeah."

"Cool. We'll just be out here. We don't have this movie channel." Knox points the remote at the television.

"Yeah, I'm not a public fucker like you, so you'll have to pay for it On Demand or something."

Knox looks offended. "I'm not a public fucker or whatever the hell that means. I'm just not ashamed of my body or my skills. If someone wants to watch because it's their kink, that's not my problem. It's not gonna stop me from doing what I want. Especially when I'm in my own apartment."

"Thanks for the Ted Talk. Now get the fuck out." I nod at the door.

Seth stands and looks around. "Where's Rian?"

She groans from the other side of the door, but neither of them hear her.

"I gotta say, the naked body is beautiful. And the shame you both have about sex makes me think you're a bunch of church ladies with nothing better to talk about," Knox continues, but Seth's clearly catching on.

"Do you two mind? I'm naked here." I knock on the door, but Rian still doesn't unlock it.

"Where's Rian?" Seth asks again, glancing around, walking toward her bedroom door with a grin on his face. "Thought she was working from home to help your sorry ass." He stops cold outside her bedroom door, probably seeing our discarded clothes on the floor. "Oh shit!"

He circles back around, and a smile as long and wide as the Brooklyn Bridge creases his lips.

"We gotta go." Seth points at the door.

"What am I missing?" Knox asks.

"Rian is the girl," Seth mouths.

"Yes, I know Rian is a girl," Knox says.

"You're really a cop, right?" I ask with a lifted brow.

Knox thinks it over, then his mouth opens in an O and he nods, looking impressed. "You could've just said that."

"Said what?" I whisper.

"'Hey, I'm fucking Rian right now. Take off.'"

I shake my head.

Knox turns off the television while Seth's nodding like a crazy man. "About fucking time. Can I say something to her?" He steps toward me.

"Fuck no. Get the hell out."

Seth nods like "yeah, that was an idiotic move" and twists on his heels to head toward the door. "Finally. I swear I think I was getting blue balls watching Dylan drag his feet."

The door shuts behind them, and I flip the lock.

"Open up for me," I say, turning to the bathroom door.

She peeks around the door, and when she hears the quiet and doesn't see the guys, she opens it all the way. "So, two down, huh?"

Rian's skin glistens in the steamy room from the humidity. I shut the door and lock it, putting my hand in the bag. She secures it with her scrunchie.

"Technically Jax too," I say.

She sighs.

"Did you want us to keep it a secret?" Maybe I pegged her all wrong. Should I have told the guys it was someone else?

"No! It'll be embarrassing the first time, but I don't want us to hide."

"Good. I think the shower's ready." My good hand snakes down her body, grabbing her ass.

"I'm ready." She takes a hair elastic from her drawer and twirls her hair into a messy ponytail on top of her head.

She steps in first and I quickly follow. My gaze follows the stream of water flowing over her body and I realize this was a big mistake.

"Let's just wash me and get the hell out of here. I cannot properly fuck you in a shower with one arm." I step under the showerhead with her, my lips falling to hers until her back hits the tile wall.

"Happy to," she says, her hands in my hair, our naked bodies pressed together. She's soft, oh so fucking soft, and she's grinding along my length.

"I can't stop touching you." Even my broken arm wants something. My fingers find their way to the seam of the bag, begging to touch any part of her.

She presses on my chest and I step back, using my time away from her to take her in. Commit the curves of her body to memory. How her tits fall like heart-shaped Hershey's kisses just waiting for my mouth to devour them.

She puddles shampoo into her hand before bringing both up to my hair. Her fingers thread through the strands and massage my scalp.

"You probably need me closer, right?" I laugh, my hands on her hips leaving us only millimeters apart.

"I really need you to dip your head. You're so damn tall."

So I do just that and take the opportunity to lick one of her breasts, sucking the nipple into my mouth. "Is this what you meant?"

She arches into me, her hands not as vigorous anymore.

"Keep washing my hair," I say, shifting my attention to her other breast.

"Trade places."

The suds from my hair drip down over her chest.

"You don't play fair," she says.

We switch so the water falls over my head. To speed up the process, I stand to my full height, dipping my head back under the showerhead to rinse my hair.

"FYI, I never play fair."

But then neither does she, because her lips attach to my nipples, her tongue running small circles around them. I grab a hold of her nipples, twisting. The harder I pull, the more she moans. I think I found a kink of Rian Wright's.

She stands up, not taking nearly enough time down there. "Conditioner."

"We can skip the conditioner."

She looks at me with mock offense. "No way. If my hands are going to thread through this hair tonight, I want it soft."

"Only if you agree to pull it." I grin. A blush travels over her whole body, and I break the distance between us. "I might just get addicted to you blushing. Tell me what you were thinking when I just said that."

She shakes her head, grabbing my bar of soap, and runs the soap over my body. "I was thinking of your head between my legs."

I put my finger under her chin and bring her face up to meet my eyes. "You better pull my hair when I'm between your legs. I plan on spending a lot of time down there."

She runs the soap over my dick, pushing her body against mine to hold me in place until she slides the soap to my back side, moving over my ass.

"You get the job of showering me every morning until this cast comes off." I kiss her nose.

She smiles. "Oh, do I? And what do I get in return?"

"You get me washing you." My hand molds around her tit, my thumb over her nipple.

"I'm not sure either one of us will make it to work." She

puts the soap down and walks me back under the shower-head. "Time to rinse off, my dirty boy."

"If I'm a good boy, do I get a treat?"

She laughs without answering, and after I'm rinsed off, I turn off the water. She gets out and pulls two towels from the rack.

"I'll dry you." I take her towel. Fuck my right hand. I won't let it fuck this up because it can't coordinate itself.

She watches me run the plush towel up both of her legs, pausing an inch shy of her pussy. I dry off her arms and torso, taking my time to make sure her tits are fully dry. Sliding the towel around her back, I make sure her ass is good and dry. With her hair up, all that's left is her pussy. I put the towel there, my hand molded to her mound, and she bucks into my hand. I need to get this girl to a bed.

Opening the bathroom door, I'm happy to find the apartment empty. We tiptoe across the room as though we're not though, and when we're secure in her room, I back her up to the bed until she falls on the mattress.

"Condom?" I ask.

She shakes her head. "I have an IUD. I'm clean."

My knees nudge her legs open. Fuck, she's killing me. Is she giving me permission to just slide right in? I've never done that before. I desperately want to and I'm clean, but I fear that with nothing between us, I'll be the minute man inside her.

"I'm clean too—just tested before the accident—but I'll be right back." I stand from the mattress and point at her. "Stay right where you are."

I run out of the room and over to my bedroom, grab a row of condoms, and return to her. Rian listened, lying exactly where I left her except she's taken out her ponytail so her blonde hair is strewn around her like a fucking angel's.

Fuck the condoms. I toss them aside and shimmy up on

the bed with my knees. "Are you sure you're okay without a condom?"

She nods. I hold myself over her on my good arm, the tip of my dick piercing her opening.

"I trust you," she says softly.

I hope she doesn't come to regret those three words.

CHAPTER TWENTY-THREE

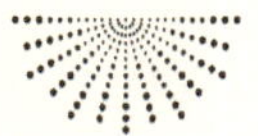

Rian

Dylan slides into me inch by inch, filling me until I gasp. He stares at me—and it's then I realize we did this all wrong.

"I should be on top. Your arm," I say.

He looks at his arm as though he has no idea what I'm talking about. "Shit, you're right."

He slides out of me, and I groan from missing him so much. The shower was some hella foreplay. I need him. Maybe after the first time, my girly parts will have more patience.

"I guess you get to ride me." He smirks and lies back on my bed, his head on my pillows, one arm outstretched and reaching for me.

Suddenly, I'm self-conscious. I've never ridden anyone. I've watched porn, but the fact that's all I have to go on is pathetic and not something I'm about to share, no matter how much I trust Dylan with my secrets.

"Are you fantasizing about cowboys?" He laughs, waiting for me.

Well, if I'm not going to tell him, it's time to hop on. I swing one leg over to straddle him.

"Put me in you." His attention is focused on the space between our groins.

Just imagine your dildos, Rian. You totally have this. I grab his base, inching up and positioning him at my opening before sinking down on his hard length.

The fact that his head is arched back with his eyes shut says I'm doing something right.

"We'll definitely be doing this when I have use of both my arms." His good hand molds to my hip.

I rock a little as his fingertips push into my skin. He smiles at me and my hands land on his chest, my gaze pouring over his tattoos to get my mind off of what I'm doing.

"Just go on feeling," he whispers.

My eyes shoot to his. He knows. *Of course he does. You've lived across from him for years and he's never once seen you bring a guy home.* I rock deeper, opening my legs farther.

He groans, his fingertips tightening on my hipbone. "There you go."

His hand ventures off my hip to my breast. He squeezes it and runs his thumb over my puckered nipple. I pause for a moment without him directing me, but the more aroused I become, the more I chase my orgasm and the thoughts about whether I'm doing it right or not are thrown out the window.

His hips raise up off the mattress, pushing him deeper inside me. The way he's stretching me isn't painful; it feels sinful and I'll never tire of this feeling. I slide up and down on him, my hands digging into his chest for stability. He's perfect.

My orgasm climbs, but I push it back because I don't want this moment to end. I want to feel like this for the rest of my life. The closeness of today, his hands scanning every inch of my body, his lust-filled eyes staring at me as though I'm the only woman who could ever satisfy him. It's all too much and I'm flooded by desire ripping through my body.

"You're fucking amazing," he says, his eyes lazily closing for a moment. "I want to tear off my cast to drill inside you until I can't see straight."

He manipulates my tit, pinching my nipple, and the dam I built around my orgasm collapses. I cry out as the waves of my climax crest over me. Dylan's hand moves to my hip and he pumps inside me from below, finding his own release with a growl and my name on his lips.

I roll off him, lying on the mattress until he seeps out of me. "I'll be right back," I say and shoot out the door to the bathroom.

I'm not in there longer than a minute when Dylan knocks on the door. "You okay?"

The concern in his voice warms my heart. "Yes. Just cleaning up."

I finish, flush the toilet, and wash my hands before opening the door to a still-naked Dylan.

He walks into the bathroom, pressing me to the bathroom counter. "I would have cleaned you."

I laugh. "Well, it took me a little by surprise."

"Yeah, I forgot that it would get messy. Which means…" He kisses me briefly and moves to the tub. "We need to take that bath now. Soothe all those parts I'm not done with yet."

I smile. "I think I have some bubble bath."

～

A HALF HOUR LATER, Dylan drains some of the water and runs the tap to add more hot water to the tub. I'm across from him, our legs tangled, our hands entwined. I can't help looking at all his tattoos again.

"Have you thought of my tattoo yet?" I ask.

A mischievous smile arises on his gorgeous face. "I have."

"Can you tell me what it is?"

He shakes his head. "Nope."

"After the cast is off, you'll sketch it though?"

He shrugs. "You let me know when you're ready."

"I'm ready now."

He nods and I know he's hiding something, but I have no idea what it could be. "You've got at least five more weeks."

He stares at me so long, I look away.

"Come here," he says. I slide so that my back is to his chest and he nuzzles his face into my neck, securing the one arm he can get wet around me, the other in plastic propped up on the side of the tub. "Have you finished that math problem yet?"

"No, but I'm getting close."

"That's my girl." He kisses my ear, his tongue twirling around the lobe. "I'm not sure you're going to get to work on it for a while though."

"Why is that?" I look at him over my shoulder.

"Because I have a lot of masturbation material and I want to make live footage with you."

I turn around fully and he takes the opportunity to get me to straddle him. "You masturbated to me?"

Stop looking for affirmation.

He laughs. "Are you kidding me? I've been masturbating to you since the first day we met."

"You're lying. That's a way to save face. You probably masturbated to Blanca and Sierra too."

He says nothing for a moment. "Truth is, I never did. I

can't really say why. Maybe Sierra scares me a little and by the time I met Blanca, you were a permanent part of my highlight reel."

"Now I feel giddy and it shouldn't matter, but…" I lean forward and press a kiss to his lips. "I'm flattered."

He holds me to him. "Wait to be flattered until you find out what we were doing."

"I think bath time is over." I pull the drain plug.

He chuckles, and I step out of the bath then help him. We remove the bag then dry off with the towels from earlier.

"We've gotten entirely too wet tonight. I'm turning into a prune." I walk in front of him to the bedroom.

"Oh, I haven't gotten you nearly as wet as I want you yet."

I'm not sure I'll ever grow tired of the dirty things he says to me. He's so open about how much he wants me physically. I wonder where that comes from when he's so insecure about showing any vulnerability. Maybe he views sex and relationships differently.

We get back to my bed and I pick up the condoms. "So we're just not going to use these?"

He picks them up and tosses them on the floor. I guess that answers that.

"Me on top again?" I ask.

"Yeah, but are you up for trying something?"

I nod.

He slides by me on the bed, lying in the same position he was in the first time. "Straddle me, but turn the opposite way so I'm looking at your ass."

"Reverse cowgirl?" I ask and his eyes narrow as though he's wondering who I've done it with. "I'm not some naive virgin. I watch porn."

A huge smile takes over his face. "Oh, that's our next thing. We're watching porn together."

"I have another idea first though."

"Do tell."

My cheeks heat, but I force myself to say the words. "A little sixty-nine before reverse cowgirl?"

He slides down the bed on his back a bit. "You are the girl of my dreams. By all means. I did skip dinner."

And let me say I haven't found one thing Dylan isn't good at. Even if he only has one good arm.

I spring up in bed and turn to my side. Dylan's asleep on his back, his casted arm on his side, half on his stomach, and his other arm above his head. He looks as tired as my body feels. Even with the use of only one arm, Dylan did a fabulous job of giving me multiple orgasms.

After pushing the covers off my legs, I grab a shirt and shorts, then I pull my books off my dresser. My mind is clearer than it's been in weeks. I grab my reading light and clip it to my book, putting pencil to paper, and the block lifts, the answer coming to me as if someone placed it in my mind.

Jax comes home, his footsteps moving through the apartment as he goes through his nightly routine of changing his clothes and having a late night snack and a beer while watching television. For a moment, I debate joining him and asking him what he told Dylan to spur the breakthrough of that wall he put between us. But then I turn to look at Dylan sleeping in my bed and I don't want to know. I'm just happy we crossed that line we've toed for so long.

Another wave of clarity washes over me and I work out another part of the equation. The rush of flying through the solution is addicting and I'm unable to stop my pencil from moving across the paper. Jax's footsteps on the other side of the door says he heads to his room, his door quietly shutting.

Dylan shifts in my sheets and steals my attention away for a second.

Picking up my books, I admire the man I'm way too invested in. He could break me, and I have to prepare myself for that. But he feels worth the risk.

I head out to the dark living room and sit at the kitchen table, working through the rest of the solution and feeling as though life couldn't get much better than this.

CHAPTER TWENTY-FOUR

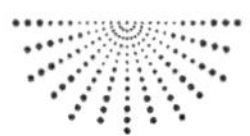

Dylan

My hand falls beside me, expecting to feel a warm body, but it lands on a cold sheet instead.

I peek at an empty spot next to me. I rarely wake up alone after a night of sex. If anything, the girl is usually begging me for another round. My heart squeezes over the idea that maybe Rian is having second thoughts. Maybe last night was too much, too fast. Maybe my mouth was way too filthy for her or my one-handed fucking wasn't stellar.

Shaking my head, I push away that notion. She was right there with me, her body instinctively knowing what to do even though her experience is limited. I tried to guide her and not make her feel inadequate because she was anything but. Hell, the caveman alpha male in me likes that I'll get to teach her some things.

I sit up, find my track pants, and after what feels like a

lifetime and I'm sweating from the effort of putting them on, I leave the sanctuary of her room—only to stop in her doorway. She's asleep at the kitchen table, her hands tucked under her head on top of the pile of papers strewn everywhere.

I slide back the veil of blonde hair covering her face and kiss her cheek. "Time to wake up, brainiac."

She stirs, swatting me away, and I laugh. My lips travel down her ear and suck her earlobe. She moans and my morning wood screams good morning once again.

"Go to the bed," I say.

When she still doesn't get up, I delve my hand under the bottom of her T-shirt and squeeze her breast, pinching her nipple.

She jolts, looks at me, and gives me one of those dick-saluting smiles. "Morning."

I chuckle and kiss her lips. "Morning."

She cuts the kiss off short and wipes her mouth.

"Should I be offended that I woke up alone?" I leave her to make coffee.

"I had a breakthrough on the problem."

"So you came out here?" I ask, shuffling between the sink and coffee maker.

Her arms reach around me as I scoop coffee grounds into the maker. "You freed my blockage," she says, her lips casting small kisses on my back.

How natural it is for us this morning. I worried we would be stoic around one another, worried what the other is thinking, but we seem to be in the same place.

I start the coffee maker and turn around, taking her in my arm. She lays her head on my chest.

"I have to go to the shop tonight," I spit out like I'm worried she's going to get upset.

She rests her chin on my chest and looks up at me. "Okay."

"You're not mad?" I expected some jealousy or disappointment over the fact that I can't spend the weekend in bed with her. I would love to, but Jax and Frankie might kill one another if I don't make an appearance.

Her hand runs up my back. "Why would I be mad?"

I shake my head. "No reason. You'll come by though?"

"If you want me to?"

I kiss the top of her head. "Definitely. I can sneak out for a late dinner."

She kisses my chest. "Deal."

We stay locked in each other's hold until the coffee maker dings. This is way too easy. I wish I could relax and enjoy it, but experience says something bad is on the horizon.

INK ENVY IS BUZZING when I show up at six o'clock. I meant to be here earlier, but Rian and I got waylaid trying out new positions with her on top. She's really finding what gets her off and I fucking love watching her sexual side awaken.

Lyle's on the bar stool by the welcome table. Jax is working on a customer and has another one waiting. Frankie's busy with a group of girls who seem to be all getting the same tattoo on their hipbone. Everything's running well, so I figure I'll head back to Rian—then my gaze stops on Mad Max coming out of the back area where the piercing station is. A woman follows him, her red face beaming. My guess is she either got her nips or pussy done.

"What the hell?" I put my hand out to him when he approaches.

"I heard you might need a little pick-me-up around here?"

"It's Saturday night. What about the place in the city?" That's where he should be. Where the money is for him. I was proud he got the job in the city.

"I'm needed here, man." He claps me on the shoulder. "I have a few more appointments set up, but I'll swing by your office to shoot the shit when I'm done."

I nod, hoping my eyes convey the words that can be hard for me to speak. But the fact he's here until I can get the business thriving again speaks volumes to me. I wonder who called him and let him know the state of things.

Jax nods at me then looks back down to his client. "I'm guessing all is peachy keen now? Or should I say you're the king of Rian's peach now?"

"Yeah, things are…" A montage of Rian and me in fifty million positions over the last twenty-four hours rolls through my mind. All our jagged edges fit together like puzzle pieces. "Good."

"Yeah, I know, I'm not deaf."

I chuckle and head to my office, passing Frankie's station.

"Hey, boss. I heard you got your head out of your ass."

I look over her shoulder to see a butterfly with three Greek letters underneath. The girl she's working on looks me over. A look that, once upon a time, would've had me sliding a chair next to Frankie and shooting the shit.

"I did. She'll be here shortly to give you all the details, I'm sure."

"Can't wait." Frankie chuckles. "Oh, I had no one for Jolie. She's coloring in your office. Sorry."

"My favorite girl." I wink to her to let her know it's okay.

As I walk away, I overhear the girl asking Frankie if we're a couple.

Frankie, being Frankie, says, "Hell no, he's my boss. He's taken by a gorgeous blonde who's a brilliant mathematician."

I smile all the way back to my office. Who would've thought the word taken would sound so calming? Not me.

I'm on cloud nine until I open my office door to find Jolie with a crayon on my wall.

She freezes. Then she gives me that sweet smile of hers. "Uncle Dylan!"

She runs to me, so I bend down. When she wraps her little arms around my neck, I pick her up and squeeze her.

"You're a lucky girl we're so free with art around here." Which is true. Our welcome table has drawings from all the tattoo artists who have come through here. "Do you want paper or a coloring sheet?" I put her down.

"I have a coloring book." She holds up a coloring tattoo book. Of course. She kneels on the floor and opens the book, choosing to color an angel tattoo.

"Can I join you?" I ask, sitting on the couch and grabbing her crayons.

"Want to pick?" She hands me the book.

I scroll through and pull out a heart with angel wings and a banner across the front. Holding the crayon in my right hand feels weird. The fact that I miss inking so much I've resorted to coloring says the next five weeks are going to be a struggle.

Jolie joins me on the couch and cringes. "You're outside the lines."

"I'm a lefty, so I don't do much with my right hand," I say. And I don't say that her angel is all blue and she's outside the lines too.

"Mommy says to stay in the outline if I want to be like her when I grow up."

I chuckle. "Is that what you want to be when you grow up? A tattoo artist?"

"I want to be Mommy," she says, coloring a line on my page with her blue crayon. She giggles.

I watch her concentrate on her picture, pressing too hard. She's such a sweet kid but hasn't had the easiest life so far. She's heard and seen way more than she ever should at her age.

"Your mommy is pretty cool," I remark, exchanging my red for gold.

"Rian too," she says. "You like Rian?"

"Man, news gets around quick in these parts."

She giggles and slides down to sit on her knees on the other side of the coffee table, leaning forward and staring at me.

"Yeah, I like Rian."

"She's pretty like a princess," she says.

I nod. Jolie's right. Rian is pretty like a princess, and instead of being with a prince, she's chosen me, the commoner who wants to brand her with a tattoo drawn just for her.

"Mommy's not pretty like a princess," she says.

I laugh. Maybe they should make a princess doll with tattoos and an edge that would challenge any prince that came her way.

"Mommy doesn't like princess stories. She says there's no such thing as a prince and I need to be able to save myself. Be strong."

Only Frankie would lecture her kid about fairy tales, but I can't say I blame her.

"I don't really believe in all that 'prince saving the princess' stuff either," I admit as Frankie opens the office door.

Jolie's eyes widen. "Really?"

I shake my head. "I think sometimes both the princess and the prince need saving."

Her small eyebrows crinkle.

"Someday you'll understand," I say.

"Lecturing my kid on fairytales?" Frankie walks in and sits in my office chair. "Finally being productive, huh?"

"Can you tell I'm itching to do anything with art?" I continue to color outside the lines, shading the wings.

"Not bad for your right hand," she says.

"Look, Mommy. An angel." Jolie hands her picture to Frankie.

"I love it. It's beautiful. Remember you have all those colors though. See how Dylan uses more than one? You can too."

Jolie snatches back the picture.

"Only you would criticize a kid's coloring page."

Frankie shrugs, not offended in the least. "It's merely a suggestion." She winks at Jolie, whose face lights up.

Jolie takes the gold crayon from my hand and puts a halo on the top of the angel's head. Then she puts the gold down and takes out the blue one again.

"Blue is her favorite color," I say and Frankie nods.

"How do you spell Jax?" Jolie asks me, and I side-eye Frankie.

"J.A.X." I write it on the back of my paper so she can see the letters.

When she writes them, it looks more like UAT, but she gave it a try. Her name at the bottom is more legible but spaced so far apart it takes a minute to figure out what it is.

"Can I go out there?" she asks, knowing she's not allowed to run through the tattoo stations. The waiting area and my office are the only places she has free rein.

"He just finished," Frankie says, and Jolie bolts out of the room.

"And you?" I stand.

"The girl brigade is complete. I have an appointment in ten though. I hate to ask this on a Saturday night, but would you mind watching Jolie?" She cringes the same way Jolie did when she told me I color outside the lines.

"Sure. What else do I have to do?" Other than take out my girlfriend. "Mind if Rian and I take her to dinner?"

"Not at all. She'll give you a good idea of what it'll be like when you have your own kids." She laughs, and I throw a crayon at her back as she leaves.

Jolie runs back in and Frankie swoops her up. "He loved it. He hung it on the wall."

Frankie turns to me and I can't decipher the look on her face, but it's not one of happiness. "That's nice."

Jolie does a little shimmy to get Frankie to set her down.

"Go work, I got this," I say.

"Thanks, boss."

As Frankie leaves and I watch Jolie, my mind wanders to kids. I'm sure it's something Rian wants, and I used to think about back when I was a teenager, probably because I never had my own family. But now that I'm a grown man I know that kids are a lot of responsibility and you have to be a good role model. That thought is terrifying.

So I do what I do best and push it aside to deal with another day.

Rian

I'm getting ready to head over to Ink Envy when the apartment door opens—thanks to someone who obviously still has a key.

"Hello?" I call.

"We're very disappointed that we had to hear about you and Dylan from Seth." Sierra barges into the bathroom, almost making me hit my arm against the curling iron.

"I would've told you. It *just* happened."

Sierra hops up on the counter and Blanca sits on the toilet.

"This is huge. It deserved a text at the very least," Blanca says. "Hell, maybe even a picture."

Sierra and I look at her.

"Not a sex pic or a dick pic, just a picture of him in your bed or something." When we still look confused, Blanca waves us off. "Never mind."

Sierra wiggles to get comfortable. "Give us all the deets."

My blush comes quickly, reflected back to me in the mirror. "It just kind of happened. He said he's liked me for a while but was afraid to cross the line."

Blanca slaps her thigh. "I knew it."

"And the sex?" Sierra asks.

"Sex is good. Great actually."

"I figured as much." Sierra rolls her eyes, a silent reminder that I'm far from his first conquest.

"What else?" Blanca asks.

I shrug, pulling another chunk of hair to curl. "There isn't much. I'm going over to Ink Envy and we're going to dinner. Nothing seemed awkward this morning. He's very handsy and affectionate with me. It's just so…"

"Perfect," Blanca says, her lovesick eyes rolling to the back of her head.

"Is that scary? I feel like it's scary." I lay the curling iron on the counter and shake out my curls.

"Why would it be scary?" Blanca asks.

"You're waiting for something like the shoe to drop?" Sierra understands where I'm coming from.

"Ahh," Blanca says. "I get that. But maybe this is all turning out perfect because it's meant to be."

I nod, not really convinced. Regardless, I'm ecstatic Dylan's admitted he holds the same feelings I've harbored for him. And I'll live this out until that shoe drops.

Sierra's hand runs up and down my arm. "I thought the same thing with Adrian. You're very invested in Dylan. You always have been. Although this is great and we were all waiting for this moment, it's a big chance. A big step."

"Not making me feel better." I leave the bathroom for some space.

"I don't mean it like that, but you guys have a lot to lose. At the same time, I think you guys are great friends who won't allow this to tear apart your friendship if it didn't work out."

"I'm not sure we should think about the negative right now. It's way too early," Blanca says. "Rian." She takes my hands in hers. "When is the last time you lived in the moment? Without thinking about the future?"

She's right. Never. Never except when I confronted Dylan yesterday. My life has always had a plan, whether it was my mom's or my own. I was taught that there's always somewhere or something I should be striving for. There's always more to achieve.

"You're right," I say. "My fear of the future could keep me from enjoying the here and now if I let it."

Blanca and Sierra smile.

"Exactly," Blanca says.

"It could be nothing goes wrong, or if it does, you get through it." Sierra opens up the bottle of wine they must've brought over. "Who would've ever thought Adrian would get the rules changed so he doesn't have to rule?"

She's right, but my worry isn't over something we'll have to face together. It's Dylan that feels unpredictable to me. He went from zero to one hundred in a night.

My friends stare at me as though they want to know my thoughts, but I'm going to keep these to myself.

"I'm good, guys, really."

Sierra pours the wine. "Then let's celebrate. You waited long enough, so enjoy that fine piece of ass."

We all laugh, clinking our glasses to toast the future.

I WALK INTO INK ENVY. Jax tattoos a girl's back as she's sprawled on his table on her stomach. Frankie works on a guy's chest, and Lyle's head is buried in his sketchbook.

"What's up?" Lyle nods and starts drawing again when he sees it's me. "Dylan is letting me tattoo him."

"That's cool. Tonight?" I ask. Lyle isn't the first to apprentice under Dylan. Everyone gets to tattoo him at some point.

He looks up with a smirk. "No. He said he had plans." His gaze sweeps over me. "I assume you're his plans."

"He's got two girls tonight," Jax says.

My heart constricts so tightly, I feel as if it's going to stop beating.

Frankie gives him a death stare. "Jolie is here," she says to me. "Way to give the girl a heart attack," she says to Jax.

"I only speak the truth."

The girl on her stomach stares lovingly over her shoulder at him. How he's able to work with some girl drooling over him like that, I have no idea.

"They're in the office," Frankie says.

"Thanks." I walk to the back.

"I do expect details at some point," Frankie says, her tattoo machine moving along the skin with skilled precision.

"We'll do lunch."

"What do you really need to know? They're fucking. I can record her moans and his grunts as proof if you'd like. I think I counted ten 'oh my gods' this morning." Jax smiles at me, not seeming upset in the least. He must see something else in my eyes though. "Relax, I'm good."

I nod and disappear down the hallway.

"You can't just take the phone," Dylan says. "You have to ask. I was on a call."

"But *Paw Patrol*," Jolie whines.

It's late for her. She's probably ready for bed.

I walk through the doorway, Dylan looks up, relief clear in his demeanor and his eyes. "Heaven sent us an angel," he says, pointing at me.

"Rian!" Jolie runs at me.

I pick her up, situating her on my hip. "I heard you had a great babysitter tonight." I tap my finger on her nose.

"Uncle Dylan won't let me watch *Paw Patrol.*"

Our gazes shift to him, and he blows out a breath. "I had Jax's client on the phone. He wanted to cancel for tonight. I'm arguing with him that he forfeits his deposit and she stole my phone to put on that talking dog show."

Jolie's head falls on my shoulder and her fingers play with my long hair.

Dylan points at her. "Don't let that sweetness put your guard down."

I hug her tightly. "I guess our dinner is takeout?" I sit down in the chair next to his desk, Jolie situating herself so she's straddling me with her head on my shoulder.

"I was hoping you'd be my dinner." He waggles his eyebrows.

"That's very inappropriate now, although I will take a raincheck."

He slides his chair over to me and kisses me.

"Ew." Jolie's hand moves to his face, pushing it away.

"See, she's sweet." I chuckle.

He kisses her forehead before falling back down into his chair. "Chinese, Mexican, or pizza?"

I shrug. "I'm game for whatever."

"Pick one." He's desperately trying to use his mouse with his right hand, but every time he has to click on something, he hits the wrong selection.

I stand from the chair, trying not to disturb Jolie since she's growing limp in my arms. "Sit down." I point at the chair I was just in.

"I like you bossy," he says, sitting in the chair.

I transfer Jolie to him. Her eyes open but fall closed again right away. Cradled in his good arm, she wraps her arms around his neck.

"Well, that was a bad move," I say, sitting in his office chair to take control of the order.

"Why? She's still asleep," he says, oblivious to how good he looks with a baby, especially a little girl, in his arms.

"Yeah. On you."

He looks down at her. "She's much more tolerable now."

Having been friends with Dylan for years, I can order our Chinese food by heart. I order some extra for the employees so everyone can eat since that's something he'll want.

"That's not it," I singsong, clicking the items he loves.

I sneak another peek at him. He scrunches his eyebrows. God, Dylan holding a child should be illegal. The image could cause ovaries to explode everywhere.

"It's you and her." I open my eyes wider at him. "Your attractiveness meter just went into overheating range with her asleep in your arms."

He smiles and looks at Jolie. "She's not mine."

"She doesn't have to be."

His smile grows. "So this does it for you, huh?"

I click the moo shu pork and sit back, examining them. His legs are spread open in a casual stance with his broken arm resting on the chair arm. Jolie's face is tucked into his chest.

"Pretty much." I slide the chair back to the computer.

"Make sure to get enough for everyone," he says, ignoring my confession.

I've never really thought about having a kid with Dylan. Mostly my time has been spent imagining him in bed, but not really as a boyfriend. I have no expectations of what our relationship will be like. There's only one stipulation I have and that's monogamy.

"I did. Are Seth and Knox stopping by?" I ask.

"I don't know, but I don't need to feed their asses. My credit card is on file."

"I see that." I click the final button and check out using his credit card. "You're a very generous tipper."

"Am I?" he asks. "Maybe I should give you a tip for doing the ordering?"

I flutter my eyelids. "Sounds promising."

"You should give me a peep show."

"No!" I point at Jolie. "She's right there."

He follows my vision. "She's dead asleep."

I stand in front of him and look at him one more time. "You have me at a disadvantage. I want to snap a picture just to relive you and Jolie like that."

He shakes his head, and his smile doesn't reach his eyes. In Dylan language, that means something is bothering him.

"Does that scare you?" I ask.

His lips purse and he shakes his head. Same reaction I got when I told him I was going out with Jax.

"I think it might," I say.

"No. But—"

I put up my hand. "Your hot level going up because you're holding her does not mean I want to have your baby."

"Really? Are you sure?"

I laugh. "What? Of course! Why would you ask me if I'm sure?"

He stares at Jolie and I step forward to take her, but he shakes his head. "I got her. Keep drooling."

I cross my arms and wait for him to answer my question.

He blows out a breath. "You're a girl who thinks about the future."

I laugh again and he gives me a blank stare. "Sorry, continue," I say.

"Now I seem like an arrogant prick."

I nod.

"It's just you're you. All life plans and timetables. I figure you've planned out our wedding and how many kids you want."

"Maybe I'm using you for your body," I say, raising an eyebrow.

A smirk indents his adorable face. "Nah, it's not that great." He crooks his finger for me to come to him.

"You think just because you beckon, I should answer your call?"

The office door opens, and Frankie stands there, watching us before her eyes land on Jolie. "I had a feeling she'd crash. I'm between clients."

She swoops up Jolie and carries her out of the room, shutting the door. Dylan takes that as his opportunity to corner me, and he successfully gets my back to the wall.

"Look, I came to you." He locks me with his hips, and his pants do nothing to hide his hard length. "So I'm wrong then?"

"I don't have us married in my mind. I'm not pregnant, and there's no white picket fence house in my head. I'm in this to see where it goes. I have no preconceived ideas. Okay?" I place my hands on his cheeks, and he nods. "So relax."

He stares at me. "One day at a time sounds good. I am slowly becoming addicted to you."

"Cheesy!" I scream.

But he swallows my yell, and we spend the next twenty minutes making out like teenagers until Lyle tells us the food is here.

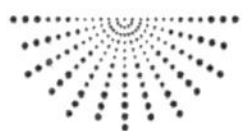

CHAPTER TWENTY-SIX

Dylan

Three weeks later, I'm on the couch, watching *Superbad* with Seth. My phone is out and I'm looking at a picture I can't stop staring at—Rian and Jolie asleep on the couch a few weeks earlier. I didn't understand why me holding a baby made Rian so gaga until Frankie and I came home that night and found the scene on my screen.

When Frankie went to the bathroom, I snapped the picture before we woke Rian. After that, my fear of having a family dissipated and I can't stop staring at the picture and thinking what if we do make it long term? A baby on Rian looks like home.

Rian's bedroom door swings open and she raises her hand in victory. "I did it!"

She's holed herself up in that room for two days trying to finish that math problem.

"You solved it?" I tuck my phone away and open my arms.

She runs across the room and throws herself into the chair with me, wrapping her arms around me and kissing my neck. "I think. I won't know until Dr. Giroux looks at my email."

"Way to go." Seth raises his beer.

She kisses me one more time then tries to slide off my lap, but I wrap my right arm—which has become strong in the past weeks—around her to keep her in place. Seth tries to concentrate on the television as though he's not witnessing our affection.

But as always, the more I have of Rian, the more I crave. Is this what all those guys who I made fun of for being pussy whipped felt like? That all they want to do is spend their time with their girl?

I capture her lips and turn us in the chair to block us from Seth, sliding my tongue into her mouth to tide me over until we're alone again. When we're done, Rian gets up and I smack her ass.

"Hey, you should know things are going south with Knox and Leilani," Seth says.

Rian stops walking toward the kitchen and sits down on the arm of my chair. I take the opportunity to slide my hand up her shirt to touch her bare back, my fingers gliding along her skin.

"What happened?" she asks Seth, sounding concerned.

Seth shrugs. "I heard them fighting. Leilani was saying she's going back home to Hawaii. Knox asked when she'd be back."

"And?" Rian asks, much more interested than me.

Knox is a great friend, but I always knew it would end this way. When a girl like Leilani breezes in and out of your life, at some point you have to see her for what she is— temporary. But for some reason, Knox is head over heels and all that rational thinking that's made him a great cop, flies out the window and travels over the Atlantic Ocean when Leilani walks back into his life. After she's gone, I'll be on the bar stool next to him once again, handing him shots to get over her.

"I didn't hear anything else, but when he went to work, she left too," Seth said. "And I haven't seen her yet today."

"She probably bailed again," I say, my hand venturing higher up Rian's back and under her bra strap. How far can I get before Seth notices? I've missed her these past two days as I gave her space to finish the problem. It's not even the sex I miss, as pathetic as I sound. It's just holding her naked body to mine. Making her laugh. And okay, I can't lie—I do miss the sex.

Rian turns to me, her forehead scrunched. "Again?"

Seth raises his eyebrows. I guess he thought all the girls knew. "They've weaved in and out each other's lives more than a crocheted scarf."

Rian's shoulders sag because she believes in happily ever afters. But Knox and Leilani don't have it in them. Rian and I might be different, but Knox and Leilani are on opposite sides of the spectrum. Something neither of them have realized yet.

"I knew they knew each other, but I didn't realize they'd gotten together and apart so many times."

Seth sips his beer. "She's run out on him before. A few years ago when he was drunk one night, he talked about her."

"They're just different," I say, not wanting to get into Knox's business.

"We're different," Rian says, her blue eyes so transparent.

"You don't want to see the world. And I'm not a black-and-white kind of guy. Leilani's a wanderer and Knox is a creature of habit. Explain how those two kinds of people can stay together." My whole hand runs along her skin now. "I believe in opposites attract, but sometimes there can be too much opposite."

Seth nods as though he understands, but Rian's lips tip down.

"I feel bad for him. Do you think she's gone for good?" Rian asks.

As she asks, the door of our apartment opens and Knox walks in, still wearing his uniform. He ignores Rian and me, his sole focus on Seth. "Did she leave a note?"

"Not that I saw," he says.

Knox nods, and his eyes meet mine. His authoritative finger points at me as if I said or did something. "I don't want to fucking hear it."

Knox slams the door behind him, and Rian turns to me.

Seth sips his beer. "Can I stay here tonight?"

"The couch is yours," Rian says.

"Or my bed," I offer.

Rian smiles. I feel bad for Knox. I saw the heartbreak Leilani left behind last time, which was why I wasn't so keen on her reappearance in his life. Still, tonight I'll hold Rian a little tighter.

I WRAP my arms around Rian's waist, swiping the chocolate frosting from the bowl and holding my finger in front of her mouth.

"You do know this is taking me twice as long, right?" she says.

I don't move my finger. She puts her mouth over it, twirling her tongue around it. Just like that, my dick pops up in my pants like a timer in a turkey.

"Let's take the bowl to the bedroom," I suggest.

"And leave the cake bare?"

The timer goes off, so she dislodges from my arm to take the cake out of the oven.

"Sure. I say we frost you instead." I swipe another finger of frosting when she's not looking and eat it myself. Damn, she really is a great baker. "Any word from that professor guy?"

"No. I got the receipt that the email went through, but he was out of the office." She puts the cakes on a cooling rack.

"I still think you should do something you love with that money if you're the first one who solved it. Like, I don't know… open up a chocolate-and-chocolate cake shop."

She laughs. "That's the only cake I make?"

I nod and steal another swipe of frosting. "Yeah, because you love your boyfriend so much. But then again, maybe you should serve everything except the chocolate-chocolate because this cake is only for me since I'm the most special person in your life."

"I think I could still sell the chocolate-chocolate cake but give you something no one else gets." She looks coy, like she wants to play.

I've never come across a game I didn't want to conquer. "Like?"

She strips off her shirt and unhooks her bra. "How much frosting can you lick off me?"

"Oh, you have no idea how much I love this frosting and your body. It's like when someone decided to put peanut butter and chocolate together. Perfection." I grab the bowl. "Let's go."

"Your bed though." She places her hand on my chest. "So we can sleep in mine afterward."

I unzip my hoodie, leaving it on the floor, and back her toward my bedroom. "I love that you can be spontaneous but still think of the aftermath."

She giggles and dips her finger into the frosting, then

traces a line down her tit and around her nipple. We open my door, she falls to my mattress, and I kick the door shut, my mouth watering and ready to work its way over Rian's body. I bring my mouth to her chest, and with the first swipe of my tongue, she shivers under me.

"Oh, Dylan," she says.

Once I'm done sucking one tit, I swipe the frosting on her other one and mimic my move. Traveling a line from her tits to the top of her waistband with my tongue, I unbutton her jeans and slide the zipper down. I help her get her jeans and panties off. Once she's naked in front of me, I stare at her, still surprised she's mine.

"What are you waiting for?" She props up on her elbows as though something's wrong. "You okay?"

I nod. "Yeah, I'm great."

After dipping my finger into the frosting, I bring my finger to her mouth and she moans around it. Instead of spreading the frosting anywhere else on her body, I fall to my knees and pull her legs over my shoulders.

"I did have plans of licking frosting off you." She watches me slide my tongue up her folds. "But we have time, I suppose."

Her back falls back on the bed.

"That's what I thought." I chuckle into her center, blowing cool air on the flesh I wet with my tongue, and she squirms.

After only the short time we've been together, I know what gets her off. She loves clit play, so I flex my tongue, using only the tip to lick tiny circles around her nub. Her hands go to her sides, gripping the sheets. At least my right hand can widen her, putting light pressure right under her clit, and her back arches off the bed.

I fucking love watching her get off.

The more pressure I use, the more she grinds against my face. My name comes from her mouth, along with praise of how great I am at this, how she never wants me to stop. I watch her chase her orgasm on my tongue, and my dick grows thick and aching between my legs.

I ramp up the speed a touch more. One of her hands grabs my hair, pulling and tugging, as her breathing labors. She's so close, so I up the speed until she unapologetically grinds my face into her pussy. She crests over that threshold and falls back down on her back.

It takes some awkward effort on my part but I remove her legs from my shoulders, ditch my track pants, and nudge her legs open. Her eyes perk up when she feels the tip of my dick at her opening. But she presses her hand to my chest.

"Oh no, you don't," she says, pushing me to sit up.

I sit back on my knees. "What?"

She grabs the bowl of frosting and swipes a smear across my chest. "I get to play too." Her gaze dips to my very erect cock.

I sit back. "By all means."

Her tongue slides along my chest, teasing my nipples. My eyes close, relishing her mouth, until she palms me, rubbing and pulling, her thumb spreading the pre-cum along the tip of my dick. As she slides off the bed and falls to her knees like I did, she urges me to the edge of the mattress. With one hand on the base of my cock, she lowers her mouth, and stars fill my vision.

Damn, is there anything Rian isn't good at? She really is a certified genius.

CHAPTER TWENTY-SEVEN

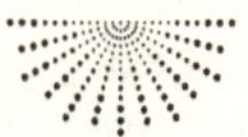

Rian

As I stare at my computer and read the message again, tears well up in my eyes.

"'Congratulations, you're the winner. Your check will be issued next week, and your name will be listed in our academic journal next month. Great job, everyone at the association is very impressed. Sincerely, Dr. Giroux, President of the Mathematics Association of America.'" I read the email out loud, still processing that I actually did it.

Jax walks out of his bedroom, spots me, and freezes. "Shit." He turns to go back but then faces me again. "Where's Phillips?"

"He's asleep," I say.

"In which bedroom?" His gaze flickers to Dylan's door then mine.

"Mine," I say, not understanding what's wrong with him.

"Thank fuck." He walks through the living room to the bathroom and shuts the door.

Odd.

I minimize the email, seeing three from my dad waiting in my inbox. Apologies for what he said mostly. I should print out the congratulatory email and go to their house and tape it to every available surface. Maybe then they'd be proud of me. But a part of me doesn't want anyone to know I won.

My phone rings and I jump in my seat.

My eyes zero in on the name. Johann must've gotten word that the problem was solved and the contest closed. Ever since that day I was going to ask him for help and Dylan talked me out of it, he hasn't contacted me. Which suits me fine.

My phone beeps that he left a message, then an email from him pings on my computer. He's probably upset that the contest has been closed and is wondering if I'm the one who solved it.

The bathroom door opens and Jax walks out in a towel. "So you're still together?"

"Yes," I say.

He nods. "Cool." He disappears into his bedroom.

What is up with him?

I look at the box of tissues next to my computer. He thought I was crying over Dylan?

I shut down my computer, walk into my bedroom, and set my phone on the nightstand, then I slide under the covers with Dylan. He stirs, sighs, and wraps his arm around my body.

"Good morning," he murmurs, kissing my forehead.

I run my hand down his chest. "Good morning."

I lay with him as he falls in and out of sleep. Peeking up, I cast small kisses to his chest.

"I won," I whisper.

He bolts up and my body falls to the mattress. Looking at me, his eyes widen. "You did?"

I nod.

Then his body is on top of mine "Congratulations! That's awesome."

I nod again but the tears well up even more this time and my throat constricts.

He stares at me in confusion. "Why are you crying?"

I sit up and rest my back on the headboard, shrugging because I have no idea why I'm crying.

Sitting next to me, he pulls me into him. "This is a good thing. A happy moment. You should be on cloud nine."

My tears run down his chest while my fingers follow an intricate tattoo on his thigh. Maybe it's because Dylan and I were friends before we got together, or maybe because Dylan is kind of a private person, but we rarely ever talk about our feelings other than toward one another. I'm not sure how he'll take me opening my heart and laying all my problems out in front of him. This might not be what he signed up for.

"Talk to me," he says.

I sigh. "I'm happy. But I'm upset too. I did it as a big FU to my parents, but I never thought I'd feel this good about doing it."

"Then why the crying?"

I sit up on my knees and face him. "When my parents find out, they're going to be so happy. Like I made their world."

"They are your parents," he says, but he doesn't understand.

"All I've ever done is disappoint them. No matter all the great things I've accomplished, it's never been enough. I think I'm upset because I did this to prove to them I could do it, but all that will happen now is they'll demand more. When will it stop? When will it ever be enough just to be their daughter?"

He takes my hands. "I know you did this for them, but be happy for yourself. And do what you want with that twenty-five grand. I'm not joking that I think you should open a bakery. But do what you want to do. Your parents will always be your parents. I don't have a lot of experiences with parents, but at some point, you have to stop looking for their praise."

"I'm not looking for their praise," I say, sitting down and loosening my hands to lay limp in my lap.

"Truth is, you kind of are. You might've done it with a middle finger, but you did it to prove to them you're smart."

I narrow my eyes. So much for him understanding. "That's not true."

My phone rings with my parents' ringtone.

He brings his knees up to his chest. "They're going to find out, and you're right, they're going to expect more from you. The question is how important is it to you?" His phone goes off on the nightstand and he slides out of bed. Staring at the name, he silences it. "I don't say it to be mean, but you chase their approval. Except for me, I imagine. They probably don't know we're dating, right?"

I sit on the bed, crossing my legs. That balloon I was floating on pops.

He leans over and kisses my cheek. "I'm going to take a shower. Call them and get it over with."

As the door shuts with his departure, I stare at my hands. Is Dylan right? Maybe he is. I slide off the bed, grab my phone, and dial my parents.

They both answer.

"Was it you? We heard that Johann didn't solve it, but someone did." My mom acts as if she's been waiting to find out if a loved one came of surgery okay. This isn't life or death.

I say, "I'd like to set up a dinner. Us and my new boyfriend."

"Sweetheart, did you not hear your mother?" my dad asks.

"Did you not hear me?" I snip.

"Fine. We'll do a dinner, but answer the question," my mom says.

"My boyfriend is Dylan. We've been seeing each other for a few weeks."

"Well, we've met Dylan, sweetheart," my dad says. "And I hoped you were dating him since you were kissing him."

"He's in a different role in my life now. I want you to have dinner with him as my boyfriend."

"This is ridiculous. Answer the question, Rian. Did you solve the problem?" My mom's last ounce of patience runs out.

Part of me wants to tell them no, that it wasn't me, but they won't stop until they find out. Then I'd have a whole other host of problems. "I did."

"You did?" my mom's shocked voice says she didn't have a lot of faith in me.

"Yes."

"Oh, my God. Okay. Okay." My mom can't get a hold of her breath.

"You okay there, honey?" my dad asks. "Are you hyperventilating?"

"I'm good. We'll call you back. I have to call the Fredericksons. Plan the dinner or whatever you want."

"Way to go, sweetheart," my dad says right before the line dies.

I turn off my phone and sit on the edge of the bed.

Dylan is right. I'm allowing them to treat me like this, and I'm the one who needs to make it stop.

DYLAN'S ACTING WEIRD. He left to go to work with only a small peck on my lips. Usually I have to push him out the door. As I enter Ink Envy with a dinner for everyone, I'm not sure what I'll be walking into. But I didn't plan on finding Dylan on a table with Lyle holding a tattoo machine to his calf. An array of girls are circled around, asking Dylan a million questions.

"Hey, babe," Frankie says, looking up as she tattoos some guy.

"Forget Phillips. I'm starving," Jax says from behind the table in the front.

I set the boxes of pizza on the counter. Dylan doesn't even notice that I walked in. A redhead on his right paws at his arm, asking questions about his tattoos. He still hasn't seen me, and it probably says something about my trust level that I prefer it that way.

"What are we doing?" Jax leans forward, putting his chin in his palm and staring at the scene.

"Just observing," I say.

Dylan moves his arm so her finger falls off, and he explains nicely about the tattoo.

"Observing if he's flirting?" Jax asks.

I look at him and his eyebrows are raised. I wave Jax off and he chuckles, sitting back down.

"Asking for trouble," he says, picking up the journal thing I've seen him carrying around lately.

The redhead blocks my view again as Dylan lifts his T-shirt to show some tattoo that they're talking about. Her hand reaches out to touch him, but he drops the T-shirt and says something to her that makes her face red. She goes to stand next to her friends.

"And you thought you couldn't trust the guy," Jax says, shaking his head. His feet fall with a thud on the floor. "Lack of trust is the number one killer of a relationship."

"Shut up. I was just…"

He raises those damn eyebrows at me again.

I sigh. "So sue me."

"Hey, Phillips," Jax calls, and Dylan peeks up. "Your girl is here."

"Come here. I'm letting Lyle tattoo me." Dylan waves me over. When I get to the table, he cradles my cheek, kissing me so deep that my knees actually weaken. "I missed you. These are Lyle's fans," Dylan says, winking at me.

I nod. Yeah, right.

After Lyle finishes the small tattoo, the girls—who found out Dylan is off the market—are chatting in the waiting area. He gets up off the table and stands in front of me.

"Can we talk?" I ask.

Dylan tilts his head, but we both know things weren't comfortable this morning. I can't help but think it has to do with my parents. One thing I know about Dylan is that the future scares him. Like when he thought I was ready to walk down the aisle and pop out a bunch of babies. Or when I flippantly made a comment about going on a vacation together next year when a commercial came on. Other than a joke about a nude beach, I got nothing.

"Sure." Dylan grabs one pizza box and nods toward his office.

"Thanks, Rian!" Frankie smiles. "And no little people in there to stop you from doing whatever you want to do."

I laugh.

Once we're behind closed doors, Dylan drops the pizza on his desk and sits, patting his lap. "What's up?"

I sit down and put my arms around his neck. "We're okay?"

"Yeah." He tucks a strand of hair behind my ear. "We're great. Why?"

"Just this morning. When I said you were wrong about my parents… it felt weird after."

He runs a hand up and down my outer thigh. "I shouldn't have given you advice. What do I know about parents?"

"You were right. When I called them and told them about us dating and how I wanted to plan a dinner, all my mom cared about was whether I won. As soon as I told her I had, she hung up to call Johann's parents."

He frowns. "I'm sorry. But I still think you should celebrate for yourself."

I nod.

"Hey." He squeezes my thigh. "I'm taking you out tomorrow. A fancy restaurant where we toast to your accomplishment."

"We don't have to." I look away.

He puts his finger under my chin, bringing my gaze back to him. "Yes, we do."

I smile and rest my head on his shoulder. "Thanks."

"You're my girl. This is boyfriend duties, right?"

I chuckle and kiss the hollow of his neck. I guess it doesn't matter how many small things come up as long as we get through them. That's what makes a strong couple.

CHAPTER TWENTY-EIGHT

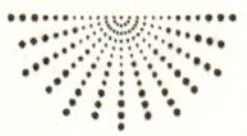

Dylan

The day has finally come. Rian and I sit in the doctor's office, waiting for him to come in and take off this damn cast.

Rian sits in a chair against the wall. "I want you to prepare yourself, because once I have use of both arms, all bets are off. You will be thoroughly fucked tonight."

She giggles and crosses her legs. "You'll hear no complaints from me."

"You might once you see what I can do with two hands." I wink, and she blushes.

Our relationship is going strong. I still can't get enough of her. She received her prize money and her name will be published in that scholar journal, which I know will be a big moment for her. We celebrated her success without talking about what she would do next. She's denied her parents' calls and emails and even told Jax to tell them she wasn't home when they stopped by. I'm trying to stay out of it because I don't know shit about parent issues.

Rian's voice draws me from my thoughts. "I say we ditch the celebratory lunch and head right home then."

"Cool. You are my favorite food," I say as the doctor knocks and then pushes the door open.

Rian purses her lips, and I chuckle. The doctor's cool enough to say a quick hello then wash his hands, pretending he didn't overhear me. The man understands what I'm talking about.

"Okay, let's get this cast off. I will warn you—your arm is going to smell pretty bad. We'll wipe it down before you leave. And you've probably lost some muscle strength that you'll need to build back up." He sits on his chair and wheels it toward me.

The nurse comes in moments later, smiling and putting on a pair of gloves.

Rian stands and comes to my side. Usually this is the type of situation where I'd be alone. Maybe Seth would've tagged along, but it's nice to have someone who cares for me. Not that Seth doesn't care, but he'd laugh his ass off if they sawed into my arm. It's a different kind of caring.

She grabs my right hand, running her free hand up and down my arm. "What do you think your tattoos look like under there?"

Fuck. How did I not think of that? "Let's hope not wrinkly as shit."

The doctor looks up over the rim of his glasses. "You'll gain the strength back right away. We'll give you some exercises to do at home."

I look at Rian and she shakes her head. Amazing how she can read my mind. But she's right—I plan on getting muscle strength back during my workouts with her. Squeezing tits, squeezing ass, finger fucking—it's all on the agenda.

As soon as the cast comes off, I gag, staring at my arm. Where is my awesome forearm with corded muscles and unbelievable ink? This scrawny, pale limb does not belong to me.

"Uh." Rian chokes on the bile that is probably running up her throat when the smell hits her. "That's horrible." But she never lets go of my hand.

"You want to wait outside?" the nurse asks.

I release her fingers because damn, that's worse than when Seth left milk in the fridge for four months.

"No." She swallows and tries to smile but fails miserably. "I'm good." She kisses my cheek then coughs in my ear.

"Man, she's a keeper, huh?" the nurse says, grabbing wipes and running them down my arm.

The doctor holds up the cast. "Do you want to keep it?"

"Hell no."

He laughs and puts it on the counter. "You'll need to head down to the X-ray department so we can have one last look, but I don't expect any issues. It was a clean break. Once you're done there, come back here and let the receptionist know you're here. If there's an issue, we'll call you back into the room. Otherwise, she'll let you know you're free to go."

"These are the instructions," the nurse says, passing Rian a piece of paper. "Like the doctor said, he'll gain strength back quickly. He's young. But in case any of these things occur, he should come back in."

I look at Rian and the nurse. "I am still here, right?"

The nurse laughs. "I've found it better to give the girl-friend the directions."

I shake my head and snatch the instructions out of Rian's hand. But Rian asks a few questions I didn't really think about. Like signs of anything bad and how much pres-sure I can put on the limb now and of course she's my girl because she asks about sexual activity and what precautions to take. She does it all without one hint of pink in her cheeks.

After I'm done, we all file out. I can't stop flexing my hand open and shut, trying to work some of the stiffness out.

"See you after the X-ray," the receptionist says.

We smile and wave, and it's clear as we walk through the waiting room to the elevators, we're a *we* now. A couple. It should terrify me. I've never liked the idea and responsibility of being a we.

But as Rian reads over the instructions in the elevator, I stare at her. That sliver of tongue rests between her lips when she's reading, and I realize that I kind of like being a we.

Who would have thought? Sure as hell not me.

A COUPLE OF WEEKS LATER, Rian walks into Ink Envy on a Monday evening. I asked her here under the ruse of helping me with my paperwork, saying I needed her math expertise. But first, I made sure to work the entire weekend—my girlfriend wasn't going to be my first tattoo after my arm finally felt better. I took the full two weeks before I felt confident enough to mark someone's skin.

"What's all this?" she asks staring at the row of candles on either side of the aisle leading to my station.

"Lock the door behind you," I say.

She turns and flicks the lock. I've already shut the blinds so no one can see what's about to transpire.

"I thought we were doing your paperwork?"

"Well, if you'd rather."

She shakes her head. "I look horrible. You should've warned me."

She pulls her ponytail out of her hair and shakes out the

strands. But I wanted her in comfortable clothes, so I'm glad she's wearing her yoga pants and T-shirt with a sweatshirt over.

"Warned you about what?" I slide my chair over to her and my hands land on her hips, my lips pressing to her stomach.

"This romantic evening you have planned."

I rest my chin on her stomach and look up at her.

Her fingers weave through my hair. "What did you plan?"

I pat my table. "Sit down."

She smiles and slides up. It's not her first time on my table. Last Saturday night after we closed, she was on the table, and let's just say I had to heavily sanitize it afterward.

"This is not a repeat of last Saturday," I say, and she pouts. I pull out my sketchbook, shielding it from her eyes. "Are you serious about wanting a tattoo?"

Her eyes light up and she stares at the sketchbook, wiggling her ass on the table. "Is that it? My drawing?"

I nod and she squeals, both hands reaching out.

"Gimme," she says like a child. I hand her the sketchbook and her jaw falls open. "But?"

Standing, I cradle her neck with my hand. "I drew this for you. I didn't have the guts to tell you that day, but this is for you. It's always been for you. It's a peony, and it represents wealth and happiness. But it also means beautiful and fragility. According to the Japanese, peonies symbolize risk taking. That you don't get big rewards without big risks. So it's you, but it's also a little reminder to spread your wings and take the leap of faith sometimes."

Her eyes glisten with moisture. "I love it," she whispers.

"It's everything I see in you. Everything that makes me more addicted to you every day. But I want you to remember forever to stand out there on your own, out of the shadows, so everyone can see how beautiful, resilient, and strong you are."

Her hand covers mine and I dip my head for a kiss. But I end the kiss because if I don't, we'll never get to the tattooing.

"Do you trust me to put it where I want?" I murmur against her lips.

"I trust you fully." A tear slips from her eye and I wipe it away with my thumb.

How did we get here? How did my life change in a matter of months? She's ingrained herself into my life and my being. There's more transforming between us. I feel it, but I can't describe it.

"Take off your shirt and sweatshirt," I say.

She grabs the hem of both at the same time and tosses them over her head.

I reach across her chest and unhook her bra, kissing her one more time. "Lie on your left side."

She follows my directions and I pull out the transparency I already did because I knew she loved the peony when she saw it weeks ago. I just had to find the balls to tell her I was drawing it for her before we were anything.

"I'm going to try to make this as painless as I can, but it's your ribs, so just tell me if you need a break."

She nods. I hook up my phone to the shop speakers through Bluetooth and hit Play on a playlist I put together. It's sappy and romantic, but I've never been good with expressing my emotions with words, so I picked others to say them for me. "Bad Things" by Machine Gun Kelly comes through the speakers.

After putting on my gloves, I go to work as I would with any client—except her tits, out there on display, are more tempting. Maybe as long as I keep my eyes off of them, I'll be okay.

Once I'm all prepared, I slide the stool over, allowing my body to be closer to her than I would another client. We're not touching, but I'm hyper aware of her proximity. "I'm gonna start."

At the first touch of the needle, she jolts.

"You sure?" I ask.

She nods. "I'm sure. Sorry."

"Don't be sorry. If you—"

"I want it, Dylan. More than I've wanted anything. Well, except for you."

Talk about a line that melts the damn heart. She has to feel what I have the last few weeks. The way her smile makes a shit day exponentially better. Waking up to her every morning fills me with happiness from the second I wake. Every day, all I think about is how to brighten her day. To let her know in a small way how much I care for her.

I press the machine back to her skin, and this time, she relaxes. The songs stream through the speakers as I move the needle along her skin. There might be silence between us, but it's a comfortable silence. I'll never forget this moment until the day I die.

"Don't I have to heal afterward?"

"I'll put some ointment on and cover it."

"So you make this big romantic gesture with candles and a playlist of love songs, not to mention drawing a special tattoo just for me, and you won't be able to have sex with me afterward? Seems a little torturous," she says.

I wipe the tattoo and take the brief break to meet her gaze. "You underestimate my abilities again."

"Oh, so I am getting lucky tonight?" She smiles wide.

I kiss her briefly. "Definitely. There's always doggie."

She chuckles. "I'd say hurry up, but it will be on me forever."

The word forever catches me for a moment. Forever as in for life or eternity. Endless.

I have no idea what will happen with Rian and me. If she'll wake up one day and decide she wants the responsible guy. But she'll look at this artwork I'm inking every day and think of me.

I'm selfish enough to smile because it means I'll be part of Rian *forever*.

CHAPTER TWENTY-NINE

Rian

I lift my shirt for the millionth time in the past week to look at my tattoo. It's a little crusty, but I can tell it's going to be beautiful once it's healed.

"You're making me jealous. I wish Ethan was a tattoo artist so he could draw on me." Blanca sips her wine.

We're up on the rooftop, waiting for the guys to return from getting stuff for a barbeque. We made all the sides, but for some reason, it's taking them forever to get the meat and alcohol.

"I think we should call the police." Sierra inspects her nails. "I'm starving."

"Knox is the police," I say, dropping my shirt and sitting down at the table with them.

"Do you think Ethan would be jealous if I asked Dylan or Jax to draw me something?" Blanca asks, scrolling through her phone.

Sierra and I exchange a look.

"Um… yeah," I say.

Blanca purses her lips and nods. "I figured."

My phone rings and it's a number I don't recognize, so I send it to voicemail, and we continue talking about Adrian being in Sandsal again. Sierra's worried that it's never going to end and there will always be a reason for him to be out there. Then she'll have to choose to leave her job in order to be with him.

My phone dings to alert me that I have a voicemail, so I excuse myself and walk to the other side of the roof to listen.

"Hello, Miss Wright. This is Dr. Ted Quinton with NASA. I understand from Dr. Giroux that you're the one who solved the problem in the contest his organization hosted. I'm very impressed and wanted to discuss the possibility of you coming to work for NASA. Please give me a call back so we can discuss further. Have a good night."

I hold the phone to my chest for a second then quickly dial back because this has to be a prank. What does NASA want with a math textbook writer?

"Miss Wright," he answers on the first ring.

"Um… hi, Dr. Quinton?"

"Yes, I'm so happy you called me back."

"Are you really with NASA?"

He chuckles. "I am." There's a pause. "I'm a good friend of Dr. Giroux and helped him make up that problem with the hopes we'd find a new recruit. It's an entry-level position, but we're always looking for new talent. I'd love to schedule a video call to talk more about it."

"You don't even know me," I say, still a little stunned that I'm actually talking to someone from NASA.

He chuckles again. "Rarely do we hear people questioning why we might offer them a job."

"I'm just surprised. I thought it was just the monetary prize. I had no idea it had anything to do with NASA."

"It didn't. But I always have my eye out for new talent. I understand you've been working at Pierson since graduation?"

"Exactly, so why would you want me?"

"Well, sometimes you find talent where you least expect to. It's why we like such contests. We find people like you."

"And where exactly is the job?" I ask.

"Houston. Is that a problem?"

My stomach drops and I grip the phone harder. "Um, no." Dylan's face flashes to mind.

"I'll tell you what. I'll have my assistant send you some paperwork that outlines the position and if you're interested we can chat a bit more then arrange a flight and stay for some time next week. I can show you what we have to offer."

"Okay," I agree in a daze.

"Great. It was a pleasure talking to you. Look for that email in your inbox tomorrow morning."

"Okay." I shake my head. "Yes. That's perfect. Thank you."

"Have a great night, Miss Wright."

"You too."

We hang up and I lower the phone, staring into the sun as it's setting. NASA wants to hire me? I remember when I had their posters up on my walls as a kid. When I thought I'd love to work there. My mom's idea, she hung those posters.

I look over the rooftop edge, far down at Ink Envy. Dylan's life is here. We've been together for such a short time; we'd never survive the distance. I'm not even sure we would try. But my heart constricts with the thought of losing him. I lift my shirt and look at my tattoo again. It brings me sadness it hasn't since I got it.

I sit back down at the table, Blanca and Sierra sit up straighter when they see my mood.

"What's up?" Sierra asks. "Who was that?"

I shake my head as the door to the roof opens and the guys file out. I force a smile, which isn't hard because Dylan pulls it from me. Now isn't the time to bring up a potential job that would make me leave Cliffton Heights anyway.

Each guy finds their girl. Ethan places Blanca's favorite wine on the table.

"Hey, babe, can you draw?" she asks him.

Ethan looks at Dylan. "I fucking hate you."

Dylan laughs, his face falling to my neck and kissing the skin there. "Sorry, man."

"I'll totally draw you a tat," Jax offers, starting up the grill.

"Yeah, no, you won't." Ethan cracks open a beer.

"Call Frankie. She'll do something," Dylan says, and Blanca beams.

"Man, you're turning all the girls on to ink now," Ethan says.

Dylan nudges me up, sits down, and pats his lap.

"Is that a no to helping on the grill then, Phillips?" Jax asks.

They've gotten along a lot better recently, even joking around, and Jax's become more comfortable in our group of friends.

"I have my hands full." Dylan whispers in my ear, "I only care about turning one girl on to ink—and all other things."

Shivers run up my spine.

"For the love of God, can we please have one dinner without the two of you making out?"

Dylan laughs. "Jealous, Sierra?"

"She's cranky because Adrian is late coming back," Blanca says.

Seth puts his arm around Sierra. "Want me to be his fill in?"

She shrugs him off and points at us. "Just be prepared—the sex does slow down at some point."

"Maybe Adrian just doesn't have the same insatiable appetite I do." Dylan kisses my neck while his hands massage any body part he can reach.

The man *is* insatiable, and I love it. But I know what Sierra is talking about. I've witnessed it with Ethan and Blanca. Not that they're not still super into PDA, but they've found a routine now—which looks nice too. I like the idea, but I'm not sure how Dylan feels about it.

"Believe me, he does. It's just the distance that sucks." Sierra leans back in her chair and pouts.

"It seems like he's never here," Knox says. "What's up with that?"

She sips her wine. "They're still figuring out how it will all work. His sister taking over, his parents' divorce. Hopefully after next month, he's here more than there."

The whole rooftop quiets except for Jax working the grill.

"Way to kill the mood, Sierra," Seth says.

She kicks him under the table as her phone dings. Fumbling to pick it up, she finally gets a hold of it, reads it, and stands, downing the rest of her wine.

"No burger for me." Sierra leans into Dylan and me. "I'm going to get nailed by my boyfriend."

Dylan laughs.

And she's gone before any of us can say anything else.

"It's like they're in a long distance relationship," Seth says.

"It's just temporary," I say, and Blanca nods in agreement.

Knox leans against the ledge, sipping his beer. From what I know, Leilani left because he said he would never do a long distance relationship. But I'm not even sure Leilani wanted one anyway.

"Fuck that. Never. I couldn't stay away from you that

long." Dylan's arms wrap around my waist and he pulls me into him, licking my earlobe.

"Sometimes there's not a choice. Would you rather lose the person than do long distance?" Blanca asks, probably because we both feel the need to defend Sierra and Adrian.

"Believe me, there's no way long distance would work," Seth chimes in. "I mean, sure at first it's probably great sex when you get together, but then week after week, month after month, you're witnessing your friends with their significant others and the longing sets in. Soon fights happen because one of you can't make the trip to see the other. You're spending a fortune on airline tickets. Phone sex becomes dull and unfulfilling. Long distance doesn't work."

We all stare at him.

"You speaking from experience, Andrews?" Jax asks.

"No. Hell, my entire life has been in this town."

"And Evan Erickson lives here, so how do you know all this?" Ethan asks.

Seth throws his beer cap at Ethan. "You guys can stop with the whole 'I love Evan Erickson' thing. I haven't been friends with her since I was nine. I like my relationships smooth as butter. Creamy as vanilla ice cream. No rocky road for me."

Silence commences until Dylan clears his throat. "I'm with Seth. Long distance would never work for me."

I turn to him. I kind of agree, but I won't say anything because of Sierra. If you love the person, maybe you make it work. Their situation is temporary, they have an end date. But some couples don't, and I wonder how they make it work.

"I need sex too much," Dylan says and laughs, most everyone joining in. "And phone sex isn't gonna cut it." He smiles at me.

"What if you actually have strong feelings for the person?

You'll throw it all away just because you can't have sex with them?"

Dylan's head rears back when he hears my tone. "Is there something you have to tell me?"

"No. I'm just saying sex isn't the be all end all for a relationship. There are a lot of other things that are more important." I stand, grab a bottle of wine, and pour myself a glass.

Dylan straightens in the chair. Jax eyes me at the cooler. Whatever. All these men who think that sex is the number one thing in a relationship annoy me.

"So you're telling me that you don't enjoy sex?" Dylan asks. "Because I think I have to call bullshit on that one. Being your boyfriend and everything, I'd know."

"Being your roommate, I can second that," Jax says. When I send him a scathing look, he turns back to the grill.

I sip a large portion of my wine. "I'm just saying there's more than sex. There are emotions, and not just the ones when you have sex. It makes me feel like all I am to you is a sex toy."

Dylan's chair slides back along the concrete and he stands.

"Whoa." Jax holds out his hand at Dylan as he makes his way over to me.

"Fuck off, Owens." Dylan takes my hands in his.

They're so warm and welcoming, tears slip from my eyes.

"Rian?" Dylan says in an authoritative voice I've never heard him use with me before.

I swipe my eyes. "It's nothing. I just want to know you're with me for more than a place to put your dick."

He draws back as though I slapped him. "I think you know you're more than that."

"But yet you wouldn't do long distance."

"I think this has gotten way too serious. We're all talking

hypothetical. This wine is delicious," Blanca says, trying to save the evening.

"Beer's good too," Seth says.

Knox is staring at us as though he knows something, but he couldn't. Maybe he just sees the demise of a relationship similar to what he went through.

"Let's go downstairs." Dylan takes my hand.

I didn't want this fun night to end like this. When I don't move, Dylan turns back around, his eyes pleading for me to tell him what's going on.

I know Dylan. Sometimes I think I know him better than he does himself. The minute I tell him, he'll shut down. The Dylan I've fallen in love with these past months could disappear forever.

He says my name again like a plea.

"I got offered a job with NASA," I say.

And just like I predicted, Dylan drops my hand. "And where's it at?"

You could hear a pin drop on the roof.

"Houston."

Darkness covers his eyes for a moment, then a smile plasters his face. Not the genuine smile I've been blessed to see every day for months. It's the one he gives customers who annoy the fuck out of him. "You should take it. NASA? Wow, that's amazing."

His arms wrap around me and he pulls me toward him in a hug that holds no emotion. His hands don't linger under the hems of my clothes, and he doesn't kiss my neck or forehead. The hug is not a boyfriend hug; it's a goodbye hug.

CHAPTER THIRTY

Dylan

Rian has no idea how much I'm struggling not to leave this rooftop right now. My pretending that I want her to go because it's such an amazing opportunity isn't a front. I do want her to go. She's magnificent and she deserves the absolute best in life.

But as she sits on my lap and the breeze wafts her perfume to my nostrils, I want to stop the pain slicing me inside. The only way to do that is get drunk or get the hell out of here and away from her—the reminder of what I'm about to lose.

We finish the dinner that her news did ruin because I'm sour and she's concerned. The others continued bullshit lines of conversation just to fill in the awkward silence.

"Let's go." I nudge her off my lap and take her hand, walking her to the roof door. I need to know where her head is at. I don't stop until we're in our apartment and I flick the lock to give us at least a warning before someone barrels in here.

When I turn from the door, she's in the chair by the couch, her knees pulled up to her chest. "I didn't anticipate this."

I sit on the couch, my arms missing her in them. "You got the call today?"

She nods. "I'm just as surprised as you. I was going to wait to tell you until we were alone, but then all that conversation about a long distance relationship came up and I kind of lost it."

I pace the room, unable to sit still because my mind begs me to grab the keys to my bike and get the hell out of here.

"Are you taking it?" The fact that it takes her longer than a second to speak gives me my answer. I hold up my hand. "You are? So it's just a will I or won't I agree to a long distance relationship? Or do you not even want one?"

"I haven't decided anything yet. He's sending me information. He's flying me down to see what the job entails."

"It sounds to me like you're taking it."

She sits up straighter. "Where do you get that idea?"

"Because it's fucking NASA. Who turns down fucking NASA?" My voice grows louder, and I clench my fists at my sides.

"Who said I want NASA? I never did."

I roll my eyes and stare at her long and hard. Her eyes puddle with tears and my anger shatters. I fall to my knees at her feet, my hands gripping her hips.

"You act like I accepted the job," she says, her voice hiccupping. "Do you really think I want to leave you?"

If she heard my answer, she'd be mad. But doesn't this go along with everything else in my life thus far? Somehow, I'm always the one in the rearview mirror.

I raise my head. "You have to take it. It's a huge opportunity and I won't let you turn it down."

I've never spoken more truth. I'd die a million deaths for her happiness. That's how strongly I feel for her.

She runs her hands through my hair. "I'm not sure it's the opportunity I want."

"You have to consider it. You have to go down there and see what they're offering. You have to."

I lift her shirt, kissing her stomach. The tattoo makes me want to grip her harder. I want to beg her not to go, to stay here with me, but I can't do that. She deserves to be the shooting star.

"Can we please just talk about it later?" She slides down, straddling me on the floor.

Our limbs are as tight as vines around one another, our lips seeking the other's in short kisses as though we're testing if this is where we want this conversation to go. My hands slide up her back and lift off her T-shirt, my mouth exploring her lips, jaw, neck. I unhook her bra and she lets the straps slide down her arms. I toss it to the side.

She bends back, and I run my hand down the middle of her breasts, flicking open the button of her jeans. When I slide my hand under the hem of her panties, she moans and rises on her knees, her lips landing on mine. Our tongues tangle with desperate urgency, as though time is short. And it might be for the future, but not right here and now. I'm going to cherish her body.

I push my finger into her. For a moment, she stops kissing me, pulling back to enjoy the pleasure. Each time her gaze falls to me, my heart turns over.

"Dylan," she whispers.

A shot of electricity zings through me as she says my name like a plea. As though all her pleasure is in my hands and I'm the only one who can push her over the cliff of an orgasm.

Running my finger through her folds, I make small circles along her clit and I manage to ease her body down on the rug. With my other hand, my fingertips skim across her bottom lip. I'm unable to stop staring at her.

An animalistic lack of control comes over me and I need her now. I'm desperate to be buried deep inside her. I fall back on my ankles, bringing her jeans and panties off in one swoop.

Her hands run up my T-shirt. "I need to feel your body."

"Your tattoo."

She gazes down and smiles, climbing up on her knees to help me undress.

As soon as I'm naked, I sit with my back to the couch and she straddles me, sinking down on my length. Her warmth fills me from inside out. How can I live my life without this? I push out all feelings of impending doom and my hand slides to the back of her head, holding her in place as I kiss up her neck to her jaw. I capture her mouth with mine, sliding in my tongue.

Her nipples press against my chest as she rocks back and forth. There's no dirty talk tonight; we're going merely on touch. Feather-light touches leave shivers in their path like waves rolling onto the beach. Each caress has a deeper meaning than any words could describe.

My knuckles skim down her spine to her ass, which I take in my hands, molding and gripping and pulling upward.

"Please don't stop," she whispers. "I want to feel like this forever."

I ignore the hitch in her voice as our tempo increases and her moans turn from a submissive whimper to a groan. Since I love watching her come, I'm relentless on getting her off once I feel the sighs of her impending climax. She rocks harder, chasing the friction of her clit along my pelvis bone.

"That's it, baby."

Her love-filled eyes gaze down at me, her hands tightening on my shoulders, her nails digging in. My hips push up off the couch to get as deep inside her as I can. She cries out and the walls of her pussy tighten around my cock. There's no holding back tonight—my own orgasm comes right after and I spill inside her.

Her body falls to mine and her arms wrap around my neck like a scared child. I run my hands down her back.

I can do this. I can be mature about this because why would I ever chance losing something so good in my life?

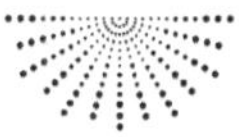

Rian

I dial up the video call to Dr. Quinton. After his assistant sent me the information on the position, I asked if he and I could talk before I headed down to Houston and she arranged this call. I purposely waited until Dylan was at Ink Envy because things are weird between us. We never talk about the job in Houston. He's quiet and withdrawn except for when we have sex, and then it's like a flood of emotions seep out of him. My heart races when he caresses my body with a longing look in his eyes as though I've already left.

Which is why I felt it was better to schedule this call when I was by myself.

Dr. Quinton answers the call. He's not at all what I pictured. I think I had an image in my head of an older version of Johann, with glasses and a thin frame. This man clearly works out and takes care of himself. Behind him is a framed picture of two blond kids and a woman who I assume is his wife.

"Miss Wright." His smile is bright and welcoming.

"Hi," I say, waving like a moron.

We exchange a few pleasantries about weather and our day. Summer is just on our horizon and I love the change of winter to spring to summer that we get in New York. When I tell him that, he says they get a different change of seasons down there.

"Have you had a chance to review the email?" he asks.

I pull out the paperwork I printed a few days ago. "I did. It's all pretty straight forward."

"Before we begin, I have a question."

"Okay." I look up from the paperwork.

The smile that's been so permanent you'd think it was sewn on his face isn't there anymore. "I wondered why you chose Pierson as your next step after your undergrad? You have some remarkable accomplishments. There are many places you could have gone. Why Pierson?"

"Um…" *Think, Rian.* If I could hit my head, I would. All I can think about is that I wanted to torture my parents, but that won't sound very mature.

"I don't mean to pry. I was just curious. If you'd rather—"

I'm not dumb—I need to answer this question if I want this job. Which I don't even know if I do. "I found Pierson at a job fair my senior year. I was unsure about going to grad-uate school, so I figured they'd be an interim."

That's the story I told my parents when my mom was appalled that I'd taken the job.

"What made you not pursue your master's? Are you still thinking about further education?" He sits straight with his fingers weaved together before he grabs a pen and poises it to paper.

"I think I got distracted but…" I got distracted by this life

I live with Sierra, Dylan, Seth, and Knox. I put more effort into developing recipes than I did looking into graduate programs. "I think I would be interested in continuing my education."

He smiles and checks something off on his paper. "That's great. We do encourage continued education so that you can advance your position within our organization."

"Of course."

We go over some more questions about my education and my ambitions. He explains the job a little more.

"How about you come on out and you can tell me yes in person?" He laughs.

"I have to think about it," I say.

He sobers up and looks me square in the eye. I hold my breath. "Can I be candid, Miss Wright?"

"Please call me Rian," I say.

He nods. "Rian, what's holding you back from accepting this position?" He scans the paperwork in front of him. "You're more than qualified, just from your background. You went to Pierson after college when there were other opportunities for you out there. I see the hesitation in your answers. I don't mean to be arrogant, but we are NASA. Rarely do we hear the word no. Especially when we come to you. I guess what I'm asking is, what am I up against to get you here?"

I blow out a breath and bite my lip. "Truth is, I'm not sure I love math enough."

He sits back in his chair. "Oh. I thought for sure it was a fiancé or boyfriend. I had a speech ready for that. This is a first for me." He chuckles.

"Do you mind if I take a few days to think about it?" I could tell him it's the boyfriend thing too, but that's only a piece of the puzzle.

"Not at all. We'd really like to have you on board, but let

me give you some advice. This life is short. Last year I went through some health issues. Before then, I was in the office all the time, never home with my kids for dinner. A typical workaholic. After I became sick and I was forced to slow down, I realized that getting sick was a blessing."

"How so?" I ask.

"Because I got the wake-up call not everyone does. I got to reexamine my life and I found that I love my job, which I'm grateful for, but it's my wife and my kids I love the most. There's truth in the cliché 'you only have one life.' I'd hate to lose the opportunity to bring you on board, but you should do what makes you happy." He smiles, and I nod that I understand. "I'll wait to hear from you, Rian. It was a pleasure talking with you."

"You as well, and thank you for the opportunity," I say.

We say our goodbyes and hang up. I close my laptop and sit in my chair. I need to really consider what I want my life to be moving forward.

The buzzer to my apartment goes off, and I jolt.

I head over to the door and press the intercom button. "Hello?"

"Rian?" It's my dad. "Can we come up?"

I sigh and look around the apartment. No reinforcements. But I need to face them eventually and I've been dodging them for long enough.

"Sure." I allow them in and open the apartment door, grabbing a soda before sitting at the kitchen table.

My mom peeks her head in. "Rian?"

"Come on in."

They each hold a coffee. My dad slides one over for me, also putting a white bakery bag in the middle of the table.

"We heard about NASA," my dad says.

My mom crosses her legs and looks at her lap.

I have no idea how they heard, but it doesn't really matter. "I haven't accepted the position."

My mom opens her mouth, but my dad puts up his hand to stop her. "May we ask why? Does this have to do with Dylan?"

"Yes and no."

My mom sits up straighter, opening her mouth to say something again, but my dad clears his throat. I guess they had a conversation before they came here.

"Can we talk about it?" he asks.

"Sure."

He opens the bag and places a smiley face cookie in front of me. The ones I would get when we went to the grocery store when I was younger. It was my prize if I calculated the groceries with tax correctly.

I smile. "Thanks. What do I need to do to eat it?"

"No conditions," my dad says.

I break off a small piece and eat the sugary goodness.

"So, Dylan… is this serious?" my dad asks.

I'm not sure my dad has started a conversation like this before. It feels odd, but it's a nice change.

"I really like him." I refrain from saying more. Although I think the feelings are there, I've yet to truly accept that I love him.

"Is enough to throw away your entire life?" Mom sneaks her own comment in, and my dad scowls at her.

The frayed thread between us snaps.

"I'm not throwing my life away. Have you ever thought that maybe I threw it away all these years you've forced me into something *you* loved? That I did math only because you forced me into a life of numbers and equations? I'm not you. I don't have the same dreams you do." I push away the cookie that did come with stipulations.

"He has no future. He's great now because you're twenty-eight. But what happens when you're thirty and you're ready for marriage and kids? That guy isn't going to stick around." Her lips purse and she looks at me with disdain.

"How do you know that?"

She shakes her head. "His type is clear as Saran Wrap. I did not bring up a daughter to be this blind. If you don't take this job, you're going to wake up one day as some single mom and saying you wish you would have listened to me."

I roll my eyes and I'm not sure they could get any farther behind my eyelids. "You do this all the time. You don't know him. You're stereotyping him because of his appearance. And regardless, he's not the reason I might not accept the job. It's the fact that I don't want a position that revolves around mathematics."

My mom paces in front of us, looking at my dad as though they're a team and he needs to tag in now.

Dad says, "Sweetheart, you're good at what you do. You're more brilliant than most and you should use that gift you were given. What will you do if you don't take this job?"

I shrug. The bakery idea sounds nice, but I'm not sure I want to put all my eggs in that basket either. "I'm not sure, but some people are lucky and find what they love. I want that."

My mind travels to Dylan and how when he broke his arm, he was depressed because he couldn't work. How many people can say that? Dylan loves what he does.

I shake my head. "You know what? It's time that you face facts. It's my decision now. Time for you to let your baby bird go."

My mom huffs.

"Sweetheart," my dad says.

"*No*! When will you love me for me? Be happy for me? Everything comes with a stipulation or a condition or a guilt trip if I don't do what you think I should." My fists pound on the table and the smiley cookie cracks into pieces under my right hand. "I'm done. You two can see yourselves out."

My mom swipes her coffee off the table. "The way you speak to us with such disrespect." She shakes her head, heading toward the door.

"Respect earns respect, Mom," I say, but she's gone.

My dad hesitates, but he's just a nicer version of my mom. "I had hopes that we could heal things between us."

"You had hopes that you could convince me. I suggest you stop coming here expecting a different result. Either you both learn to love me for me or stay out of my life." The words are hard to say, but I mean them. I can't be on this merry-go-round anymore.

My dad's shoulders fall and his eyes lock on mine. Probably to figure out if I'm bluffing. But there's no bluffing. I should've had the backbone to say this a long time ago.

He nods and stands, following my mom out the door. The click of the door shutting brings a finality I'm not sure I was prepared for.

Once they're gone, I grab my purse and leave my apartment, needing the security of Dylan's arms. His reassurance that I did the right thing.

I open the doors of Ink Envy with my tears barely held in check. If he's with a client, I'll wait in his office.

Lyle is at the front desk and glances up from his sketchbook like every other time I've been here. Frankie's station is empty, and Jax's tattoo machine is aimed on some woman's pelvis. He nods to me, pausing because he's just as perceptive as Dylan when it comes to people's feelings.

I see no sign of Dylan and ask Lyle, "Where is he?"

Lyle looks to Jax to answer the question and sourness fills my stomach.

"He's in the back doing a discreet tattoo." Jax tips his head toward the back room. I start down the aisle between stations. "Maybe wait in the waiting area or his office."

He's right. I can't very well barge in there.

"Lyle, go tell Dylan that Rian's here," Jax says.

Lyle drops his sketchbook on the table. A minute later, he returns from the back room. "He said he's finishing up. You can wait in his office."

I head to the office, but on my way, the door of the room Dylan's working in opens. When I look in, I spot a girl still straightening her clothes. Whatever they're talking about, they're laughing, and Dylan wipes his mouth with the collar of his shirt.

He sees me and says, "I'll be right with you," as if I'm a customer.

The girl who's flushed from head to toe looks me up and down as though I'm her competition.

Instead of going into his office, I hang out in the hallway, watching him check her out. He allows her to run a fingernail down his bicep. She hands him a piece of paper, and he slides it into his back pocket with a smile.

All those tears that were threatening to come out dry up with the anger twirling around my body like a tornado.

She leaves after kissing him on the cheek and gives him a pat on the ass.

Lyle stares at me in the hallway, and Dylan catches sight of Lyle before turning toward me. I have two choices: get the hell out of here, or stay and demand answers.

Why would I waste a night when I feel so feisty? I open his office door, go in, and slam it shut, preparing for the hurricane that's about to hit landfall.

CHAPTER THIRTY-TWO

Rian

I knew he wouldn't dodge the confrontation, so when he opens the office door two minutes later, I'm not surprised.

"What's up?" He nods to me as if I'm an acquaintance.

I cross my arms. "Care to explain?"

He releases a breath. "Explain what? You know it's my job to tattoo people in private places and that means private rooms." He sits at his desk. "I'm actually done early today. Want to go get dinner?"

"Dinner?"

He swivels in his chair. "Yeah. You know, when we put food in our mouths, chew, and swallow. Third meal of the day?"

"Don't."

The smile falls from his face and that hurts worse because

he knows what he did out there. What I want to know is if he did it only for my benefit.

"Don't what?" he asks.

"You took her number."

He huffs. "You know how many numbers I get on a nightly basis?" He digs it out of his pocket and tosses it in the trash. "You know this relationship won't work if you don't trust me." He swivels back around, looking something up on his computer. "I could order and we could pick it up and eat at home, or if you want, we can hit up a restaurant."

"*Stop it!*" I yell.

His chair slowly turns, which reminds me of the movie *The Godfather* that Dylan made me watch a few weeks ago. Like I don't want to mess with him right now. But I desperately do. It's time we hash this out.

"What is your problem?" he asks.

"How would you feel if you witnessed what I just did?"

He shrugs, and my hand itches to slap his don't-give-a-shit attitude off him. "I threw it away. I had no intention of calling."

"Let me call Lyle in here so he can pat my ass then. That's okay?"

A condescending laugh erupts out of him. "Lyle wouldn't do that unless he wants to get fired."

"See? There's a problem that you allowed her to."

"She's a client."

I blow out a breath. "You're sabotaging us, aren't you?"

"I have no idea what you're talking about. Now do you want Italian or Mexican? I kind of feel like eating a taco." He waggles his eyebrows.

I throw my hands in the air. "Stop acting like there's nothing wrong. Just stop."

His jaw clenches. "You're seeing things. You can't be insecure if you're my girlfriend."

All that fight in me crumbles. The Dylan I know is gone. "So that's the way we're going to play this? You're going to shut me out?"

"Babe, I have no idea what you're talking about." He stands to approach me, but I put up my arm to stop him.

"*Babe?*" He's never once called me that. He always says my name, or calls me brainiac if he's teasing me. "You want me to break up with you?" I almost whisper, unable to meet his gaze.

He says nothing.

"Just be straight with me, Dylan. If you're done with me, say so. If you don't want to continue this, please don't play games with me. Just be straight. Is this because of the job in Houston? Are you scared? You have to talk to me."

His face softens and his shoulders sag. Finally we're getting somewhere. But then his cell phone rings, and he turns around to grab it.

"Please don't pick it up," I say.

"It could be a client." He answers it.

I have no idea what he even says because my thoughts are on how he's chipping away pieces of my heart. When I leave this office, I have a feeling we'll be done.

He tosses his phone onto his desk. "Are you sure you're not seeing things so you have an excuse to go to Houston?"

Every cell in my body heats with anger. He did not just say that. "Are you sure you're not trying to push me away?"

"Why would I push you away?" His face distorts into a "you're crazy" look.

"Oh, I don't know, look around your office."

He actually scans the room and looks back at me, waiting for me to explain.

I say, "You don't have one personal effect in here."

"You want me to put up a picture of you? Is that what this is about?"

My frustration is so great, I want to scream at the top of my lungs. I settle for digging my nails into the palms of my clenched fists. "You keep everyone at arm's length, and I thought we were over that. I thought you were all in. One roadblock and you're doing everything you can to push me away?"

He scoffs. "You being jealous of a girl whose tits I had to tattoo isn't me pushing you away. It's me paying the bills."

"Come on, you know what you're doing here. I know you do. I'm not even sure I want the job."

Like a cord snaps, his back goes ramrod straight. "I gotta go."

"What?" I run to the door, blocking it. "We're talking this out."

He pockets his cell phone, grabs his jacket off a hook, and puts his hand on my hip, nudging me out of the way. "Take the job."

"Is that what this is about?" I ask. "You think you can force me to leave? Pretend that you made out with some girl in the back room, get me pissed, and I'll go to Houston? And what? It'll prove your theory about life?"

His gaze locks with mine. I shiver at the chill it sets off, but I won't shy away at this point.

"I know you didn't do anything with that girl," I say. "You wiping your mouth with your shirt to pretend like she kissed you isn't the Dylan I've fallen in love with. You did that for your own benefit so you can blame me for leaving."

He tears his eyes away from mine, his hand landing on the doorknob. "You have no idea what the hell you're talking about."

"You're not that guy, and I will not run off to Houston because of some lame attempt to force my hand. I know you would never cheat on me."

A cruel smile crosses his lips and he turns the knob, but I

use every muscle in my body to keep the door shut. If he gets out, he'll be gone. "You have no idea the man I am. You think you love me? You love an illusion."

"You have it wrong. That is the man you are. That is the man I'm in love with. You're the one who's scared of him. You created this illusion for yourself so you can always be the victim. It's easier that way, right? It's never your decision, never your fault. Everyone else leaves."

He scowls and turns the knob, pulling forward. My body loses all strength as he opens the door and flees. I slide along the wall and sink to the floor, my face buried in my knees.

The door slowly opens, and when I peek up, Jax is there, eyes closed, shaking his head. He crouches, pulls out his cell phone, types out a message, and puts it back. He doesn't say anything to me, just sits in a similar position, his arms wrapped around his propped up knees.

"I don't understand." I rest my chin on my knee. Jax has known him the longest. Shouldn't he have an answer for me?

He shrugs. "The way we grew up... it comes with a lot of fucked up beliefs."

"But we were doing so well."

He nods. "I thought for sure you were in it for the long haul."

"Were?" My voice cracks. "Past tense?"

He blows out a breath. "Don't listen to me. Phillips isn't one who runs forever. He'll be back, but..."

He doesn't have to finish. I know exactly what he's saying.

I put my forehead to my knees again and tears seep out of me like a faucet. Still Jax sits with me, offering no words of consolation. I prefer it that way. He's not making any promises he knows to he can't keep.

What feels like ten minutes goes by before a soft knock lands on the door. Jax stands. I don't even look up. It's probably Lyle.

Blanca sits down on one side and Sierra on the other side of me. I offer Jax a soft smile before he nods and shuts the door behind him.

"Oh, sweetie," Sierra says, putting her arm around my shoulders.

There's nothing they can say, so I allow them to do what girlfriends are supposed to do in situations like this. Tell me bullshit lines like I'll get through this and he's not worth my time. I see now what Dylan was so scared about. These two have already turned on him. He's right—we were stupid to risk our friendship for something more.

But my heart aches as I walk out of his office with a friend on each arm, knowing I'll probably never be back to Ink Envy. Jax sees us and follows.

"You can't leave me responsible for the place," Lyle frantically says to Jax.

Jax pats him on the shoulder. "Sure, I can. Tell any of my clients I had an emergency." Jax tosses his key to Lyle. "No parties, and don't burn the place down."

Lyle laughs. "You sound just like a dad."

Jax scowls. "Fuck you. That's an insult."

Ethan walks in and gives Blanca a kiss on the cheek.

"Where are you going?" she asks.

"We're going after Dylan."

"Let him rot," Sierra says.

I squeeze her hand for being a protective friend, but I don't want Dylan suffering out there by himself.

"Do you know where he would've gone?" I ask.

Jax eyes Ethan as Knox, Seth, and Adrian join the party in the waiting room.

"You're going too?" Sierra asks Adrian.

"Take me with you," I say, leaving the arms of my friends.

Knox steps in front of me, blocking my way. "Let us talk to him first, okay? We'll text you when we find him."

I nod.

"Who rides with who?" Seth asks.

"What do you mean?" Knox asks, putting on his leather coat.

"Whose bike am I on?" Seth adds.

Knox looks at Jax.

Jax raises his eyebrows. "You are not riding bitch on my bike."

"You three can go in Adrian's fancy car," Knox says.

Seth's shoulders deflate. "You guys get to act all cool on your motorcycles and I ride in the back of a Range Rover?"

Knox nods. "Get your motorcycle license and a bike and you can ride with us."

Seth rolls his eyes. "Whatever."

Adrian and Ethan say goodbye to their girlfriends.

Seth hugs me before they leave. "I'll bring him back to you." He winks.

Jax and Knox roll their eyes because I'm pretty sure they're the ones who know where Dylan might have gone. I mouth a thank you to Jax and he nods like always. A man of few words. We watch them leave.

"Um, Rian, can we call Frankie?" Lyle distracts me as they disappear around a corner.

"I'll run to the liquor store," Sierra says and runs her hand down my arm.

No way we can leave Lyle in charge of Ink Envy even for a half hour. He's clearly not ready.

As I sit on the couch in the waiting room, I remember all the times I came in here and dreamily looked at Dylan. It feels as though we've come so far since those moments, but now I'm lost on where we'll end up. One thing is certain—I don't belong in Texas. Even if Dylan returns and sells Ink Envy and disappears forever, or if we find some new normal for our friendship, or if we work out as a couple, I'm meant to be in Cliffton Heights. It's where everyone I care about lives.

I pull out my phone and email Dr. Quinton my decision to decline the job. Just like math, I'll narrow down my choices one by one. Eventually I'll find the solution to my problem.

CHAPTER THIRTY-THREE

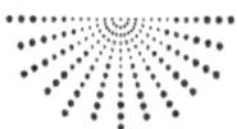

Dylan

The headlight from my bike shines on Joyland's closed sign; the S is tipped upside down. I ride down the long driveway and through the vacant parking lot that's overgrown with weeds and grass.

Once I weave through the opening where I used to witness thousands of families anxiously waiting to get in, I stop at the pool that's now dried up. No one has been here in years. The park was abandoned after they closed their doors due to bankruptcy. I continue on past the merry-go-round that's missing some animals and poles over to the children's area. I park my bike by the bumper cars and game booths, then sit up on a concrete ledge.

Rian's blazing eyes are all I've seen since I left Ink Envy. Truth hurts, and Rian knew what she was talking about. I can't deny it. What she expects from me isn't feasible. I'm not the guy she thinks I am. And I'm sure as hell not gonna be the reason she misses out on a once-in-a-lifetime opportunity.

The sound of two bikes rumbling through the park alerts me that my friends have found me. I had hoped they wouldn't search me out or would overlook this place. I guess our time here meant a lot to them too. They stop near my bike, each cutting the engine and taking off their helmets.

"Funny meeting you here," Jax says, climbing off his bike and hitting the kickstand.

"Why did you follow me?"

Jax sits next to me on the concrete ledge. "Someone has to talk some sense into you."

I desperately want to ask how Rian is. Is she crying? Is she packing her bags? But I leave those questions where they should be—far out of my concern.

Knox leaves his helmet on his bike and joins us. The three of us sit in line, just like when we were younger. We'd come here for an entire day and always end up on this piece of concrete, watching the families wind down for the day as the sun set. I'd see kids fall asleep on their dads' shoulders, or mothers cleaning faces and hands after buckling them up in the stroller. The parents exhausted but with smiles as they looked at each other with happiness in their eyes. I always envied them.

"Remember that time that dad had his son's arm twisted behind his back?" Jax says. "The kid was, like, nine."

I nod. "Knox jumped down and surprised him, told him if he ever saw him do something like that again, he'd find him out and cut off his dick." I glance at Knox.

He shakes his head. "I was such a punk, but hopefully nothing else happened to that kid. What about that time a mom hit on Jax?" We all laugh. "And you told her she should be watching her kids and not hitting on a high schooler unless she wanted to be arrested."

"She just left them for anyone to kidnap," Jax says. "What kind of mother is that?"

We saw so many different versions of parents while we sat on our perch, judging. We intervened more than we ever should have.

"Then you have Phillips, always giving his stuffed animals to the kids." Jax's hand clasps the back of my neck and squeezes.

"What was I gonna do with them?" I shrug as though it wasn't a big deal, but I loved the way the kids' eyes would beam and the parents didn't look at me as if I was trash.

"You always were a family man." Knox nudges me with his elbow.

I shake my head.

"Phillips, don't even try to deny it. How many times did you say that you wanted what those people had?" Jax says.

I jump down from the ledge. "Because I was a foster kid. What foster kid doesn't want parents? A family?"

They jump down and join me walking around. It's sad and desolate and depressing here now.

"You wanted your own family," Knox says. "I remember you saying, 'I'd never treat my kid like that,' and 'My wife is going to be smoking hot with a great pair of tits.'"

I huff out a laugh. We really were punks. "I was young and stupid."

"You knew what you wanted, so what changed?" Knox asks. "I see the way you look at her, man."

I clench my teeth. "She's better off in Houston. She has so many possibilities for her life and I want her to realize all of them."

"Bullshit. Come on. Own it, Phillips." Jax's voice echoes through the empty park as we all hang on metal beams from a ride that's half rotted away.

"Own what?"

Jax looks at Knox and shakes his head. "You fell in love with her and you're scared because what happens when you love people?"

"They leave you," Knox fills in for Jax.

"You two are psychologists now, are you?"

"Maybe she doesn't want to leave? Maybe she doesn't want the job." Jax walks up to me. "Maybe she doesn't want to leave you." He jabs me in the chest.

"Do we really have to give you the 'you are worthy' speech?" Knox puts his arm around my neck and rubs his knuckles along my skull. "People have been assholes and yeah, maybe your dickhead parents abandoned you, but that doesn't dictate everyone's actions."

I get out of his hold. "My head is all kinds of fucked up right now. She called me out on all my shit. She figured me out."

Jax laughs echoes in the night. Only the moon lights our path as we continue along. "You're not a Rubik's cube, moron. And I should kick your ass for that stunt with the client."

I nod. He should. It was low. "What if I fuck this up?"

Knox slaps me on the back. "Too late for that."

He's right. I have fucked this all up. When Lyle said she was there, I purposely got Colleen out quickly so she would still be adjusting herself. Wiping my mouth on my T-shirt was playing dirty.

"I guess we're all gonna wait around for her to meet that accountant, huh?" Jax jumps up on a concrete ledge and walks it. "Watch her pop out a few perfect kids. Sit on the sidelines and let some other fucker get the life you want? Just like we used to watch those families here when we were kids." Jax jumps down in front of me and I rear back. "It's time to grow up. You love Rian and she loves you. Shit, I've witnessed so many gooey moments the last few months that I need five root canals."

Knox nudges my shoulder with his. "He's right. It's time you take what's yours and fight what's holding you back. We all have our demons. Everyone grows up with them. You and Jax were dealt a shitty hand, so toss the cards back into the deck and reshuffle. Or better yet, pluck out your cards so that you end up with a royal flush. It's in your hands. You're the one in control, not that jealous boy who used to watch all the families here."

"Man, Whelan, I'm impressed," Jax says.

Jax is right—Knox did good. He's wrong about one thing though. The jealous boy inside me is the one I should be listening to, because he's the one who said fuck this life he was given, he was gonna have the wife and the kids and the whole family. He wasn't scared.

"Where is she?" I ask, my hand digging into my pocket for my keys.

"She's packing for Houston. Leaving on a red-eye, I think," Jax says.

"Fuck." I turn and run back to my bike.

They follow suit.

"I'm not sure you're going to catch her," Knox says.

All three of us climb on our bikes, and with me in the lead, we head out of the park—except we come upon three guys using their cell phones as flashlights when we reach the merry-go-round. I stop the bike, and my friends stop on either side of me.

"Fuck, guys, you knew we couldn't get Adrian's Range Rover through those openings," Seth says.

Jax and Knox shrug.

"Sorry, we weren't thinking," Knox says.

"I gotta go." I rev my engine.

"This is bullshit, I wasn't able to give him his 'come to his senses' speech." Seth holds up a piece of paper. "I wrote down notes on the way here."

Jax inches forward on his bike. "All taken care of. Now we need to stop her from getting on the plane." Jax pats Seth's back.

"Thanks for coming, guys, but my head's on straight again." I wheel by them and out of the park, right to the highway.

I zoom and weave through traffic with confidence and ease. We pull up to the apartment, all of us killing our engines. The guys tell me they'll park my bike.

I run up the stairs of our apartment building, winded when I bust open the door to nothing but darkness. I slam the door and run down the stairs. Jax and Knox are still parking my bike curbside.

"She's gone!" I yell. "Give me back my helmet. I have to go to the airport."

As the words spill out, the door of Ink Envy opens and Rian steps out. Her arms are wrapped around herself in protection.

I know then, more than I've known anything in my whole life, that I'll do whatever I have to in order to fix this. I will not lose the woman I love.

CHAPTER THIRTY-FOUR

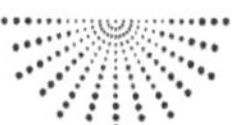

Rian

We all heard the motorcycles coming down the street. Sierra and Blanca looked at me. Hell, even Lyle peeked up from his sketchbook.

When a few minutes pass and no one walks in, I figure I'll go outside to save Knox and Jax from having to tell me in front of everyone that Dylan isn't coming back. But as I open the door, Dylan tears out of our apartment building, demanding the guys give him back his helmet. Until he looks up and our eyes lock.

My feet stop. I wait for him to cross the street, holding his hand out for a car to stop.

"Rian," he says.

Just hearing him say my name does things to me. No matter if he's here to tell me it's over or tell me he messed up, I feel better seeing that he's okay.

"Hi," I say.

"I'm an idiot. I didn't do anything with that woman. I swear. I just…" He looks at me, tucking his hands into the pockets of his jacket. "You were right. I was scared. Scared you were going to leave me, because all the people in my life that I love leave me. But I should have trusted you. I should have fought for us. I should have done anything but what I did. And I'm sorry. I'm so sorry."

The truth of his words reflects in his eyes, but the thought of him trying to push me away stings. "I should torment you. Make you grovel."

He falls to his knees and puts his hands in prayer pose.

"I was kidding. Stand up." I don't want him to beg or grovel. I just want him to love me.

He stands. "I was thinking about it, and I could close Ink Envy and open up in Houston. Or do a branch. Maybe Frankie runs this one, I don't know. Or I can tattoo in someone else's shop down there. I can find clients. I'm talented."

"You'd move to Houston?" A warm feeling fills my chest.

He nods. "I can't do long distance. I don't want to be away from you, so if you'll let me, we'll move in together. Or we can get our own places. Whatever you want." He looks around, then down at my hands. "Shit, are you leaving? Let me pack a bag and hopefully I can get a seat on the same plane." He backs up from me and turns to run across the street.

"Dylan!" I yell.

Jax and Knox are hanging on the street corner, Adrian dropping off the guys before going to park his car. Dylan turns around in the middle of the street.

"I'm not going to Houston," I say.

He looks over his shoulder. Jax and Knox laugh so loudly, they startle the people walking by.

Slowly, Dylan crosses back to me. "You have to. You're too smart."

I put my finger on his lips. "My life is here. In Cliffton Heights, with you and all our friends. I'm trying to figure out what will make me happy, and one thing I know for sure is that a big part of that is you and everything else I have here. Maybe part of the fun is figuring it all out, I don't know."

"You can still have me. I'll go with you. We'll make new friends." He takes my hands.

"Hey now!" Seth yells from across the street. "You have free bagels for life. You won't find that in Houston!"

We both laugh.

"I like us here. This is where we fell in—" I stop because I'm fully aware that I told him earlier I loved him and he still ran out on me.

"Love." He cradles my cheeks and steps closer. "We fell in love."

My eyes water and I nod. I inch up on my toes. "Don't ever run away again."

He bends down, bringing his lips closer. "I promise."

Then he seals that promise with a kiss. And like a cheesy romantic comedy movie, all our friends clap and cheer around us.

Problem officially solved.

EPILOGUE

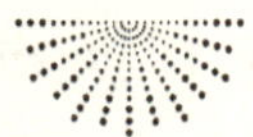

Dylan

Today is the day I prove to Rian how serious I am about us. That I'm not going anywhere unless she's next to me.

"You're being secretive today. What gives?" she asks, coming out of our bedroom wearing a sundress. Although it's early fall, we've been lucky to have an extended summer.

Jax moved in with the guys, so the apartment is officially ours alone. It's weird to have two empty bedrooms, but we turned one into an office with a futon and the other into a guest room.

"It's something we should've done a long time ago, but we've been so busy, I haven't had the time. This is your first weekend without a function to bake for."

Rian finishes putting in her earring and sits on a kitchen chair, sighing. "I never would have thought I'd be in the sweets business."

Rian quit her job at Pierson months ago. It didn't take her long to get her baking business off the ground, and she's doing better than I think she ever expected. She makes anything from cookies to cupcakes, to cakes for people and businesses.

I slide a piece of paper in front of her and massage her shoulders from behind. "You think you're ready to start your own bakery?"

Rian's rents out an industrial kitchen space, where she takes orders online or by word of mouth. She's not ready to put all her eggs in one basket until she knows she'll be happy. Forever the girl with a plan.

She leans back in the chair and her eyes roll shut. "Maybe. I think it would be easier in some regards. I don't much like the hours I have to keep at the industrial kitchen space. But that's a lot to take on. Being an entrepreneur."

I get what she's saying. I'm fortunate that with Jax coming on to Ink Envy, we're back in the black. I'm surprised he's stuck around, but I'm happy he has. It's given us time to rebuild our friendship.

"Take a chance," I say. "I heard there's an open space by this amazing tattoo parlor who will pimp out your goods. Supposedly the owner is really hot."

"Oh, maybe I'll have to check it out, but my boyfriend might get kind of jealous."

"Your boyfriend *is* a little protective when it comes to you. But I get why. He was lucky enough to find a girl like you, so he's right to be afraid to lose you."

She tips her head back and smiles at me.

I lean down and place a kiss on her lips. "Look at the paper."

She picks it up to read it. "What is this?"

"It's my in case of emergency for my insurance," I say.

I take a seat beside her and watch her read the paper.

When she's done, she puts it down, comes over to me, and straddles my chair.

"Seth is going to be upset," she says.

"I don't give two shits about his ego." My hands find their way to her ass like they always do. "So what do you say? Will you be my ICE?"

She kisses me. "I say yes."

I squeeze her ass and pull her closer. "I love you." Never have truer words left my lips.

"I love you. Is that what you were planning this whole time? You didn't even have to ask me. I wouldn't say no." She moves to stand, but I hold her to my lap.

"I have another surprise. I think it's definitely get-me-laid material."

She narrows her eyes. "Are you complaining about our sex life?"

Visions of us all over this apartment run through my mind like a movie reel. "Never. Maybe I should say blow job material. Deserving of a swallow." I grin and wink.

"Hmmm… you have my curiosity piqued."

I pat her ass to get her up. "Then let's go."

We leave our apartment, and I walk her down the street toward the gazebo where the event is taking place. How she hasn't already bothered me about coming to this, I have no idea.

She cringes. "You're not planning some surprise with my parents are you?"

"Never."

Her mom didn't talk to her for three months after Rian declined NASA, but last month, we had them over for dinner. I let her mom's ridicule roll off my back, and when we shut the door on them at the end of the night, we agreed that another dinner wouldn't happen for a very long time. Maybe with time things will improve, but since they both act like assholes and make my girl doubt how brilliant she is, I'm not a fan of them being a part of our lives until that changes.

"Good."

We pass Las Tacos and all the activity in the park up ahead is chaotic. Luckily, I already called in our reservation.

"What is this?" she asks.

"It's an adoption fair." Her eyes widen, and I hold up my hand. "Now, I've already reserved one from a litter for us, because God knows I can't see you down again if we got here and all the dogs were gone."

She laughs, but I don't find it funny. I don't want to see her disappointed like that ever.

"We're getting a dog?" Her smile beams like sunlight in my direction.

"We are." I pull her across the street by her hand and walk her over to the booth set up by the no-kill shelter I talked to on the phone. "Hi, I'm Dylan. This is Rian, my girlfriend. We spoke on the phone."

The woman shakes our hands and points at the pen. "Your boyfriend is very persuasive. You get to pick before anyone else."

Rian looks at me as though I just granted her queen for the day. I'll never stop striving for that look on her face.

She bends down and picks up one of the puppies. He has black and white spotted fur and squirms in her arms. She holds him out to me. "What do you think?"

Five other puppies push on the metal fence, eager for attention. A few kids come over and squeal, giving the puppies enough attention that they shift their attention to them.

"Is something wrong with that one?" I point at the one in the back, curled up in a ball on the grass, not interested in the kids, just chilling.

"He's the runt of the litter. Never demands a ton of attention but loves to snuggle." She picks him up and hands him to me.

He curls up in my arms, nuzzling his face between my arm and rib. Rian coos and puts the other dog back down.

I chuckle. "Is this like when I hold Jolie?"

She nods, pulling out her phone and snapping a picture.

"Remember what I said earlier." I wink at Rian.

She turns to the woman. "We'll take him."

"Oh!" Her surprise has me wanting to ask more questions. Maybe people don't normally want the runt? "Let me get the paperwork."

"Are you sure?" I hand him to Rian and he puts his face on her breast, staring up at her. I pet his head. "That's my favorite spot too, buddy."

"I love him. He's so sweet and quiet." She looks at the pen filled with all the high energy dogs. I guess we're on the same wavelength.

"I did this so you can pick one out, not me."

"And I did." She bends down and kisses his head. "Now we need a name."

"And about a million other things."

We fill out the paperwork, now officially co-owners of a dog without a name, and head to a booth that sells everything we'll need.

Rian

I NUZZLE BABY Winston in my arms as we leave with all the puppy supplies.

"You will have to put him down eventually." Dylan kisses my cheek, his hands full of bags.

"He can't walk on a leash yet."

"We could try to train him on the way home," he says.

Seth and Knox walk out of Las Tacos, spotting us.

"You got a dog?" Knox asks.

Seth pets Winston and Winston eats up the attention. "What's his name?"

"Winston," I say.

Seth looks at Dylan. "Is that your dog or hers?"

"Ours," Dylan says with a smile.

"You gave your dog an old man name," Seth says.

"It fits him." I shrug. "You not a dog person, Knox?" I ask since he's quiet.

He meets my gaze. The poor guy is still sporting heartbreak, although he's been trying to heal it with an array of women.

"I'll be right back," he says and crosses the street.

We all watch him head over to the gazebo, where there's an open area for the dogs to play.

"Isn't that Evan Erickson?" Dylan asks, nudging Seth.

Seth looks around as though he can't locate her. As if her dark curly hair is hard to miss. With the wind today, it's blowing all over her face. She reaches into her purse and grabs a ponytail holder. The guy she's with pulls it back for her, securing her hair into a low ponytail.

"Who's that?" Dylan asks.

"You guys need to stop. It's probably her boy..." His eyes turn murderous. Not a common look for Seth. "You have to be fucking kidding me."

"What?" I ask, looking at Dylan for some backstory.

"That douchebag she's with is my brother's drug dealer. Fuck." Seth turns away, clenching his fists at his sides.

"Well, that sucks," Dylan says.

"Do you think she knows?" I ask.

"Fucking A. Goddamnit." His hands go behind his head and he weaves his fingers, staring at Evan and the man, blowing out a breath. "To answer your question, no. I'm sure she doesn't. She would never, which means…"

"What?" Dylan bit his lip to stop from laughing because we all know Seth. He's too good of a guy, regardless of their history.

Seth steps off the curb then steps back on. "See. This is why"—he points at Dylan—"I like it smooth as vanilla ice cream. I don't need a bunch of shit to muddle through. And now." He's already in the middle of the street, his hands out to his sides. "I gotta go deal with rocky road."

"Stop making excuses and go save the girl," Dylan yells.

Seth flips him off but continues on his path toward Evan.

My back rests on Dylan's chest, and I turn and look up at him. The love of my life. He bends down and kisses me.

"I fucking love our life," he says.

I giggle and nod. I couldn't agree more.

"Let's go home," he says.

And we do, the three of us, to start a life together that might have a little rocky road. But as long as we charter those peaks and valleys together, that's all that matters.

The End

COCKAMAMIE UNICORN RAMBLINGS

Oh, Rian and Dylan. This was one of the rare times we planned everything out ahead of time and the fact so many of you were dying to get your hands on their book (which we'll add can sometimes make it terrifying to write) we were proud that we put those bread crumbs in My Bestie's Ex and A Royal Mistake.

We figured readers would be anticipating Dylan's book when we began this series. Who doesn't love a tatted up guy with an unknown past that gave him the chip on his shoulder? He of course needed to be paired with our sweet and innocent Rian who admired him from afar and baked for him as way to show her affection. Could it be any other way?

Some fun facts about writing this story…

First, we knew that the final guy would move into The Rooftop Apartments in this book. Obviously, the title says it all. And we knew the guy would be interested in Rian and would spur Dylan to make his move. But it didn't turn out to be a childhood friend of Knox and Dylan's until we were writing the end of A Royal Mistake. Rayne sent Piper a message after she had Knox be the one to come in and tell Rian he had a roommate for her. The way she wrote Dylan's reaction she knew whoever this Jax Owens was he had to be more than just a buddy of Knox's. And that's what spurred the backstory of the three of them (Knox, Dylan and Jax) and Dylan's in particular. Amazing how stuff we don't immediately realize when we're plotting comes out in the writing and editing process.

Second, the minute Rayne wrote Jax in a scene she quickly realized he stole it. The more she wrote him, the more she was falling for him which was a bit of a problem because we didn't want to make this a serious love triangle and have readers rooting for Jax. We wanted to use him more as a push for Dylan to make his move. Rayne messaged Piper right away and conveyed her worries. And after the manuscript went to Piper for editing, she was quick to message Rayne after she read the first scene with Jax to say she was loving him too. I guess you never know who will steal the show as you write, but hopefully if you're a Jax lover, it makes you want to get your hands on his story because Rian isn't the girl for Jax. Can you guess who is?

Again, Thanks to our team who if not for them, we'd never be able to finish these books!

Danielle Sanchez and the entire Wildfire Marketing Solutions!
   Cassie from Joy Editing for line edits.
   Ellie from My Brother's Editor for line edits.
   Shawna from Behind the Writer for proofreading.
   Hang Le for the cover and branding for the entire series.

Regina Wamba for the great picture of our Rian and Dylan.

Bloggers who consistently carve out time to read, review and/or promote us.

Piper Rayne Unicorns who shout from the rooftops about our new releases and love our characters like we do.

Readers who took a chance on our book with so many choices out there.

Up next? Seth and … we're sure you've guessed it—Evan. Oh we have a feeling Seth is in for a long ride and he's got three friends who have coupled up that will be more than happy to give him unsolicited advice. The problem is, he's got two single guys living in his apartment who might steer him the wrong way. Then again, we're not so sure Evan will be very easy to win over anyway.

XO,
Piper & Rayne

ABOUT THE AUTHOR

Piper Rayne, or Piper and Rayne, whichever you prefer because we're not one author, we're two. Yep, you get two USA Today Bestselling authors for the price of one. Our goal is to bring you romance stories that have "Heartwarming Humor With a Side of Sizzle" (okay...you caught us, that's our tagline). A little about us... We both have kindle's full of one-clickable books. We're both married to husbands who drive us to drink. We're both chauffeurs to our kids. Most of all, we love hot heroes and quirky heroines that make us laugh, and we hope you do, too.

www.piperrayne.com
Amazon
Goodreads
Facebook
Instagram
Pinterest
Bookbub

The Rooftop Crew
My Bestie's Ex
A Royal Mistake
The Rival Roomies
Our Star-Crossed Kiss
The Do-Over
A Co-Workers Crush

The Baileys
Lessons from a One-Night Stand
Advice from a Jilted Bride
Birth of a Baby Daddy
Operation Bailey Wedding (Novella)
Falling for My Brother's Best Friend
Demise of a Self-Centered Playboy
Confessions of a Naughty Nanny
Operation Bailey Babies (Novella)
Secrets of the World's Worst Matchmaker
Winning My Best Friend's Girl
Rules for Dating your Ex

The Modern Love World
Charmed by the Bartender
Hooked by the Boxer
Mad about the Banker

The Single Dad's Club

Real Deal

Dirty Talker

Sexy Beast

Hollywood Hearts

Mister Mom

Animal Attraction

Domestic Bliss

Bedroom Games

Cold as Ice

On Thin Ice

Break the Ice

Box Set

Charity Case

Manic Monday

Afternoon Delight

Happy Hour

Blue Collar Brothers

Flirting with Fire

Crushing on the Cop

Engaged to the EMT

White Collar Brothers

Sexy Filthy Boss

Dirty Flirty Enemy

Wild Steamy Hook-up